Praise for Anne Stuart

"The very talented Ms. Stuart once again gives
readers a truly rich story. Her characters are
beautifully developed and very real, placed
in a tale that can't be put down."
—*Romantic Times* on *The Widow*

"There are very few authors who write
to the level of excellence displayed by Ms. Stuart.
She takes intrigue, adventure and excitement,
adds a hot romance...and comic relief,
and the result is pure joy."
—*Romantic Times* on *Shadows at Sunset*

Praise for Day Leclaire

"Day Leclaire ensures that a good time
will be had by all!"
—*Romantic Times*

"A pure delight!"
—*Affaire de Coeur*

"Day Leclaire leaves the reader
with a smile and a warm heart."
—Debbie Macomber

ANNE STUART

has written over sixty books in her twenty-five-plus years as a romance novelist. She's won every major award in the business, including three RITA® Awards from Romance Writers of America, as well as their Lifetime Achievement Award. Anne's books have made various bestseller lists, and she has been quoted in *People, USA TODAY* and *Vogue*. She has also appeared on *Entertainment Tonight,* and according to her, done her best to cause trouble! When she's not writing or traveling around the country speaking to various writers' groups, she can be found at home in northern Vermont, with her husband, two children, a dog and three cats.

DAY LECLAIRE

and her family live in the middle of a maritime forest on a small island off the coast of North Carolina. Despite the yearly storms that batter them and the power outages, they find the beautiful climate, superb fishing and unbeatable seascape more than adequate compensation. One of their first acquisitions upon moving to Hatteras Island was a cat named Fuzzy. He has recently discovered that laps are wonderful places to curl up and nap— and that Day's son really was kidding when he named the hamster Cat Food.

ANNE STUART

Kissing Frosty

Day
Leclaire

The Boss, the Baby and the Bride

HARLEQUIN®

TORONTO • NEW YORK • LONDON
AMSTERDAM • PARIS • SYDNEY • HAMBURG
STOCKHOLM • ATHENS • TOKYO • MILAN • MADRID
PRAGUE • WARSAW • BUDAPEST • AUCKLAND

ISBN 0-373-83524-8

HARLEQUIN SPECIAL Vol. 4

Copyright © 2002 by Harlequin Books S.A.

The publisher acknowledges the copyright holders
of the individual works as follows:

KISSING FROSTY
Copyright © 1996 by Anne Kristine Stuart Ohlrogge

THE BOSS, THE BABY AND THE BRIDE
Copyright © 1994 by Day Totton Smith

This edition published by arrangement with Harlequin Books S.A.

® and TM are trademarks of the publisher. Trademarks indicated with
® are registered in the United States Patent and Trademark Office, the
Canadian Trade Marks Office and in other countries.

Visit us at www.eHarlequin.com

Printed in U.S.A.

CONTENTS

Kissing Frosty

Anne Stuart

Prologue

"All right, what are we going to do now?" Megan Mc-Graw demanded, staring out over the frosty, moonlit scene in front of them.

Nadja Commorski blinked owlishly through her over-size glasses. "What do you mean?"

Meggie shrugged. "We've eaten too much pizza and ice cream, drunk too much wine, cried over that stupid movie, lusted over Brandon Scott, and it's still not even midnight. I thought we were going to celebrate our latest disaster. All we've done is make ourselves sick."

"Maybe Roebuck will change his mind?" Nadja suggested, in her soft, timid voice.

"I doubt it. My natural-foods restaurant and your new-age store don't bring in the kind of money he'd make if he buildozed our building and put up condos. Which is exactly what he'll do, as soon as we depart."

"He can't make us leave."

"Sure he can," Meggie said bitterly. "We had a gentleman's agreement with him, not a lease. Unfortunately, none of us are gentlemen. Which leaves us up an icy creek without a paddle. And at the advanced age of thirty-two, I'm getting tired of wandering around. It's time I settled down."

"I thought you had."

Meggie glanced fondly at her young friend. "My biological clock is ticking, Nadja. I want a baby. I want a docile, nonthreatening, handsome husband to pay the bills and keep me in style. Is that so much to expect from life?"

"Not for most people," Nadja said. "I wouldn't have thought you'd settle for something so tame."

"I can do tame," Meggie said in a meditative voice. "So what have you got in your bag of tricks?"

Nadja looked faintly guilty. She was almost ten years younger than Meggie, with a skinny, sparrowlike body, a small, pointy face, frizzy hair, and an air of gentle anxiety. "What makes you think—?"

"Come on, Nadja, we've been sharing business quarters for a year and a half now, struggling together. I know that somewhere among your crystals and potions you have a magic spell or two. You've already told me that tonight's the night of the winter solstice, a night when magic happens. Let's make some magic."

"Meggie, I sell these things, I don't use them. At least, not most of them," she added, endearingly honest.

"You must have something to summon forth a man. A love potion?"

"There are dozens of them in the shop," Nadja said wryly. "They're my biggest sellers, though they've never worked for me. Besides, you've kept away from romantic entanglements for as long as I've known you. Who did you want to summon?"

It was a cold, frosty night in the tiny ski town of Watson Hole. The town was decorated for the Christmas season, and each shop had lights, ice sculptures, wreaths and trees galore. Even Nadja's and Meggie's. Meggie sauntered across the snow-packed street to the corner of the alleyway, where a huge, somewhat disreputable-looking snowman she'd helped build early that afternoon sat. He was suitably rotund, but there was something about the composition of his coal eyes and his carrot nose that suggested a certain cynicism. "How about we find a magic hat and turn old Frosty into the perfect mate?" she suggested, slinging her arms around his icy middle.

It took her a moment to realize that Nadja hadn't responded. She turned, one arm still around the snowman, to see her friend's speculative expression.

"There is an incantation," Nadja said slowly.

Meggie pulled away. "I'm kidding, Nadja. He'd melt in bed."

"No, I mean he could be used as an oversize poppet. Something to transfer energy. It wouldn't do any harm to try."

"What are you talking about?"

"We can use Frosty to summon your true love. If you've got something belonging to him."

"Nadja, I don't have a true love. Maybe Brandon Scott, if he weren't five years younger than I am, and much too pretty..." she added with a laugh.

"I don't think you really want to marry a movie star, Meggie," Nadja said disapprovingly.

"Probably not. Still, he is awfully nice to look at. And there are plenty of pictures in that old *People* magazine you have under the counter. Where they call him the sexiest man in the world. Let's use that."

"I don't want to rip up my magazine," Nadja protested. Her face screwed up as she thought about it. "Oh, what the hell…it won't do any harm to try."

"That's the spirit," Meggie said. "Shouldn't we do it by midnight? That only gives us fifteen minutes."

Nadja sighed. "You get the picture, I'll get the stuff. Just promise me you'll invite me to Hollywood and introduce me to Tom Cruise."

"He's married."

"Well, find someone who isn't," Nadja said. "Or I'll take Brandon, if you get tired of him."

"Who could get tired of someone who looked like him?" Meggie said soulfully.

It took them less than ten minutes to get what they needed. They searched through Nadja's new-age shop, giggling like naughty children, and when they were finished, Nadja was loaded down with candles, herbs and unguents and Meggie had a photograph torn from a magazine. "I didn't have to defile your *People* magazine," she assured Nadja. "I found a picture of him in an article about the Oscars."

"Pin it to his chest," Nadja said, lighting a dark blue candle. The flame shivered in the cold night air, but, fortunately, there was no wind.

Meggie did as she was told, vaguely hoping that the police wouldn't choose this moment to patrol the narrow Swiss-style streets for mischief-makers. Not that they'd be arrested—they'd lived in Watson Hole long enough to be known. But Meggie didn't relish the thought of explaining exactly what fool thing they were doing.

"Okay," Nadja said, setting the candles in the snow at various points around the rotund snowman. "Now step inside the pentagram and put your arms around Frosty."

"Brandon," Meggie told her, doing as she was told. "He's cold, Nadja. Maybe you better hurry this up."

"Hey, I'm not experienced at this sort of thing. If you'd thought of it earlier, we could have called one of my customers…"

"I have some dignity," Meggie said, resting her head against Frosty's. The packed snow was icy beneath her cheek, and the chill soaked through her clothes. "Go ahead."

Nadja sighed. "Close your eyes and kiss him," she said, lighting a tiny pile of leaves that smelled like sausage. "I'll take care of the rest."

Meggie closed her eyes. Frosty was too fat for her to reach all the way around, and the chill of his packed form, instead of numbing her, felt oddly burning. She pressed her lips against the icy face, and for a strange moment it felt as if she were kissing real lips. A man's mouth, firm and hard. She tried to summon forth the celluloid features of the world's sexiest man, with his mane of streaked blond hair, his pouting lips, his gloriously sorrowful eyes. But someone else kept interfering, a shadowy figure, dark and disrupting.

"It's done," Nadja said abruptly.

Meggie opened her eyes and released her grip on Frosty. She glanced up at him speculatively, but he didn't move. "I don't think it worked, Naddie," she said doubtfully. "He hasn't turned into a movie star."

"These things take time," Nadja said reprovingly. "You can't expect instant results."

"We don't have a hell of a lot of time, Nadja. We're supposed to be out of here by New Year's Day."

"This isn't Federal Express, Meggie. Things happen in their own time," Nadja intoned.

"Oh, God, don't go all new-age on me, Naddie," Meggie begged. "Tell you what—let's go back home. At least I can dream about Brandon Scott carrying me away to Hollywood. It's probably all for the best. I don't have the highest opinion of men in the first place, and even perfection, in the form of Brandon Scott, would probably have its drawbacks."

"I could learn to live with them," Nadja said wryly. "Don't confuse me by talking about reality, Meggie."

"Reality is the pits," Meggie said in a mournful voice. "What about the picture? Do we leave it stapled to Frosty's heart?"

"Tuck it in your bra."

"I don't sleep in my bra, Nadja," Meggie said severely.

"Well, tuck it under your pillow, then."

"That's part of the spell?"

"I'm making it up as I go along. It can't hurt," Nadja added.

"No, it can't hurt." She pulled off the ice-crusted page from the magazine, folded into a tiny square and tucked it inside her bra. It burned against her skin. "Night, Nadja. See you in the morning."

Chapter One

Frosty had developed a decided tendency to smirk at her, Meggie thought days later, as she was cleaning the counter of her café. It was past closing time, dark outside, and only the remaining holiday lights illuminated his hefty shape. She'd stared at him for the past few days, some small, foolish part of her half hoping he'd disappear, and that Brandon Scott, the hottest thing of the nineties, would set foot in her store. But so far, the damned fat snowman had stayed put, smirking at her.

Nadja was back in the kitchen, finishing up the pots and pans. It had been a busy day, but then, most of their business was between Christmas and New Year's. Three more days till that old skinflint Roebuck closed them down, and Meggie still didn't have the faintest idea what she'd do.

There were other natural-foods restaurants in the small, trendy village, and she was a good cook. But she'd lost the taste for working for someone else. Besides, she'd done cooking. Just as she'd done her stints as a paramedic, rodeo clown, country singer, executive secretary, hospice worker, carpenter, journalist, bartender and chambermaid. Hell, she'd even done a stint as a litter-bearer at Lourdes. She'd packed enough careers, enough lives, into her thirty-two years to keep her memories busy for the next fifty. Always moving on, ever since she'd left college, midway through her junior year. Her dependent, widowed mother had died, the money had been gone, and Meggie had been free for the first time in her life. Free to walk away from entanglements and other people's smothering needs, free to walk away from the demands of her possessive, unimaginative boyfriend. Free as she'd been ever since. And she'd never been bored.

That freedom was beginning to pall. It was time to decide whether to try stability again. Relationships. Or spend the rest of her life alone.

Doubtless she'd find the answer if she just relaxed and waited for something to happen. If she was just patient enough, an opportunity would present itself.

"Someone just drove up," Nadja called from the kitchen.

"Didn't you put the Closed sign up?"

"I did."

Meggie quickly snapped off the lights. She wasn't in the mood for stragglers looking for a bean-sprout sandwich. If money wasn't so tight, she'd be sorely tempted to sneak into the only place in town that served red meat and get herself the biggest, rarest steak in the world. But Saucy Jack's astronomical prices didn't include a professional discount for his fellow restaurateurs, and Meggie needed to hoard every penny.

The car lights outside flicked off, and she heard the slamming of two car doors. "Whoever they are," she said, "they don't take a hint."

Nadja appeared in the kitchen door, her thin face anxious. "You want me to send them away?"

"I can do it," Meggie said wearily, crossing the small dining room. Someone was pounding at her door, a fact that didn't particularly please her, and if the noise wasn't so irritating she'd have been tempted to ignore them.

But she couldn't ignore the rattling of the doorknob. She switched on the outside light and yanked open the door, fully prepared to send her unwanted customers on their way.

She took one look at the two men who were standing there and began to scream.

"What the hell's wrong with you, lady?" O'Leary demanded, shoving the door open all the way. The idiot creature just stood there, screeching, and he reacted instinctively, shoving her against the wall and clapping his hand over her mouth, shutting off that infernal yowling. "You got a problem?"

She'd stopped making any kind of noise. She had gorgeous eyes, staring at him above the hand he'd clamped over her mouth. There was no way he could have missed them, even though they were glaring at him with a mixture of fear and shock. "That's better," he muttered, dropping his hand, releasing her. Though, for some reason, he didn't really want to. "Aren't you a little old to be acting like a groupie?"

The eyes were a golden brown, and they slid over him with only a brief glance, going instead to the man behind him. O'Leary was used to it. Traveling with Brandon Scott got a man used to feeling invisible.

"Oh, my God!" There was another woman in the dimly lit restaurant, younger, plainer, just as horrified. For a moment, John James O'Leary wondered whether they'd wandered into a mental colony. "It worked!"

The woman close to him opened her mouth, and he half expected her to start shrieking again, but she seemed to have pulled herself together. She kept looking at Brandon in disbelief, but that was normal enough. Brandon, as usual, didn't even seem to notice the reaction he was causing.

"The restaurant's closed," she said in a hoarse voice. And it was no wonder she was hoarse, O'Leary thought cynically.

"Don't be ridiculous, Meggie!" the young one said, flicking on the lights, illuminating the small, cozy place.

"Yeah, Meggie," O'Leary said, getting his first good look at her. "You got a couple of hungry customers here."

She was quite a luscious handful, though he hated to admit it. She was taller than average, rounded in all the right places, with a mane of wild, honey-streaked hair that tumbled around her shoulders. Strong shoulders—he liked that in a woman. She had a big, stubborn mouth to go with her gorgeous eyes, and an air of wariness that didn't even hint at vulnerability. She was a scrapper, a fighter, a survivor. Like he was.

She was also fool enough to be smitten by America's sweetheart, Brandon Scott, the darling of just about everyone missing a Y chromosome and a hell of a lot who weren't. The prettiest, sweetest, dumbest male on the face of this earth, and for the past three days he'd been O'Leary's constant companion. It was enough to make him want to scream as loud as the transfixed Meggie.

The plain one scurried from behind the counter, blinking through her thick glasses. "What can we get you, Mr. Scott?" she asked, practically wringing her thin hands.

Brandon gave her his usual smile, and O'Leary half expected her to swoon. She managed to keep upright, by sheer effort, but O'Leary had played a variation on this scene almost every place they stopped, and it had gotten old, fast.

"Look, lady," O'Leary said, "we've been driving for five hours, we're tired, and we're hungry. Just give us something to eat, some directions, and we'll be out of here."

"Of course," the skinny one said, ushering Scott to a table. O'Leary followed, vaguely aware that the voluptuous Meggie was still standing there in blessedly silent shock. He glanced back at her, expecting her to be staring at Brandon with a besotted expression on her face. Oddly enough, she looked more horrified than entranced.

"Ginseng tea," Brandon murmured, in the soft, rich voice that made millions swoon. "And a sprout-and-tofu sandwich on whole-grain bread."

"And I'll just have a cup of coffee," O'Leary said, leaning against the counter. He'd been sitting for too long—he wasn't in the mood to fold his long frame into one of those delicate-looking chairs. He glanced over at Meggie. "You wanna get it for me, sweet-heart?"

He knew that would galvanize her. She came to with a jerk, glaring at him. "We don't have coffee," she said. "This is a natural-foods restaurant.

"You telling me coffee's not natural? It's grown in the mountains of Colombia, picked by Juan Valdez, and brought here just for my delectation. Don't tell me you don't have any."

"We carry several grain beverages—"

"Coffee," he insisted. "Loaded with caffeine."

She had a magnificent glare, one that went well with her generous, heaving bosom. He was old-fashioned in many ways—he liked a woman with curves and breasts. "I'll see what I can find," she said, stalking through the swinging doorway.

"I'll bet you will," he muttered under his breath. She'd probably come back with rat poison. If he was real lucky, she might find an old jar of instant coffee with enough powder left to make a weak cup. He might prefer the rat poison.

She was back suspiciously quickly, and the hand-thrown earthenware mug she slammed down in front of him was filled with a dark, delicious-smelling liquid.

"Goat's milk or soy?" she said with spurious sweetness.

"Black," he said, bracing himself for a huge swallow.

She'd already turned away from him when he set the half-empty mug down on the counter again. "Hey, Meggie," he said.

She glanced back at him, her long hair swinging. "You have a problem with the coffee?" she said frostily.

"You know damned well I don't. This isn't just coffee."

"I couldn't find any rat poison."

Since he'd just been thinking the very thing, the phrase startled him. "Are you some kind of witch?" he demanded.

She looked momentarily guilty. And then it passed. "Do you believe in witches, Mr.—?"

"O'Leary," he said. "And you made it quite clear you know who my friend is. No, I don't believe in witches. I just wondered how a place that claims not to have coffee manages to serve a truly great cup of it. These are freshly ground beans, probably fresh-roasted, as well."

"Life is full of little mysteries," she said.

"Yeah, well one of those mysteries is how we find a place called Madame Rose's Palace."

He'd managed to surprise her again. "You're staying there?"

She was relaxing, just a tiny bit, and he decided to take advantage of it. He slid onto one of the stools, taking another sip of the finest damned coffee he'd had in months. "That was the best the studio could arrange for us on such short notice," he said.

"This was an unexpected trip?" The question was innocent enough, but he couldn't rid himself of the feeling she had a hidden agenda in asking it.

"America's sweetheart and I were supposed to be at a film festival up in Montana. For some reason, we both had this stupid need to take a detour to Watson Hole, so we decided to go together.''

"You mean you're not his bodyguard?" she asked incredulously.

She was one of the most annoying women he'd ever met, he thought. Even if she did make great coffee. "Do I look like a muscleman? I'm not his bodyguard, his publicity agent or his keeper. As a matter of fact, I'm a screenwriter. Since we've worked on several pictures together and we were headed in the same direction, I decided to give him a ride." And regretted it every living moment of the way, he added silently.

"Why didn't he want to drive?" she asked.

"He can't. He lost his license last year for speeding. So he's forced to rely on the kindness of strangers. Fortunately, all he has to do is smile and bat his lashes over those baby blues and people will lie down and die for him."

"And you resent that?"

His head jerked up at that caustic remark. "Hell, no, Meggie," he said lazily. "It keeps them off my back." He reached into his pocket absently, looking for the cigarettes he'd given up two weeks, three days and thirteen hours ago. Empty, of course. He reached for his coffee instead, draining it. "So, where's Madame Rose's Palace? And what the hell is it, for that matter?"

"It's a historical landmark, just up the street," the woman said, a wicked smile curving her full lips, which he found a hell of a lot more enticing than

Brandon Scott's famous pouty smile. "It's redbrick, with red lights in the window. You can't miss it."

"Why is it a historical landmark?"

"It's the oldest building in town, and it's been renovated so that it looks exactly the way it did in the late 1800s. Without the women, of course."

"The women?"

"It's a whorehouse, Mr. O'Leary. I imagine you'll feel right at home."

Damn, he thought. He liked this woman. "You spend a lot of time there, do you?" he inquired in a silky voice.

He liked her laugh, as well. "Finish your coffee, and Nadja will show you where it is."

"Why not you?" He wasn't sure why he was asking. She'd probably just hang all over Brandon.

But then, she hadn't done more than glance at Brandon since he'd sat down. "I've got things to do," she said briskly. "Don't worry, if you stay here long enough you'll be bound to run into me. How long are you staying?"

"I don't know."

"Why are you here?"

"Beats me," he said lazily. "Got any ideas?"

And he watched, with utter fascination, as the color drained from her face.

Chapter Two

Megan was having a difficult time of it that late winter afternoon. Not only had Brandon Scott actually arrived on her doorstep, looking even more glorious in real life than he did on the screen, he'd been accompanied by an evil-tempered troll.

Not that O'Leary looked like a troll, she thought fairly, glancing at him. If Brandon hadn't been around, he might have seemed quite attractive. For one thing, he was tall, and rangy with a kind of muscly leanness that was a far cry from Brandon Scott's carefully bulked-up physique. His face wasn't pretty—at some point during his life, his impressive, beaky nose had been broken, and his high cheekbones, narrow, clever face and strongly marked eyebrows made him look faintly satanic. Clever men irritated her. She preferred them cute and passive.

He had hair so dark she wondered whether he might have some Native American blood in him. His wide mouth might have been considered sexy if it wasn't twisted in a mocking smile, but there was no denying he had extremely fine eyes. They were very dark, almost black, and yet there was something about them that drew one in.

All in all, it was a lucky thing the sexiest man in the world was sitting in her restaurant, or she might be spending far too much time watching this mocking stranger in the rough cotton sweater and the faded black jeans that hugged his long legs, and not concentrating on Brandon Scott, who was wearing...

She didn't know what he was wearing. The realization horrified her. She had summoned him through supernatural forces, he had arrived just for her, and all she could do was argue with his friend.

"I have no idea why you'd want to show up here," she finally said, shrugging, turning to look at her heart's desire.

Brandon Scott was eating his sprout sandwich with single-minded concentration. Meggie should have been pleased that he liked her cooking, but there was something about sprouts that gave her the willies. She would have to expand his culinary choices.

Nadja was hovering over him, like a doting mother, but when she felt Meggie's eyes on her, she looked up, flashing her a look of excitement.

"You finished with your sandwich, Brandon?" O'Leary asked, in the patient voice one usually reserves for children.

Brandon immediately pushed back his chair, touching his perfect, pouty mouth with his cloth napkin. Meggie made a mental note to save the napkin. If things didn't work out, she could always sell it to some deranged fan for a fistful of money.

"Nadja, would you show them where Madame Rose's Palace is?" Meggie moved forward to clear the table. For some reason, she wanted to move away from O'Leary, and his dark, observant eyes.

Nadja's expression would have been comical if it wasn't so blatant. "No," she said flatly. "I can't."

Meggie wanted to throw the dishes at her. If she pushed it, Nadja might just come right out with the reason Meggie should take them to Madame Rose's. After all, Brandon Scott had come for her, not Nadja.

"All right," she said in her most annoyed voice, dumping the dishes back down on the table. "Wait a moment while I get my boots and coat."

"I hate to put you to any trouble." It was Brandon Scott's famous rich, deep voice, directed at her for the first time. It came accompanied by a slow, sexy smile and those incredible blue eyes. Meggie stood motionless for a moment, waiting to melt in delicious response.

Nothing happened. Except for O'Leary, moving between them. "Come on, sweetheart," he drawled. "You can moon over him later."

It took no effort at all to pull her attention away from Brandon's dazzling smile. "You know, O'Leary, I think you've been watching too many Humphrey Bogart movies," she said sweetly. And as she disappeared into the back room, she heard the unsettling sound of his laughter.

He had a damned sports car. A two-seater, and O'Leary was already behind the wheel, looking at her out of his wicked eyes, when she joined them outside. "I'm afraid you're going to have to force yourself to cuddle up with Brandon for the ride," he said.

"It's not that far. I can walk."

"You can sit on my lap," Brandon murmured.

Yeah, sure, Meggie thought. He'd probably never had one hundred and thirty-five pounds of mature female flesh on his lap, and she wasn't about to introduce him to the experience. There was a limit to just how effective Nadja's brand of magic was. "I don't think so," she said.

"Let him sit on your lap, then," O'Leary growled.

Her immediate thought was obscene enough to still even her runaway mouth. Brandon just smiled sweetly and held the door for her. "There's plenty of room for both of us, if we squeeze," he said. "I know I'm kind of beefy, but I'll try not to crowd you too much."

Since Meggie knew perfectly well that her hips were at the very least six inches bigger than Brandon's, she started to melt, only to be brought up short by O'Leary's derisive snort. "Get in the damned car, will you?"

It was clear that Brandon wasn't going to get in first and let Meggie cuddle up to the door handle. Gritting her teeth, she scrambled inside, glaring at O'Leary, who watched her with impassive malice as she tried to make herself as tiny as possible in the leather bucket seat before Brandon climbed in.

She had no choice. Brandon might have skinny hips, but the car was minuscule, and she found herself with her butt on the emergency brake, her thigh up against the gearshift.

"This is a damned stupid car for a grown man," she informed O'Leary bitterly as Brandon settled himself next to her.

O'Leary put the car into Reverse, his hand sliding along Meggie's thigh. "Tell it to Brandon," he said cheerfully. "It's his car. I drive a Jeep."

He had long fingers, and she'd have sworn he was

letting them linger against her thigh, just to try to
disturb her. She tried to move, then realized she
couldn't. Brandon was pressed up against her other
side, quite solidly. And it was with another start of
horror that Meggie realized she'd barely noticed him.
He was warm, solid and male. He was the sexiest man
in the world. And she'd been too busy paying attention to the irritating man in the driver's seat.

Fortunately, the drive to Madame Rose's Palace
was brief. Unfortunately, Meggie couldn't manage to
drum up too much enthusiasm for her first cuddle
with her intended. She blamed it on O'Leary's damp-
ening presence.

The place was dark and deserted, only the framed
red lights glowing from several of the upper-story
windows, when O'Leary pulled the ridiculous car in
front of it. "You're lucky they're letting you stay
here," Meggie said as he cut the engine. "They usually only let CEOs, and the like, use the apartments."

"You don't think I qualify, Meggie?" he murmured. "I think we'll feel right at home in a bordello."

"I imagine you will," she said sourly. "The two
guest apartments on the third floor come with all the
amenities, even if they are decorated in period style."

"All the amenities? I thought you said it didn't
include ladies of the night."

"I'm sure we can find someone willing to put up
with you. For a price," she said sweetly.

"And what's yours?"

It was just another of his gibes, one that Meggie
should have responded to in kind. Except that sud-

denly there was a strange, underlying heat to his words. A heat that reached out and curled inside her....

Until she realized the door was open. Brandon had already disappeared into the house, and she hadn't even noticed.

"More than you could afford," she snapped, scrambling out of the car and slamming the door behind her. That was another problem with sports cars, she thought bitterly. The doors didn't make a satisfying crash when you slammed them. Just a piddling sort of thunk.

O'Leary was standing beside her in the frosty night air, looking up at the place. "Why'd you get out of the car? Don't you want a ride back to your restaurant?"

"No thanks. I can walk. And I won't bother showing you around Madame Rose's Palace. It's easy enough to figure out where to go. Just don't be too shocked at some of the pictures on the walls."

"Naked ladies?" O'Leary murmured. "I can't wait. Which reminds me. I wouldn't set your sights on America's sweetheart in there."

"What are you talking about?"

"Brandon. The sexiest man alive, remember?"

"You aren't going to tell me he's gay?"

"Nope. But I know from experience, he likes his ladies just past the age of consent, bordering on the anorexic, and not a brain in their heads. Sorry, sweetheart, you fail on all three counts."

"I beg your pardon?" She could be as frosty as

the night air. "I'd like to know what business it is of yours?"

"Just doing my neighborly duty," he said with spurious concern.

This day had not gone well, and the sudden appearance of the man of her dreams was turning out to be less than enthralling. She looked at the man looming over her, and said, in her sweetest, calmest voice, "The bottom line is, I'm too long in the tooth and too broad in the beam for him. Is that what you're so tactfully trying to tell me?"

"In a nutshell."

There was an icy snowbank behind him, on the left. There were thick shrubs decorated with tiny white lights behind him on the right. She opted for the shrubs, taking him off guard. She was halfway down the snow-packed street by the time he'd struggled out of them, and she could hear his curses floating after her.

And she found she could smile after all.

Madame Rose's Palace was like something out of a movie set, O'Leary thought as he followed Brandon up to the third floor. The studio had had to pull strings to get them a place to stay there, and since neither Brandon nor O'Leary could come up with a reason why they suddenly had this overwhelming need to go to Watson Hole, it had made things a little more difficult.

But they were here now.

"This place is cool," Brandon said, stretching the syllables of the word. O'Leary controlled his instinctive wince. It wasn't that Brandon wasn't a perfectly nice kid, it was simply that he was about fifteen years younger than O'Leary and about ten bricks shy of a full load. It only made sense—the boy was blessed with extraordinary good looks, a beautiful voice, an undeniable acting talent and a sweet nature. There was no reason he should have brains, as well.

"Very nice," O'Leary grumbled. Actually, he kind of liked the gilded tawdriness of his room. The fat, cavorting cupids on the brass bedstead. The red flocked wallpaper and velvet bed hangings, the erotic paintings on the walls that were an odd mixture of quaint and arousing. But the bed was too big, even for a man as tall as he was. It needed someone soft and luscious sliding between the sheets.

"What did you think of her?" he asked abruptly, leaning against Brandon's doorjamb. Brandon's room was similar, though done in shades of dark blue velvet.

"Who?" Brandon pulled off his sweater and shook his long blond hair with the casual abandon of a fashion model.

"The woman at the restaurant."

Brandon's perfect face scrunched in thought. "She wasn't very pretty, was she?" he said after a moment.

For some reason, that offhand dismissal infuriated O'Leary. It made no sense, but then, not much had made sense during the past few days. "It's a question of taste," he growled. "Some people might prefer their women to have curves."

"Yes," said Brandon. "She had very kind eyes, didn't she?"

O'Leary thought back to Meggie's eyes. They were a rich brown, shrewd and challenging. "I wouldn't say so. Anyway, she's not your type."

"I didn't know that I had a type," Brandon said.

"Maybe not. But if you do, she wasn't it," he said firmly. He wasn't quite sure why he was so determined to warn Brandon away from her. But he was.

Brandon smiled. "I didn't think you even noticed her. You were too busy arguing with the other one."

It took O'Leary a moment to comprehend. "I thought we were talking about the other one. Meggie."

"I was talking about Nadja. The skinny one, with the frizzy hair and the glasses."

"Oh," said O'Leary, suddenly deflated. "Well, what did you think of Meggie?"

Brandon Scott's smiles were as famous as his long blond hair. He had several versions—the slow, sexy one, the gentle one, the male-bonding grin. It was that last one he gave O'Leary. "I think you'll be very happy together, Jay." And he closed the door between them, quite gently.

Meggie's mood had done a nosedive by the time she returned to the restaurant. Nadja had already closed up and gone, and Meggie was half tempted to drive over to the tiny apartment she shared with two other girls on the top floor of an old Victorian house on the edge of town.

She didn't. She went straight upstairs to her own rooms, dropped her rented video on top of the VCR and headed into the kitchen. She kept her stash of diet

Coke behind the bottles of organic carrot and raspberry juice. She kept her bags of taco chips hidden behind the dried banana flakes. She assembled a junk-food feast, complete with guacamole, hot dogs, cinnamon buns for dessert—enough cholesterol to choke a horse—plunked herself down on the mattress in front of her TV and started the video.

Winter of the Heart was Brandon Scott's most famous movie so far. Nadja and Meggie had seen it three times in the movie theater and twice on tape, and it never failed to transport the two of them into a state of weak-willed adoration. She was counting on its having its usual salubrious effect.

The opening frames weren't much of a help. For the first time, she noticed the writing credits. Screenplay by John James O'Leary, based on a novel by Nathaniel Harris. She shoved a chipful of guacamole in her mouth, snarling.

By the time she was halfway through, she knew she should turn the tape off, but she couldn't help herself. Brandon Scott in glorious buffed Technicolor had lost his magical effect. Meggie watched the familiar scenes unfold, and all she could think about was the annoying predictability of the plot.

By the end, when all the women and half the men lay dead amid the gorgeous scenery, her mood hadn't improved. She snapped off the TV and went in search of ice cream.

She must have dreamed about him, of course. When she woke the next morning, she was covered with a fine film of sweat, her body tingled, and she knew her dream had encompassed one of the finest sexual encounters of her life, far better than anything she'd ever actually experienced. The problem was, she couldn't remember anything about it.

The first thing she saw when she came downstairs was John James O'Leary, sitting at her counter. She almost turned around and walked out again, but she steeled herself. She'd never been a coward, and she wasn't about to start now.

"We're not open for breakfast," she said.

It was amazing to her, how a grin could be condescending, infuriating, mocking—and utterly charming, despite it all. "And a good morning to you too, Meggie. Yes, I slept well, thank you for asking, and I'd love a cup of coffee."

"Did Nadja let you in?"

"She did. I sent her up to Madame Rose's with a sack of nuts and twigs for Brandon. She seemed to think you should be the one to deliver his breakfast, but since she said she couldn't make coffee, I didn't give her any choice."

"We don't do take-out service."

"Not even for the sexiest man in the world?" O'Leary taunted.

If there was any way she could possibly survive without coffee, she would have done so, but some things were simply beyond her. "You're really starting to annoy me, O'Leary," she muttered, heading back out into the kitchen.

She should have known he'd follow her, looming over her as she ground the beans, lounging against her refrigerator. "There are other places to get coffee, O'Leary."

"Yeah, but none of them with such charming company," he shot back. "By the way, where do I buy a pack of cigarettes in this place?"

"You smoke?"

"I'm trying to quit."

The day was looking up. She couldn't keep the wicked smile from her face. "The problem has been taken out of your hands, O'Leary, at least for now. Cigarettes are outlawed in Watson Hole. You can't buy 'em, you can't smoke 'em."

He stared at her in shock. "You're kidding."

"Nope. This is the most politically correct town in the entire United States. You can't wear fur within the city limits, you can't smoke cigarettes, you can't use foam cup or paper napkins or wood heat. You can only buy nonalcoholic wine and beer, you get fined if you use more than a certain amount of gasoline per month, and you get free condoms everywhere you go. They were trying to outlaw red meat, as well, and they've almost succeeded."

"Oh, God," O'Leary said.

"She's allowed, but She has to be multicultural and multigendered."

"What the hell am I doing here?" he murmured to himself.

"You tell me."

They stood in contemplative silence, watching the coffee drip. "I watched *Winter of the Heart* again last night," she said casually. "I noticed that you wrote it."

He looked at her warily, clearly not duped into expecting lavish praise. "So?"

"So how come all the women die in the movie? And how come they have all the personality of a fly-swatter, and how come they're just on screen to give Brandon a chance to take off his shirt or look depressed?"

"Didn't you appreciate Brandon taking off his shirt?" he countered.

"I didn't think a woman had to die for it."

"I gather militant feminism isn't outlawed in Watson Hole. Listen, sweetheart, I didn't write the book, just the adaptation. For which, I might mention, I received a Golden Globe and an Academy Award."

"You must be very proud," she said with spurious sweetness.

He glared at her. "You're very annoying, you know that? If it weren't for your coffee, I'd be half tempted to take you outside and dump you in a snow-bank."

"You and what army?"

He let his eyes run down the length of her, slowly, and it was all she could do not to react. She was wearing black sweatpants and a T-shirt that said The More I Know Of Men, The More I Love My Dog, and her long hair was screwed up in a knot on the top of her head. She seldom bothered with makeup, and today was no exception. He could hardly be impressed.

"I might enjoy trying to give you a taste of your own medicine," he murmured.

Sudden, unexpected sexual heat was in his voice. A heat that curled between her breasts and traveled downward. She took an instinctive step away from him, unsettled. "Yeah, but I make great coffee," she said, pouring him a mug. Hoping he didn't notice that her hand was shaking. "So when are you leaving?"

He took the mug, his hand brushing hers. Hands that were long-fingered, elegant. She cursed inwardly. She'd always been a sucker for beautiful hands. "In a hurry to get rid of us, Meggie? You haven't had a chance to fling yourself at America's sweetheart yet."

"Who says I want to?"

"Everyone wants to, Meggie," he said flatly.

She smiled at him over her own mug of strong, wonderful coffee. "Oh, poor O'Leary. I'm sure there are some women in this world who would settle for you. Don't give up hope."

She was hoping to infuriate him. Instead, he merely gave her a measured look. "I won't, sweetheart."

He set his mug of coffee down on the counter. He took her coffee away from her, as well, setting it down beside his. And then, to her absolute astonishment, he kissed her.

Chapter Three

He tasted like coffee. He tasted like winter, and tooth-paste, and an icy heat that was like nothing she'd ever felt before. Somehow, her body had gotten pressed up against his, his hands were around her waist, holding her, and he was using his mouth like an instrument of the devil, seducing her into a brainless mass of bean sprouts marching toward destruction.

Oh, Lord, and she wanted to go! She wanted to sink into that dizzying mass of need and elusive ful-fillment, she wanted to let her brain go flying free and concentrate only on her body and the powerful, churning reaction he was coaxing from her. He'd pushed her up against the counter, he was using his tongue, and she was just about ready to put her arms around his neck and kiss him back with all the fierce, burning need that had been banked inside her for too long when she heard the front door of the restaurant open.

The shock of it made it easy to shove him away. "It's too early in the morning, O'Leary," she said. Summoning her last ounce of self-control and taking her coffee, she strode past him into the dining room of the restaurant. Before he could see just how badly he'd shaken her.

Nadja was busy hanging her parka on the row of wooden pegs across the back wall, and for some reason her gaze slid away from Meggie's with an almost guilty furtiveness. She knows, Meggie thought.

"How's Brandon?"

Nadja threw back her head and smiled brightly. "Gorgeous, of course. If you'd only woken up in time, you would have been the one to see him. God, Meggie, he's enough to make your teeth ache."

"Too many sweets tend to have that effect," O'Leary drawled, sauntering out of the kitchen.

Nadja's pale skin turned a bright red. "I didn't realize you were still here."

"I'm on my way out," he said. He didn't touch Meggie as he moved past her, and she could almost sense the faint stirring of air currents against her body as he walked by. It felt like a caress.

She said nothing, waiting until he'd left. She could see the street from her vantage point, and she stared after him until he was almost out of sight, halfway up the hill to Madame Rose's. And then she turned to Nadja.

"Something is very wrong," she said in a doleful voice.

"What do you mean?"

"We screwed up. Did the spell backward, summoned an evil twin. I don't know—it's just wrong!"

"Don't be ridiculous. I followed the directions. We used the snowman as our poppet, we cut out a picture of Brandon Scott and stuck it to his chest, I lit the candles, burned the sage and did the incantations. You pictured him in your mind, didn't you, while you were kissing Frosty?"

"I tried," Meggie said.

"And here he is. Five days later, the man of your dreams arrives in town for no discernible reason, he doesn't even know why he's here, and you think something's wrong?" Nadja said with a trace of irritation. "Sometimes you don't know how lucky you are."

"I just wish he hadn't brought O'Leary with him," Meggie said in a small voice, perching on one of the wooden stools and dropping her chin into her hands.

"Why not? I've never known a man to get the better of you, and while O'Leary might come close, I'd still put my money on you anytime." Nadja joined her at the counter, shoving a hand through her frizzy hair. "Besides, he didn't happen to just show up here, any more than Brandon did. There must be some reason why he chose this time to come here. Some destiny he has to fulfill."

"That's what I'm afraid of," Meggie muttered.

"You think he'll come between you and Brandon?"

"Sort of."

"Well, don't let him," Nadja said in a bracing voice. "If you want Brandon Scott, you fight for him, with every fiber of your being. Don't let anything get in your way—not friendship, not second thoughts. Just do it. And don't waste your time with regrets."

There was an odd note in Nadja's voice, one that pulled Meggie out of her self-absorption to stare at her oddly. "You're ten years younger than me—how come you're sounding like Obi Wan Kenobi?"

Nadja's pale mouth curved in a ghost of a grin.

"Age doesn't necessarily equal wisdom, young Sky-walker."

"Too true."

"So what are you worried about? Besides O'Leary trying to throw a monkey wrench into your future?"

She couldn't bring herself to confess the truth. That she was having a hard time even noticing her heart's desire when O'Leary was anywhere around. And O'Leary's unexpected kiss hadn't helped her equilibrium one tiny bit. It was nothing more than hormones run amok—she hadn't been kissed in years, and it was only natural she'd react to it. If it had been Brandon Scott kissing her, with that rich, pouty mouth of his, she probably would have climaxed on the spot. Instead of simply coming perilously close to it.

"I just want to make sure we did it right," she said stubbornly.

Nadja sighed. "Okay, we'll check tonight."

"Why not now?"

"If you want to draw another pentagram in the snow, light candles and have you wrap yourself around Frosty in broad daylight…"

"Tonight will be soon enough," Meggie said hastily. She glanced around the empty restaurant. "I suppose I should start getting ready for the lunch crowd. We've only got two more days of this."

"Maybe we'd be better off closing the place now and concentrating on packing up."

"Then what in God's name would I do with all that leftover tofu and bean sprouts?" Meggie asked.

"Eat it?"

"You're sick, Nadja," she replied, insulted, pushing away from the counter and heading back into the kitchen. The scent of coffee was rich in the air, and O'Leary had left his coffee cup on the counter, where he'd kissed her. She scooped it up, ready to dump it in the sink, but something stopped her. She stared at it for a moment, meditatively. And then, almost without realizing what she was doing, she put her mouth against the rim, where his mouth had pressed.

The realization of what she was doing hit her with a shock, and she dropped the mug on the floor, watching it shatter at her feet. Once again the knowledge hit her, certain and sure. They'd screwed up that incantation. They might have summoned Brandon Scott, but all she could think about was John James O'Leary.

O'Leary was everything she didn't want in a man. Strong, demanding, bad-tempered, forcing himself into her consciousness when she'd rather be dreaming about Brandon Scott. She'd spent almost ten years of her life ignoring men, but O'Leary wasn't a man to be ignored.

And it scared the living hell out of her.

O'Leary would have been all right if he hadn't made the mistake of taking a nap. He'd brought his laptop with him, and once he'd managed a decent breakfast and a gallon of coffee that was far inferior to Meggie's brew, he concentrated on getting some work done. He missed his cigarettes, damn it. Almost as much as he missed seeing Meggie McGraw snarl at him.

Speaking of snarling, he'd had to stay in the

kitchen long enough to pull himself together. If her plain little friend hadn't come in, he would have gotten her to open her mouth to him. He would have lifted her up on the counter, moved in tight between her legs and worked her into the same mindless, lustful, irritated state he was in.

He'd just felt her begin to respond when she pulled away, and he'd kept his reaction to himself as she escaped—there was no other word for it—from the kitchen. He didn't want her knowing what she did to him. Not when even he couldn't figure out why.

Two flights beneath, tourists were trooping through the bordello, giggling at the naughty oil paintings, fascinated by the rough-and-tumble life of times gone by. Up here, all was peaceful, with only the painting of the voluptuous creature over the desk disturbing his thoughts.

He wondered if he could talk the Watson Hole Historical Society into parting with that painting. He doubted it. According to the guidebook, the lush creature reclining on the red velvet sofa was thought to be none other than Madame Rose herself. No one could tell for certain, because her face was hidden, turned away from the artist.

He stretched out on the bed, only planning to rest for a moment or two before he went in search of something decent for lunch. He stared up at Madame Rose, at her creamy white flesh, her thick tumble of honey-streaked hair, and he wished he could see her face. For some reason, she reminded him of Meggie. Though, on second thought, that wasn't so odd. Anything sexual made him think of Meggie.

She came to him in a dream of gaslight and whiskey and the rich, seductive smell of cigarette smoke. Her face was still hidden, her body draped in diaphanous silk, and she looked like an erotic dream come to life. She moved out of the shadows and knelt on the bed beside him.

"Nothing but the best for Madame Rose's private customers," she murmured, reaching for the brass buckle on his jeans. And as her hand trailed over him, he looked up into Meggie McGraw's wickedly gorgeous face.

He woke up with a start, alone on the bed. The darkness of early winter had settled down around the place, and the reconstructed gas lamps outside the front of the building glowed beneath the lightly drifting snowflakes.

There were no cars on the streets, and no electric lights, and for an odd moment he had the sense that he'd traveled through time. That if he stepped outside of his bedroom he'd be stepping into the past, into the time of Madame Rose. He stood leaning on the windowsill, letting his imagination drift. Until he saw Brandon pull up in that car he shouldn't be driving.

He had someone with him, and O'Leary peered down, trying to see who the blonde du jour was. He recognized Meggie's skinny little friend with a sense of shock. There was no mistaking the frizzy hair beneath the scarf, the thick glasses. No mistaking Brandon's effortless charm, even from this distance.

O'Leary pushed away from the window. Brandon always insisted he adored women, all women, but up until now his taste had still seemed to run to perfectly proportioned goddesses.

He went back to his computer, switched it on and stared at the screen in brooding silence, his fingers tapping on the cherrywood table. It was none of his business if Brandon wanted to seduce and abandon Meggie's innocent little friend. As a matter of fact, he ought to be grateful Brandon had set his sights on Nadja, rather than Meggie. O'Leary had yet to meet a woman who was immune to the world's sexiest man.

Though why gratitude should have anything to do with matters was beyond him. Why should it matter whether Brandon slept with Nadja and Meggie?

Because he wanted to sleep with Meggie, he admitted to himself. And the thought of Brandon Scott putting his perfect hands on her gave O'Leary a tension headache.

He switched off the computer and rose. He needed to warn Meggie, he decided. Her best friend was in danger of getting her heart broken, and Meggie would want to know about it. Yes, that was what he would do, he thought. And then maybe he'd look a little harder for a place that sold cigarettes.

He met Brandon walking up the snow-packed street, snowflakes speckling his blond mane. "I don't think you want to go down there, Jay," he said. "You won't be welcome."

"What have you done this time, Brandon?" O'Leary demanded wearily.

"Had a wonderful day with Naddie," he said sweetly. "It doesn't have anything to do with me, or with you, either, I expect. They're doing some sort of Wiccan incantation, and testosterone would upset the balance of nature.''

O'Leary just stared at him. "Oh, my God," he said in disbelief.

"Actually, it's probably 'Oh, my Goddess,'" Brandon said. "They should be finished soon enough. Nadja and I are going out for dinner at the natural-foods restaurant up the mountain. You're welcome to join us.''

O'Leary didn't bother to hide his shudder. "What about Meggie?''

"She can come, too, but Nadja says she hates health foods.''

"Then what's she doing running a health-food restaurant?''

"You hate Hollywood. What are you doing writing screenplays?" Brandon replied with maddening, unanswerable logic.

O'Leary snarled, then started past him down the snow-packed road.

"I really think you ought to leave them alone," Brandon called after him.

"I'm not going to bother them. I'm looking for cigarettes.'' It wasn't an actual lie. He *was* looking for cigarettes. And he had no intention of bothering Meggie and her little friend as they danced naked around a campfire, or whatever it was they were doing. He simply wanted to watch.

It took him a while to find them. They were out in back of the restaurant, in a small side street, and the light from the candles surrounded the odd tableau.

O'Leary ducked into the shadows, watching, and forgot all about cigarettes for the first time since he'd quit.

"Don't you think we should have waited until after midnight?" Meggie demanded, looking over her shoulder uneasily. The alley was deserted, as usual, and overhead a sliver of moon hung crooked in the sky. A witch's moon, Meggie thought, shivering in the icy breeze.

"I need to find out what went wrong." Nadja's fierce quiet was uncharacteristic. She moved around the pentagram, lighting the candles as she sprinkled sage over each one. "I'm not willing to wait."

"Why not?" Meggie was more than willing to wait for an answer she wasn't sure she was ready to have. She didn't want to know that they had screwed up somehow. Strangely enough, she was even more unwilling to find out that everything was as it should be. That Brandon Scott was here for her, and it was just taking both of them a ridiculously long time to realize it.

Nadja shrugged her skinny shoulders. She had a hat pulled down close to her hair, and her brown hair frizzed out the sides. She squinted at the candle, and though Meggie couldn't see behind the thick lenses of Nadja's glasses, she almost suspected that Nadja was crying.

But Nadja was sane, grounded, and had no earthly reason to cry. Whereas Meggie was feeling as if she had a bad case of PMS, when logic and her calendar assured her she didn't.

"All right," she muttered, reaching into her bra for the crumpled page from the magazine. "Let's get it over with." She unfolded it and pressed it against the snowman's bulbous chest, securing it with a tack. "How do we do it this time?"

"The same way," Nadja said. "Put your arms around the snowman, press your breast against the picture, and picture him in your mind. The way he looks in the picture. And then kiss him."

Meggie smoothed the crumpled sheet against Frosty's icy chest. "I'll try," she muttered. "I didn't have too easy a time visualizing him..." Her voice trailed off.

"What's wrong, Meggie?" She heard Nadja's voice coming to her from a distant place, and for a moment she wondered whether she'd fainted. She stepped back from the snowman, bringing the magazine page with her.

She wasn't sure whether to laugh, to curse, or to cry. She looked at the piece of paper clutched in her fist. It was a picture of Brandon Scott, all right, looking tanned and gorgeous at last year's Academy Awards. When she ripped the page out of the magazine, she'd barely noticed the couple standing with him. The Oscar-winning screenwriter John James O'Leary, and his far-too-gorgeous date for the evening.

"I think I found our problem," she said in a dull voice. She passed the damp, wrinkled paper over to her friend. Nadja squinted at it for a moment, then carried it over to one of the candles that were stuck in the snowbank, squatting down to get a better look at the picture. And then her eyes met Meggie's.

"You didn't notice this before?" she asked in a quiet voice.

"It was darker that night. Midnight, in case you'd forgotten, and I think we'd had too much wine. We must have, otherwise we never would have done anything so incredibly stupid in the first place."

"How did you know? How did you guess?" Nadja demanded.

She sounded upset, and Meggie knew she should rouse herself, comfort her best friend over the failure of her first attempt at spell-casting. But right then she was too busy feeling sorry for herself. "I knew," she said in a small, bitter voice. "Blow out the candles, Naddie. We have our answers. Unless you know how to undo it?"

"Meggie, it was a joke. A parlor trick. Don't you remember what it says on everything I sell—'These items are for entertainment purposes solely'? It was nothing but a coincidence that he showed up here."

"There are no coincidences—isn't that what you're always telling me?"

"Well, this time there are." Nadja bent over and blew out the candles, scurrying around the deserted alleyway. "There's a perfectly logical explanation. And the fact that there's another man in the picture shouldn't have any bearing on the matter. You know what you want. Go for it."

"Go for it," Meggie echoed dully. Except she didn't know what she wanted. Her hormones, her heart, were at war with her brain. And she'd made it a policy never to be unduly swayed by common sense.

"I'll take this stuff back to the shop. Brandon's asked us to go up to Zach's for dinner. I told him we'd be ready by seven."

"Zach's?" Meggie echoed. "He'll feed us seaweed for dinner."

"It's entirely natural and full of nutrients."

"It's entirely horrible and full of sand," Meggie shot back. "I'll stay home."

"Meggie, you wanted him..." Nadja said, and there was no missing the sound of desperation in her voice.

"Past tense, Nadja. The spell backfired, and right now I don't give a damn about Brandon Scott, gorgeous as he is. You go and eat seaweed with him. He won't even notice I'm not there."

For a moment, Nadja didn't move. "Are you really certain, Meggie?" she asked, an odd expression on her face. "You really don't want him?"

"After all your hard work? I'm afraid not, kid." Meggie ran a hand through her thick hair. "You go ahead and have a good time. I have to do something about exorcising my particular demon."

Nadja hesitated a moment longer. And then she was gone, disappearing into the starry night with a swirl of her handwoven poncho, leaving Meggie alone in the darkness.

She'd called both of them. And when she put her arms around Frosty, closed her eyes and summoned him, it hadn't been the perfect California beach bum who arrived. It had been someone darker, leaner, meaner.

"O'Leary," she said in a bitter voice, "why in God's name did it have to be you?"

"Just lucky." His voice floated out over the still night air, and for a moment Meggie thought she'd dreamed it. She turned to look at Frosty for one long, uneasy moment, but the great white monolith didn't move. She wondered just how much O'Leary had heard. When the shadows shifted, he stepped forward into the murky moonlight and Meggie's heart stopped beating. "You want to tell me what the hell's going on here, Meggie?"

And for one brief moment, Meggie considered ripping Frosty's head off and heaving it at her unwanted eavesdropper.

Chapter Four

Meggie looked furious, which was no surprise. She was always looking pissed as hell when she looked at him, and O'Leary had grown used to it. This time, however, she looked oddly stricken, as well. As if she'd been told her dog had died.

"Eavesdropping, O'Leary?" she said in a deceptively even voice, kicking out the traces of the pentagram from the snow. "Don't you have any other way to get your jollies?"

"Not in the land of the politically correct," he said.

"You come from L.A. You should be used to political correctness."

"Actually, I live on an old ranch in Montana. The kind of place where you can find a good steak and a pack of cigarettes when you need them. The kind of place where men are men and women are glad of it."

"The kind of place where half of Hollywood has descended and bought up the land at inflated prices from people who've been there for generations. Just who did you rip your place off from, O'Leary?"

"My father. And his father and grandfather before him."

He'd finally managed to shut her up, though he knew it wouldn't last long. There was a meditative expression on her face that he could recognize even in the darkness, as if she was considering whether he might not be the devil incarnate, after all. "What's it like?" she asked in a marginally nicer voice.

"Five hundred acres of hills, rocks and the sweetest little waterfall you've ever seen. My parents sold it to me when my father retired. The two of them drive around the country in an RV the size of Rhode Island, and they told me they weren't coming back to Montana till they had some grandchildren."

He could have sworn she'd turned pale, but it was really too dark to tell. "I didn't know you were married," she said.

"Haven't been for eight years."

"She couldn't put up with you, eh? I can't say I'm surprised."

That was the Meggie he knew and loved. "Yeah, but I've mellowed over the last few years," he said.

"You're a regular pussycat."

He considered crossing the packed snow and kissing her again, and then thought better of it. If he kissed her now, he wasn't going to stop, and he really didn't feel like dropping his jeans in the snow. He'd been hard-pressed to think of anything but her mouth since he'd kissed her that morning, and the longer he waited, the more overpowering the very thought became.

He could wait a few more hours. Until he got her someplace warm, dry and secluded. And he could see whether he'd really flipped out and he was imagining the hot thread of longing in her belligerent eyes whenever she looked at him.

"So where do we find a truly great steak in this crunchy-granola town?" he drawled.

"Saucy Jack's, just up the road from Madame Rose's. And what's this *we,* white man?"

"You aren't going to make me eat alone, are you? With only my dubious self for company?"

"Why would I want to do you any favors?" she said warily.

"You wouldn't. You'd want to pick on me and fight with me some more, and I wouldn't be surprised if you wanted to do it over a good steak." He waited. She was wavering, and he had absolutely no intention of letting her say no. He couldn't rid himself of the feeling that time was running out, and if he didn't move soon, it would be too late, and she'd be gone.

She wasn't in any particular hurry to put him out of his misery. He stood there in the chilly moonlight, waiting, and he had a sudden, strange notion. He could see himself down the years, waiting for her while she tried to figure out the best way to annoy him. And for some reason, that bizarre vision was strangely enticing.

"Are you by any chance asking me out on a date, O'Leary?" she said, her voice laced with suspicion.

"Lord, sweetheart, what if I am? It's not much of a commitment, is it? I'm not asking you to bear my children."

Now he'd really managed to startle her, and he couldn't figure out why. For some reason, she was treating this as if the fate of the world, or at the very least, the rest of her life, rested on the answer. If she tried to say no, he'd just start kissing her.

"Okay," she said, in such a small voice that for a moment he doubted he'd heard her correctly.

There was something odd going on. The cool night air was dry and sparkling with electricity, and for some strange reason he glanced over at the snowman, wishing he'd heard more of Meggie's conversation with Nadja. Frosty just squatted there impassively enough, but for some reason O'Leary could almost imagine an expression on that bulbous face. One of sly amusement.

"Okay you'll go to dinner with me?" he asked. "Or okay you'll have my babies?"

He wanted to see if he could push her far enough to find out why she'd panicked, but she'd already gotten past whatever was troubling her. "For a great steak, I'd go out with Newt Gingrich," she said. "And Saucy Jack's has great steaks. As for the kids, if you want your parents to visit that badly, then maybe you'd better rent some."

"Don't you want kids?"

For some reason, she glanced at the snowman. "All in good time, O'Leary," she said. "All in good time."

This was a major mistake, Meggie thought as she walked beside him up the hilly street. Behind her she could just imagine Frosty, watching them as they headed toward the steak house.

None of this made any sense. She didn't believe in magic spells, she didn't believe in snowmen, she didn't believe in summoning people or love at first sight. And most of all, she couldn't believe how much she wanted O'Leary, the bad-tempered swine, to kiss her again.

She'd been presented with a choice back there, a simple enough choice. She'd wanted Brandon Scott, who was rich, famous, gorgeous and sweet. She'd summoned him, and ever since he'd arrived all she could think of was his traveling companion, who wasn't nearly as pretty, rich or famous. Not to mention the fact that he was singularly devoid of sweetness.

There was no use reasoning with herself, berating herself, or hiding in her apartment over the store any longer. The moment she kissed the snowman, she'd put these events into motion, and she couldn't fight them anymore. It was time to give in and see what happened.

Saucy Jack's was packed. It was December 30, the night before New Year's Eve, and like most ski resorts, the town was crowded to capacity. O'Leary made no effort to help her with her coat, which was a good thing. She probably would have smacked him. The bar and anteroom were jammed with people. "Looks like we're in for a long wait," he said.

"Not necessarily." She started back toward the kitchen, and he followed.

"Meggie, darling!" the burly, bearded chef called out to her from across the madhouse of a kitchen. "You've been a stranger!"

"Not tonight, Jack," she called back. "Anyone in the Vegetarian Room?"

"It's yours, Meggie. Who's your friend? Do I smell love in the air?"

Saucy Jack was well named. Fortunately, Meggie had her back to O'Leary, so he couldn't see her uncharacteristic blush. "You smell burning steak, Jack," she said severely, as she started up the winding metal stairs.

She was oddly breathless by the time she got to the private dining room, and she told herself it was the steep climb, rather than the man who followed close behind her. The first floor of the restaurant held the public rooms, and the second held a series of smaller private dining rooms. Most of them were filled, as well—she could tell from the noise of muted conversation. She opened the door to the Vegetarian Room and then almost closed it again.

It was too late to back out. "Here we are," she said brightly, strolling in.

She'd forgotten that the room looked like something out of Madame Rose's Palace—forgotten the huge overstuffed sofas, the candlelight, the decadent Victorian lushness of the place.

But O'Leary was already closing the door behind them. "I hope this doesn't mean we eat vegetables tonight?" he murmured, leaning against it. Barring her escape.

She didn't want to escape, did she? "The Vegetarian Room is the most private of all Jack's private dining rooms. It's for those clean-living souls in town who don't want to be seen when they eat red meat and drink whiskey."

He glanced at the overstuffed sofa. "Are those the only sins people indulge in around here?"

She knew what he was thinking. She knew, because she was thinking the same thing. "Most people have their own bedrooms, O'Leary," she said sharply.

He moved away from the door, starting toward her, and she took a deep breath, waiting. She liked his face. It wasn't pretty, like Brandon's. It was narrow and clever and dangerously intelligent, and his dark eyes held secrets that enticed her. She didn't even dare look at his mouth, for fear that she'd fling herself against him.

She liked his body, too. She liked tall men, men who were lean and strong, rather than bulky. And his hands made her hot and cold at the same time.

She wanted his hands, and his mouth, on her. And she wasn't used to this feeling, this wanting. She took a tiny step backward, coming up against the table. Then the door opened and the waiter appeared.

She didn't realize her sigh of relief was audible until she saw the faint, ironic grin on O'Leary's face. O'Leary's mouth. "It's only delayed," he murmured under his breath, holding her chair for her with mocking politeness.

They ate red meat and drank wine. They had coffee and cognac and sinfully wonderful cheesecake. They talked, and they laughed. And Meggie could feel herself fall deeper and deeper under Frosty's spell. Or was it O'Leary's spell? She could no longer tell.

They'd ended up on the sofa. A dangerous move, but so far he'd kept his distance, lounging in one corner while she curled up in the opposite, her hands cradling the glass of cognac. "So are you going to tell me what was going on with the snowman?" he asked lazily, and she was too warm and too comfortable to be wary.

"I suppose so. Do you believe in magic?"

"No."

She smiled into her cognac snifter. "Spells? Crystals? Incantations?"

"I don't even believe in destiny," O'Leary said.

"Then it would be a waste of time trying to explain to you what happened."

"Try me," he murmured. And she told herself there was no double meaning.

"It was the night of the winter solstice. A night of great magical power," she began.

"If you say so."

"Don't interrupt me if you want to hear this." Her voice was stern.

"Sorry."

"Nadja and I decided to see if we could work a little magic. The restaurant was closing, I'd had enough of Watson Hole, and I decided I needed a handsome prince to rescue me."

"Oh, let me guess," he said. "Brandon Scott."

"It's half your fault," she protested, still feeling stupid. "If you hadn't made him so appealing in that sexist movie..."

"If *Winter of the Heart* was so sexist, why did you even bother to see it?"

"After the seventh time, it began to annoy me," she said with great dignity. "But you've got to admit, the boy is devastatingly pretty."

"He's not my type," O'Leary drawled, watching her.

"I don't think he's my type, either," Meggie admitted mournfully.

"You're getting sidetracked," he said, but she thought his dark, dark eyes looked vaguely pleased.

"We decided to see if we could summon Brandon to Watson Hole. Nadja works with me, but she also runs a new-age bookstore, you know. She has access to everything—crystals, incantations, herbs and candles. And I must admit we'd had a little too much wine with our pizza. So we decided to see if we could turn the snowman into Brandon Scott."

"You've been listening to too many Christmas songs," he said. "Obviously it didn't work. Frosty's still there."

"But so is Brandon. He showed up a week later, for no particular reason. He just arrived at my doorstep, as if he'd been summoned."

He stared at her. "That's why you screamed."

She nodded. "It was unnerving, to say the least. I hadn't really believed it would work. Even when I kissed Frosty..."

"You kissed the snowman?"

"It was part of the spell." She couldn't help the defensive note in her voice.

"And how do snowmen kiss?" He'd somehow moved closer. He'd finished his own cognac, and his tanned, beautiful hands were free. She clutched her own glass more tightly.

"Not as well as Brandon Scott."

He froze. "When did you kiss Brandon?"

"I haven't. But I've seen all his movies, even the bad ones. He's one of the all-time great kissers."

"And you're one of the all-time great idiots," he shot back. "Don't you know that screen kisses are all show? There's a technique to them, and it has nothing to do with real kissing.''

Meggie shrugged. "I'll take your word for it.''

"No, you won't." He took the glass of cognac out of her hand and set it on the table in front of the couch. She considered fighting him for it, but then she decided it would be undignified. If he was going to kiss her again, and she strongly suspected he intended to, then she was determined to be cool and unruffled.

He slid his hand along her neck, tilting her face up to his. "With a screen kiss," he said, "you put your mouth at a slant, alongside the partner's mouth. Depending on how passionate it's supposed to look, you grind your jaw up and down a lot.''

"It sounds painful." Her voice was no more than a whisper.

"It's not very arousing." His voice was low, too, persuasive. Dignity, she reminded herself, staring at his mouth. "Whereas a real kiss is an erotic feast in itself." His thumb brushed across her lips, and they parted, trembling. "One open mouth against another," he whispered. "Tongue and teeth, heart and soul.''

He still didn't move closer. Meggie felt hot and cold at the same time, and light-headed with longing. Her heart was beating so loud and so fast, she wondered that he didn't hear it. "It sounds very... pleasant," she whispered.

His smile was slow, and incredibly erotic. "Pleasant?" he echoed in a soft voice. "I could make you come just by kissing you."

She stared at him, transfixed, breathless, waiting. Only to have him move away from her, leaving her unkissed. "So you really believe you brought Brandon Scott here by kissing a snowman?" he said.

It took her only a moment to pull herself out of the trance. "There was more to it than that. We had to put a picture of Brandon on Frosty's chest. And that's where we screwed up."

"Oh, yeah?"

"You're beginning to annoy me, O'Leary," she said, reaching for her cognac and draining it.

"Beginning to? I thought it was hostility at first sight."

"Exactly."

"So how did you screw up?"

"I put the wrong picture on Frosty's chest. It was Brandon, all right. But you and some blond bimbo were in the picture, as well."

"Blond bimbo?"

"Someone with enormous breasts, clinging to your arm and looking at you like you hung the moon."

"Oh, Annabelle," he said, remembering. "Actually, it was the bra she was wearing. I don't think she's any better endowed than you are."

"I might hit you, O'Leary," she said in a meditative voice.

"You've had too much cognac." He reached for the empty glass, but she clung to it tightly. "So you ended up summoning both of us?"

"Obviously."

"Obviously," he echoed wryly. "And you expect me to believe that?"

"You're here, aren't you?"

She'd managed to startle him out of his obnoxious superiority. "A coincidence."

"There is no such thing as coincidence," she intoned.

"You've definitely had too much cognac." He rose, stretched, and she looked up at his lean body with confused, disgruntled longing. "Come on, Meggie, a little fresh air will do wonders. I'll walk you home and put you to bed so you can sleep it off."

He reached down, caught her hand and hauled her to her feet. She stumbled against him, and his arm came around her to steady her. Their faces were close, dangerously close.

Meggie knew exactly how much she'd had to drink. One glass of wine and a snifter of brandy. She could drink most ski bums under the table when she was in the mood, and it wasn't the alcohol that was making her dizzy and irrational.

She wasn't about to tell him that. "Such a perfect gentleman," she said coolly, pushing him away. "Let's go."

He caught up with her halfway down the snow-packed street. A light snow had begun to fall, but Meggie was ignoring it. Ignoring him, even though he had her jacket in his hand and it was probably in the low twenties. "You're going to freeze to death," he said as he caught up with her.

"It'll sober me up," she managed to say.

"You still haven't explained why you haven't flung yourself at Brandon since he arrived."

"I told you, we screwed up."

"So you got me, as well? What's the big deal? Just ignore me."

She stopped, glaring up at him in the moonlight. "Don't you think I haven't tried? You are amazingly obtuse, aren't you, O'Leary? I didn't get you, as well. I got you instead. Brandon is the one who came along for the ride."

He stared at her. Without a word, he put her coat around her, pulling it tight. Pulling her against him. She didn't fight him or pull back. She simply let him put his hands on her.

"You're telling me that Frosty didn't turn into Brandon Scott? He turned into me?"

"You got it," she said. "Though I think he kisses better."

"I doubt it," he said. And finally, finally, he put his mouth against hers.

Chapter Five

She was cold, so cold, but where her body pressed up against his, she was burning hot. His mouth against hers was cold, as well, tasting of snow and cognac and coffee. She was trapped against him, imprisoned by the coat flung over her shoulders, and she had no desire to escape. She tilted her head back, closed her eyes and let him kiss her, fighting the overwhelming urge to kiss him back.

If she kissed him back, she'd be lost, forever. She didn't believe in magic, in spells, in summoning forth spirits, and she certainly didn't believe in snowmen. O'Leary lifted his head, and when she opened her eyes she could see him looking down at her.

"I'm still in one piece," she said. But her voice shook slightly, and some of the grimness vanished from his eyes.

"Yeah," he said, "but you had to fight it."

She wanted him to kiss her again, but he didn't. He simply pulled the coat more closely around her, threaded his arm through hers and continued down the snowy street.

They stopped outside Madame Rose's Palace. There was no sign of Brandon Scott's sports car, and the building was almost dark. O'Leary glanced up at the place, making no effort to release Meggie's arm.

"I thought you were going to walk me home," she said in a deceptively even voice.

"This is as far as you're going tonight," he said.

"Says who?" As a response, it lacked a certain sophistication, but right then Meggie wasn't feeling sophisticated.

"Me," O'Leary said. "Come inside and I'll ply you with cognac."

"You told me I'd had too much."

"I lied."

"I'm not going to sleep with you, O'Leary," she warned him as she climbed up Madame Rose's front steps.

"Fine," he said. "I'll do my best to keep you awake."

She should turn and run. She wanted to. He wasn't holding her that tightly, and he certainly wasn't going to coerce her. If she wanted to leave, to run away, all she had to do was pull her arm away, wish him goodnight and walk away.

She stepped inside the perfumed parlor of Madame Rose's bordello and let him close the door behind her. He locked it, barred it, but he didn't bother to turn on the lights. The tiny, decorative white lights from the shrubbery cast a pale glow inside, enough that she could see his face. She backed up, instinctively, not sure why she did so, coming up against the solid hardwood door.

"If you put the chain on, how will Brandon get back in?" Her voice was low, hushed in the dim light.

"He's already found someplace else to spend the night."

Meggie made a little grimace. "I don't imagine Nadja will be too happy about that," she said. "She seems to be reacting to him the way I was supposed to."

"I think she'll be very happy. No one's ever said Brandon isn't good in bed, and he's sleeping with her."

She accepted that information calmly enough. "Good for her. I hope," she added, honestly enough. She glanced behind her at the barred door. "And how am I supposed to get out?"

"Just lift the chain, Meggie. No one's forcing you to stay here," he said, as he pushed the coat from her shoulders. It fell in a pile on the floor, and she shivered.

"I don't think this is a good idea." She couldn't keep from watching his big, beautiful hands as they stripped off his jacket.

"Why not? It's fate. You summoned me, you say, whether you wanted to or not. So here I am, primed and ready."

"You don't believe that."

"I'm here, aren't I? And I want you. I believe that much."

The flat honesty of his words shook her. "Listen, all you have to do is drive up to the ski resort, and you can have your pick of dozens of women who look just like…like that woman in the picture," she said, somewhat desperately. Why the hell had she come in with him? What had happened to all her carefully honed self-protective instincts?

"I don't want a woman like Annabelle. If I did, I would have stayed in Hollywood. I want you."

"Stop saying that!"

"Why not? It's true." He seemed more fascinated than offended by her protest.

"You don't even know me. You know nothing about who I am, my hopes, my fears, my dreams…"

"Sweetheart, just because I want to strip off your clothes and screw your brains out doesn't mean we need to get involved. I'm talking a one-night stand here, not a lifetime commitment."

Her outrage finally vanquished her nervousness. "You despicable cretin," she said furiously, pushing away from the door. "You slimy, sexist, brain-dead pig. You have the soul of a turnip and the moral standards of a water closet. You—"

He caught her, pulling her up against him, and she could see that he was laughing. "And you have a way with words, Meggie. I'd much rather have you pissed at me than scared."

She should have ripped herself out of his arms, but for some reason she couldn't. "I don't get scared."

"Bullshit, Meggie. You say I don't know you? Wrong, lady. I know you more intimately than people I've known for decades."

"I'm so glad I'm that easy to figure out," she said bitterly.

"You're not at all easy. You're a bundle of contradictions. It must be that your magic snowman is giving me a little help."

"I never should have told you," she muttered.

He threaded his long fingers through her tangled

hair, the gesture unbearably intimate, as he tilted her face up to his. "Shall I tell you about yourself, Meggie? Prove how well I know you? I know you're impatient, too smart for your own good, trying damned hard to be a cynic and losing because you've got a dreamer's heart. You're loyal, generous, and self-sacrificing, and deep underneath your tough exterior you're scared to death."

"I'm not afraid of anything," she protested in a hoarse voice.

"You're afraid of everything, Meggie. You're afraid of commitment, of being alone. You're afraid of downhill skiing and tofu and bean sprouts, you're afraid of magic, and you're afraid of men. And most of all, you're afraid of me and what I might make you feel."

It was a good thing the hallway was dark. He wouldn't be able to see that her face had drained of color. She couldn't see it, either, but she could feel it. The stricken expression that no amount of defenses could keep from her face as he summed her up so damned accurately.

She made one last effort. "You're ridiculous. If I'm afraid of men, how come I tried to summon Brandon—?"

"Because he's a fantasy. A mindless, pretty little boy who wouldn't threaten or challenge you in any way. He's someone perfectly safe. And for some reason, you're looking for safety."

"Obviously I'm not going to get it with you," she managed to say.

"Obviously not. But I'm not convinced it's what you really want."

"You are egocentric, aren't you?" she said with a respectably cool tone, despite the fact that his long fingers still cradled her face. "Why don't you let go of me, and I'll take myself back home to my apartment? Alone."

"I can do that, Meggie," he said. "If you kiss me."

She rolled her eyes. "I've already kissed you, O'Leary. Twice. And, frankly, the earth didn't move."

He ran his thumb across her lower lip, and despite her best efforts, it trembled. "Meggie, Meggie," he whispered, bending toward her. "You stood still, patient and well behaved, while I kissed you. That's not the same as you kissing me back, and if you haven't realized that by now, then you're even more innocent than I thought."

"I'm not innocent," she protested, deeply offended.

"Prove it, Meggie. Kiss me, and then walk away."

He knew her too well. How he'd managed to see right through her well-disguised fears was a mystery, but she wasn't going to give him the satisfaction of realizing he was right.

"Certainly," she said in a brisk voice, sliding her hand up the side of his neck and pressing her lips against him. Hard. And then she backed away, and he released her, his dark eyes watching her.

"There," she said, ready to leave.

"Surely you can kiss better than that, Meggie," he

taunted her. "You're such a connoisseur of screen kisses, I'd think you'd had a little more practice."

"I've had plenty of practice."

"Prove it."

"O'Leary..." she protested.

"Kiss me again, Meggie. Do a thoroughly indecent job of it, and I promise never to taunt you again."

"Promises, promises." But she made the very foolish mistake of stepping up to him again, putting her hands up on his shoulders and tilting her mouth up to his. He didn't move, didn't do anything to help her, and she knew perfectly well that a fast, hard kiss wouldn't help her vanquish her fears and this annoying man.

"Kissing is a highly overrated activity," she said severely.

"You obviously haven't been kissing the right men."

She put her mouth against his, softer this time. His lips were firm, well-defined, and she allowed herself a tentative nibble with her own. He still didn't move, just stood there, patient, as she slowly explored the outside of his mouth.

She touched his lower lips with her tongue, and he opened his mouth to her, with far more patience than she would have thought O'Leary capable of. He waited for her, and she advanced, carefully, ready to retreat at the first sign of aggression. But he simply stood there, letting her learn the contours of his mouth.

She liked it. Oddly enough, it was almost as if she'd never kissed anyone in her life. Maybe kissing

Frosty had opened up a whole new realm in the heretofore unappreciated world of kissing.

She grew a bit more enthusiastic, sliding her arms around his neck, pressing her body up against his. His hand stayed at his sides, not touching her, a fact that she found vaguely annoying and insulting, until she happened to rub against his groin and discovered just how aroused he was.

She broke the kiss, meaning to step back, but she couldn't. She simply took a deep breath and moved closer, pulling his head down so that she could kiss him again, and this time he kissed her back.

His hands slid up her thighs, bringing her loose skirt with him until he cupped her hips, pulling her tight against him. She shivered slightly in the cool night air, and when he broke the kiss she felt as if she were going to explode.

"Are you going to run away, Meggie?" he whispered. "Or are you going to come upstairs with me?"

"I'm coming upstairs with you," she said.

If he wasn't so damned turned on, he would have laughed. She sounded like someone facing her execution, and she put her ice-cold hand in his and let him draw her up the two flights of stairs so many couples had traveled, for exactly the same purpose, with all the enthusiasm of an early Christian martyr.

Who would have thought fierce, fiery Meggie would be shy and uncertain? Who would have thought someone who aroused such lusciously sexual feelings inside him would herself be sexually timid? It was all part of the enigma of Meggie McGraw, and before he'd even realized it, the stakes had risen tremendously. He had to go about making love to her with the dedication of an artist. One wrong move and he could cause irreparable harm.

He shouldn't feel uncertain. He was a sensual man, talented and creative in bed. He knew tricks, moves, ways to arouse the most stubborn woman. But tricks wouldn't do with Meggie. He refused to consider why, but the rest of his life depended on the next few hours. And if he wasn't so turned on, he'd be almost as scared as fearless Meggie McGraw.

He didn't bother to turn on the light. He closed the door, took her cool, limp hand in his and placed it against his chest. Against his pounding heart. "Tell me, Meggie," he whispered in a calming voice, "did someone do something to turn you off?"

"No." The word was almost inaudible. It was also a lie.

For some reason, he decided to push it as he began unfastening the tiny buttons of her sweater, starting at her throat. "No one hit you? Forced you? Raped you?"

She jerked her head up, staring at him, that heartbreaking mix of fear and courage in her eyes. "Life isn't always that simple, O'Leary," she said. "I'm sorry, but I just find all this a highly overrated activity."

Relief swept through him. "Not like in books or the movies, is that it? No waves crashing?"

"No."

"And exactly how many lovers have you had, Meggie?"

"Four hundred and thirty-seven," she snapped. "Is that enough?"

"Obviously not." He'd finished unbuttoning the sweater, though she didn't seem to have noticed. She was wearing a soft, lacy bra, God bless her, with a front clasp. He undid it, and for a moment she panicked, wrapping her arms around her chest.

"Change your mind, Meggie?"

For a moment, she didn't move. She glanced over at the huge, rumpled bed where he'd spent the afternoon napping, dreaming erotic dreams of her. And then she looked at him.

"No, I haven't changed my mind," she said in a small voice.

"Then let me see your breasts."

After a moment, she dropped her arms, still looking like a martyr. He moved closer to her, pushing the sweater off her shoulders, pushing the bra with it, so that she stood in front of him in her long, full skirt, her thick hair tangled around her shoulders, like a Pre-Raphaelite beauty.

Before he could touch her, she put her hands out, and he half expected her to push him away, to grab her discarded clothes and run. Instead, she reached out and began to unfasten the buttons on his soft denim shirt, staring at them with single-minded determination, as her beautiful breasts rose and fell with her labored breathing.

Her hands touched his skin, cool against his heated flesh, as she pushed the shirt from him. And then her eyes met his, defiantly. "Next?" she said.

"Your smart mouth won't protect you, Meggie," he said.

"It won't?"

"You don't need protection from me." And he kissed her so softly on her mouth that he felt her soften and melt.

Never in his life had he had the faintest desire to carry a woman to bed. Without thinking, he scooped Meggie up, holding her tight against his chest, skin to skin, and moved across the room with her. He laid her down on the bed, covering her body with his, covering her breasts with his hands, pressing his groin against the cradle of her thighs, as he kissed her, slowly, letting her accustom herself to the feel of his mouth against hers, his chest against her breasts, his erection pressing against her belly.

She kissed him back, sooner than he could have hoped. He felt her fingers trace the muscles on his shoulders, down his arms, and he let his mouth descend the side of her neck, nibbling, tasting.

She stiffened when he put his mouth on her breast, then leaned back, determinedly patient. Something else she didn't like, as well as kissing. Something else he'd have to teach her to appreciate.

She was a quick student, a fact that clearly surprised her. Her hands, which had lain passively against the sheets, reached up and caught in his hair. Within moments her back was arching and her hips were moving restlessly, as he moved his mouth to her other breast, feeling the nub harden against his tongue.

He was going to take it slow, spend the entire night

carefully seducing her into a state of mindless oblivion, despite the cost to his own well-being, but she was already racing past him. He could feel her tension, her astonishment and her need, and he could only thank God he wouldn't have to risk insanity by waiting much longer.

He tore the button on her skirt, yanking it off her, taking her lacy panties with it. She'd closed her eyes, and he knew he could unfasten his jeans and take her like some Edwardian bride. And he could make her enjoy it.

But it would be cheating. He took her hand in his, and she opened her eyes, wary, some of the haze of bewildered desire fading. He put her hand on the stiff bulge beneath his zipper, half expecting her to pull away.

She didn't. She stared at him for a moment, and then her long fingers stroked down the length of swollen denim, so that it was he who closed his eyes with a groan of impossible longing, ready to explode.

But she deserved better than that. He pushed her onto her back, very gently, and used his mouth on her, nibbling at her breasts, kissing her navel, putting it between her legs until she was beating at his shoulders, gasping with frustrated need that he could fulfill so easily.

But he wasn't going to make her come that way. Not without him. He shoved off his pants, then moved up over her, filling her with one thick, sure thrust, holding very still as she convulsed around him.

He waited until the first wave passed, and then he began to move, pushing in deep, pulling out and then thrusting deeper still. At first she could barely respond. She simply lay beneath him, accepting, her body still shaken with the aftermath of her climax.

But she was capable of more, and he knew it, even if she had her doubts. He felt the rise of tension once more, the occasional soft cry. He buried his head against the side of her neck, lost in the scent and texture of her, of Meggie, learning her delight and his, and when he heard her cry out in choking need, he put his hand between them, touching her.

Her cry drained his soul, drained his body, and he poured himself into her, lost, his teeth on her shoulder, his heart in hers.

He wasn't sure who regained some portion of sanity first. It should have been him. He should have taken it all in stride—he was used to the transcendent pleasures of lovemaking.

Ah, but he wasn't used to the transcendent pleasures of making love with Meggie McGraw. The way she curled up against him, hiding her tear-damp face against his chest, oddly, endearingly shy, tore at his heart. Her faint, watery sigh made him long to tighten his gentle hold on her, and the feel of her smooth, warm skin made him hard again.

She slept, exhausted, against him, curled up trustingly. In the warm room, he cupped her breasts, and they hardened instantly against his skin. He stared down at her, at the salty streaks of tears that ran down her pale face, and he told himself to ignore the strange burst of joy and panic that battled inside him.

He could leave. He could always leave. Hadn't he told her it was a one-night stand?

Chapter Six

When Meggie awoke, she was alone in the rumpled bed. A murky twilight filtered in the window, and she burrowed deeper into the feather bed, deciding it had to be near dawn. She closed her eyes and breathed in the scent of him. Of them.

Her body tingled with the afterglow of all the things he'd done to her. All the things she'd done to him. He'd lied to her—he'd let her sleep, but not for long. She would drift off, sated, replete, and then awake, to find him wrapped around her, inside her, just as she was ready for him.

She hadn't been kissing the right men, he'd told her, and the truth of that was unavoidable. None of her options were particularly appealing. Either she was extremely difficult to please, or the magic she and Nadja had conjured on the winter solstice had been powerful indeed. Or the third, most terrifying possibility of all. That, by some twisted joke of fate, O'Leary was her destiny. A destiny he said he didn't believe in.

She didn't want O'Leary. She wanted someone safe and nonthreatening, someone who could give her children and freedom and leave her alone. She expected that making those children would be the same slightly uncomfortable, slightly ridiculous situation it had always been before, but it was one she was willing to put up with.

But not after O'Leary.

She could still feel his hands on her. His mouth covering her body. The feel of him, inside her. She could feel him, and she wanted him again, needed him.

She opened her eyes in the semidarkness, wondering where he'd disappeared to at the crack of dawn. And then she focused on the carriage clock by the bed in disbelief. It was half past nine in the morning.

She stumbled out of the bed, dragging the sheet with her, and headed for the window. She knew what she'd find before she got there.

A storm had blown up during the night, something very close to a blizzard. The visibility was so limited she couldn't even see the street outside Madame Rose's. But she knew what wouldn't be there. O'Leary's car.

Except that it wasn't O'Leary's, she reminded herself absently. It was Brandon's. And he was probably gone, as well.

She turned and looked over the room. He'd managed to pack everything without waking her, an amazing feat, considering how lightly she usually slept. But then, she'd had far more than her usual share of exercise the night before—she probably could have slept through a herd of elephants.

No note to be seen. O'Leary had left after his one-night stand, just as he'd warned her. If she'd had any sense at all, she'd be relieved.

After all, if she'd enjoyed sleeping with one man,

she could probably find another who'd be as good, or better. Someone with a sweeter nature than O'Leary, which wouldn't be hard to find.

It took her almost half an hour to make the ten-minute walk back to the health-food restaurant, battling the weather. It was no surprise that the place was dark and deserted, with no sign of Nadja. After all, New Year's Eve was technically their last day of business, but their customers had already found new places to patronize, and the weather was hardly conducive to impulse shopping.

She headed straight upstairs to her apartment, to her shower, marveling at her wonderful calm. Nothing could touch her, she thought as she used up every bit of hot water, scrubbing her body. Her defenses were back in place, no one could hurt her. Her interlude with O'Leary had been…instructive, but it was a fortunate thing he'd up and disappeared without any embarrassing morning-after scene. Now she could get on with her life, without his annoying presence. She had plans to make, places to go.

She found the note lying on the counter when she wandered out into the dining room, a cup of coffee in one hand, and for a moment her heart leaped inside her, and the coffee trembled in her hand. She set the mug down carefully on the counter. Reaching for the paper, she told herself that Nadja's scrawling handwriting was a relief. And who else would have left her a note?

Meggie—I've gone to California with Brandon. Please don't be angry with me. You're right—

we must have screwed up on the incantation. All I know is I can't help myself.

I couldn't find you to tell you we were leaving—we wanted to get out before the blizzard hit. Brandon says to tell O'Leary that he can keep the car for now. Don't be mad at me.

I'm sorry about the snowman. Nadja.

Meggie set the paper down again. It was past noon by now, and that strange, eerie light continued as the storm battered the village. It was going to be a hell of a New Year's Eve she thought. And then the last sentence registered.

She ran outside into the deep snow, with no coat and only her canvas sneakers on her feet. The storm was too thick for her to see more than a few feet ahead of her, but she didn't hesitate. She stumbled toward the side alleyway, searching for the rounded shape of the magic snowman.

He lay in a pile of snow, smashed to pieces, already covered with a thick layer of new snow. Someone had driven into him, most likely, or some teenage hooligan had taken a shovel to him. It didn't matter. He was gone, as surely as if he'd melted in the bright sun. For a moment, Meggie stood there, unmoving, as the snow coated her hair and eyebrows.

"What the hell you doing out here, Meggie?" The snowplow driver leaned out the window and shouted through the whirling snow. "This stuff's gonna keep up for another five or six hours. Best go get warm."

She shook herself, and the snow went flying.

"Thanks, Danny," she said numbly, turning away from the ruins of her one brief bout of magic.

"Sorry about your snowman," he called as he rolled up the window. "You can always make another, if this snow keeps up."

She didn't even bother to give him a reassuring smile—he wouldn't have seen it through the whirling snow. Instead, she just waved at him.

The power went off just as she reached the restaurant. She'd left the door open in her mad dash outside, and already snow had drifted into the front entrance. She slammed the door shut against it, kicked off her shoes and walked barefoot on the cold, wet floor.

She sat down at the counter, picked up her coffee and burst into tears.

Life certainly was a pain in the butt when you least needed it to be, O'Leary thought furiously, reaching automatically for the cigarettes that were never there. It was always two steps forward and one step back. Sure, he'd gotten to spend the most earth-shattering night of his thirty-seven years with a woman who fascinated him almost to the point of obsession. But after that his mental processes had melted entirely.

It had made perfect sense to him at four-thirty in the morning. He'd throw all his stuff in the back of Brandon's stupid little car, make the four-hour drive north into Montana in three hours flat, pick up the Jeep, tell Marge to expect visitors, and be back before she even realized he'd left town.

Of course, he'd reckoned without a blizzard clamping down over the highway once he'd reached the halfway point. And top-of-the-line all-weather radials didn't do diddly-squat in deep, drifting snow. He made it to the ranch—or, more exactly, to a snowdrift half a mile away from the main house, in just over six hours. Only to find that the phone was out once he got there.

He kept telling himself that Meggie was a reasonable woman, and he knew he lied. Her very lack of reasonableness was part of her dubious charm.

He told himself she had to know him well enough to realize he wouldn't have just taken off. And he knew that was exactly what she'd believe.

He paced the old pine floors of the sprawling ranch house, staring out into the storm with mounting frustration and something oddly akin to panic. Three times he tried to leave, only to have the wind whip up the fallen snow into a cloud of zero visibility. The fourth time, just after five o'clock in the afternoon, he kept going, headlights piercing the swirling snow and the pitch-black night.

The snow turned to a mushy kind of sleet sometime in the middle of the afternoon. Meggie sat alone in the deserted café, listening to the most lugubrious country music she could find on the battery-powered radio, and stared out into the storm. She was drinking lukewarm diet Coke now, and eating everything in sight as she waited for the power to come back on. For the snow to stop. So she could get the hell out of there.

Not that her ancient Toyota was all that good in deep snow. It didn't matter. As long as she was out of Watson Hole by the New Year, she'd be all right, she promised herself. She could put the past behind her.

And never, ever, would she kiss a snowman again.

Oddly enough, she mourned Frosty. Instead of brooding over O'Leary's expectedly faithless ways, she concentrated on the tumbled pile of snow that had once embodied her romantic dreams. Of course, they'd been the wrong romantic dreams, summoning the wrong man to interfere with her carefully arranged life-style, but nevertheless, she mourned him.

The lightweight snow from the blizzard would have been worthless for packing. Once it warmed to a wet sleet, Meggie pulled on ski bibs that had never seen a ski slope, tucked her feet into her warmest pair of boots and headed out into the afternoon light. The wet snow plastered her face and hair, soaking through her down parka. She didn't care.

It took her almost an hour to finish building the new snowman, on the very spot where Frosty had stood. The new version was a sleeker one, taller, with a rakish tilt to his head that somehow reminded her of O'Leary in one of his baiting moods. As she worked, she hummed under her breath, a tuneless little hum that was part "Frosty the Snowman" and part "You Can't Get a Man with a Gun." When she finished, it was fully dark, the lights were still out around town, and the sleet had turned to a sullen rain.

Meggie looked up at her snowman with a jaundiced eye. "I'm going to keep away from cold climates, kid," she said aloud. "At the very least, I'm going to avoid snow." She leaned forward, putting her arms around his middle. "In the meantime, take care of yourself, Frosty. And thanks for O'Leary. Even if he is a son of a bitch."

She pressed her mouth against Frosty's freshly ice-packed face. And then she headed back to the café, determined to get the hell out of Dodge before she asked the snowman to bring O'Leary back to her.

It shouldn't have taken her long to pack. She was a woman who traveled light, and even if some inexplicable part of her had started longing for some kind of permanency, she hadn't yet started acquiring the things that made moving a royal pain.

Within an hour, working by candlelight, she'd managed to pack up her clothes, books and CDs and drag them downstairs to the front door. She glanced back at the kitchen, strongly tempted to walk away and never look at another bean sprout, but she couldn't do that to Nadja. Sooner or later she'd be back, once she realized that all men, Brandon Scott included, were pigs, and she wouldn't want to deal with a refrigerator full of moldy health food.

Meggie yanked open the refrigerator and stared inside in dismay. Blocks of tofu filled the second shelf, sitting in slimy bean water. On the shelf above, bean sprouts grew, their little tentacles stretching down toward the tofu as if they were separated lovers.

With a shudder, Meggie started hauling out the tofu, dumping it in the trash. A big block slipped out of its protective wrapper, landing on the butcher-block counter with an ominous splat, and Meggie just stared at it, wondering if she could steel herself to pick it up with her bare hands.

She was so engrossed in her battle of self-will that she didn't hear the front door open. She'd just managed to force herself to touch the gelatinous mass when O'Leary sauntered in the door, looking cold, ice-coated, and gorgeously smug.

If it wasn't for the smugness, she would have dropped the tofu and run to him, and the hell with good sense and self-preservation. If he'd said something apologetic, or sweet, she would have forgiven him anything.

Instead, he leaned against the doorjamb, his dark eyes bright and mocking, and drawled, "Miss me?"

She looked down at the glop of aging tofu in her hands, then looked up at him. A moment later, the mass was winging its way toward his head.

His reflexes were impressive. He ducked, and the stuff smacked against the doorway, then slid down into a gelatinous puddle on the floor.

"Yes," he said meditatively, staring down at the mess. "You missed me."

She dived for the refrigerator, searching for more ammunition, but he was too fast for her, pulling her away and slamming the door shut. She yanked her hand free, glaring at him as she backed away across the candlelit kitchen. "What were you expecting?"

"I've only been gone a total of fourteen hours, Meggie," he said, in a voice of perfect reason. "Don't you think you're overreacting?"

"It depends on what fourteen hours we're talking about. Why did you leave?"

"I had to get a couple of things."

"What?"

"My Jeep. I figured I couldn't fit all your stuff in the back of Brandon's toy car."

Her hands were sticky from the tofu. She rubbed them on her thighs, staring at him in disbelief. "Why would you want to put my stuff in your car?"

"I thought you could come back to Montana with me." He sounded almost casual about it, and she considered picking up the tofu from the floor and trying another shot.

"Why should I want to do that?" she said suspiciously.

"Beats me. Why should I have shown up here in the first place? No one ever said it made any sense."

She considered it. She considered him. There was no way she could look at him and not feel the pull, the need that twisted her insides. It wasn't as simple as lust or desire, as pure as liking, as easy as love. It was a tangled knot of angry, needy emotions, and whether she liked it or not, she was caught.

"How long would I be staying?" she asked him, her voice just as casual.

"Oh, it'd be up to you. I was thinking maybe fifty, sixty years."

She stared at him. "This is crazy."

"Yes."

"You think I'm going to do it?"

"Yes."

She scowled in frustration. "I can't be in love with you. I've only known you for three days, and I'm not someone who falls in love." She took a step closer to him, away from the tofu. "Are you in love with me?"

"Yes."

She shook her head. He was leaning against the refrigerator, seemingly at ease, staring at her out of dark, watchful eyes. "You're expecting me to throw common sense away, to just toss my stuff in your car and go with you without even considering the future? I suppose you expect me to marry you and have babies, as well?"

"Yes," he said.

She glanced back at the tofu longingly. "Can't you say anything but yes?" she snapped.

"Yes," he said. "Come here, woman, and take a chance."

"Oh, hell," Meggie said. And she flung herself against him, before wisdom and fear could prevail. His arms came around her, tight, and he was warm and strong and real, and she could feel the layers of ice melt around her. Outside, she could hear the church bells toll midnight, as the New Year broke around them. Inside, Meggie started to cry.

And she was home at last.

* * * * *

The Boss, the Baby and
the Bride

Day Leclaire

PROLOGUE

"IT'S BEEN over two years," Reed Harding snarled into the phone. "You're the top PI firm in the state. All you have to do is find one woman. How difficult can that be?"

"Mr. Harding, the woman in question clearly doesn't want to be found. That makes our job a little tough."

Reed shoved a stack of papers to one side, fighting the frustration these calls always stirred. The papers tipped over, spilling to the floor in a multicolored waterfall. He ignored the mess. Secretary number twelve could deal with it. Or was it lucky thirteen? "I need to ask her one question. That's all. Just one simple question and then she can crawl back under whatever rock she's currently occupying."

"I understand, Mr. Harding. But I'm forced to assume it's a question she doesn't choose to answer."

Brilliant deduction! Reed clamped his jaw shut so he wouldn't utter the scathing response. "What about relatives?" he asked instead. "I remember her mentioning a mother."

"Have you remembered the mother's name?"

"No."

A telling silence followed that one, bitten-off word. "We'll keep looking, Mr. Harding. She's bound to surface one of these days. We'll be in touch again next month, as usual.''

"You do that.''

Reed dropped the receiver onto the cradle and kicked back his chair as he stood. Dammit! Why couldn't he find out the truth, to know for certain whether or not Emily had borne him a child? That's all he wanted—his one desire in the whole world. Heaven above, was that too much to ask?

"Angie Makepeace. Please report to your supervisor. Angie Makepeace to Supervisor Goodenkind.''

She heard the whispers start the moment she stepped onto the gilded path. They always whispered about her, even though it meant a spot of tarnish tainting their golden halos or an alabaster feather or two thinned from their magnificent wings—or even a sooty smudge clinging with leechlike ferocity to frost-white robes. And it was always the same question they asked....

"What's an angel like *her* doing in a place like *this?*''

Of course, such uncharitable thoughts didn't belong in heaven, either. She'd made that point a time or two—made it with a few blistering invectives and a basic willingness to wade right in where most angels feared to tread. Not to mention a powerful left hook. Angie smiled broadly at the memory, as well as the resulting ruckus. Boy, had the thunder pealed that day. More than one mouthy angel had emerged from the altercation with rumpled robes, dinged halos and a severe attitude adjustment. Too bad she couldn't have enjoyed the results a wee bit longer. Instead, she'd been trotted off to Goodenkind to "account" for her misbehavior.

"We haven't seen such a display since Cleopatra tried to force her way in here," her supervisor had trumpeted in a rare display of wrath. "You're not on earth anymore, Angie Makepeace. Deal with it or you and your tarnished halo will find yourselves on the wrong side of the Pearly Gates!"

Angie sighed. And here she stood, called on the gilded carpet yet again for having failed her twelfth angel mission in a row.

Well, he— *Heck!* What did they expect? She'd only made it into heaven by the very tips of her inch-long formerly red fingernails. Do-gooding wasn't exactly her forte. That one soul-saving incident had been…an aberration. A mistake. If she'd thought first, she'd never have jumped off the dock and saved that little girl.

Especially if she'd known she'd end up drowning. Sh— *Shoot!* It had been a royal pain in the a— *acorns* to kick off with wet, stringy hair and makeup smeared over half her face. Not to mention what the salt water had done to her Donna Karan original.

"Miss Makepeace?" Supervisor Goodenkind stood in the open doorway. "How kind of you to finally join me. Do come in."

Angie sauntered into the office and glanced over her shoulder at the head angel. "Sarcasm, Good? I thought that was banned along with all the other fun vices."

His brows drew together. "Let's just say you bring out the worst in me."

"I'm not surprised." She laughed—a deep, husky, come-to-my-bedroom sort of laugh. It didn't fit in around here any more than she did. "I seem to have that effect on most of heaven's denizens."

"Yes, we've noticed." He waved a hand toward a gilded chair. "Oh, sit down, Makepeace. You know I've never been one to bother with formalities."

"Which is why you're stuck with me, I suppose." She reclined in the chair he'd indicated. "I assume I've been called up so you can yell at me some more."

"We don't yell."

She grinned. "Sure you do. You just do it with righteous anger." She tilted her head to one side and fixed her big baby blues on him. In another life they were guaranteed to bewitch the most saintly of humans. Unfortunately they weren't quite enough to bewitch the most saintly of saints. Too bad. "I screwed up again, didn't I?"

"We've sent Dotty DoGooder in to clean up the mess you made of that restaurant."

"Oh." Angie crossed her legs. "Did Chuck have the day off?"

"It's Charles. And Mr. CrosstoBear is still recovering from your last mission."

"The hotel *was* in a bit of a shambles."

"My dear young angel, it was an unmitigated disaster."

"I excel at disaster," she confessed with a charming smile.

"Yes, you do." Goodenkind sighed. "Which brings me to our current dilemma."

"Am I kicked out?" She managed to say it casually. After all, she'd known it was only a matter of time before they realized their mistake and sent her...wherever.

"Not yet."

She inspected her fingernails, oddly shaken by his pronouncement. It was ominous, but not a total disaster. "So what's the deal?"

"The deal is... You have one last chance to accomplish your mission."

"Lucky thirteen?" She gave a careless laugh. "What happens if I blow this one?"

"You'll be put outside the gates."

Blunt and to the point. She'd always liked that about her supervisor. She sensed how badly it disturbed him, though, which seemed so unfair, considering she was the one at fault. "It's all right, Good. You did your best," she encouraged. "But I'm used to being a stray dog."

He— *Heck!* She'd spent her entire life living on the outside of people's gates, hoping against hope she'd be taken in and accepted. Loved. When she'd been young enough to believe in dreams, she'd longed to experience a forever kind of love. She'd wished for that special someone with all her heart. She'd never found him, though. Certainly not on earth. Why had she expected heaven to be any different?

"Heaven is different," Goodenkind said gently.

''The angels you've associated with are in training, too. That's why their flaws are so visible.''

She cocked an eyebrow. ''Reading my mind? Isn't that against the rules?''

''Sometimes wishes speak so loudly, angels hear. Especially when those wishes are your true heart's desire.''

''Really? I've never heard any wishes.''

''Maybe you haven't been listening.'' He waited a beat, then asked, ''Shall we get down to business?''

''Okay. What's my latest assignment?''

''His name is Reed Harding and your job is very simple. You're to find him a wife.''

That sounded easy enough. Still... Knowing Goodenkind... ''So, what's the catch?'' she questioned suspiciously.

The supervisor smiled. ''He has to love her—the forever kind of love.''

The painful irony of his demand kept her silent for a long moment. ''Anything else?'' she finally managed to ask, relieved that her voice sounded almost normal.

''That's it. Find him a wife he can love and you've completed your assignment.'' He paused—always a bad sign.

''Come on, Good. Spill it,'' she prompted. ''What else?''

''Since it's your last chance, I'm giving you some extra help on this one. I've decided to send a Guardian Angel along with you.''

''No! Not—''

''''Fraid so. Scratch goes, too.''

CHAPTER ONE

REED HARDING heard the whispers start the moment the woman stepped through the front door of the office building housing Harding Construction. It began as a low buzz of curiosity and rose in intensity as she made her way across the reception area. What's someone like *that* doing in a place like *this?*

He turned, leaning against the receptionist's desk, and watched, impressed. She was a gorgeous creature, he acknowledged. Not his type—platinum blondes might appeal to some, but he preferred a more earthy woman. Certainly, one less aware of how to manipulate the male half of the population. Still… She had the sweet face of an angel and a figure wicked enough to tempt a saint.

She'd painted on a short, vivid red dress, and accompanying her—disbelief rippled through him. A dog trotted alongside, his clipped nails echoing the staccato tap of her high-heeled shoes against the oak floor. It was a dalmatian, no less, a red leather collar encircling its neck and a mischievous glint shimmering within its odd, pale eyes.

"Find out what she wants and take care of it," Reed ordered. He had no time for women at this point in his life—even an angelic blond in a tight red dress. A truckload of work awaited him, the sheer volume a serious threat to the stability of both his desk and his sanity. "I'll be in my office."

He heard the receptionist intercept the woman with a quick, "May I help you?"

Then he heard a laugh—a laugh that caused every head in the office to turn, had every man stopping in his tracks and gravitating toward reception, and every woman grinning at the sheer predictability of the male animal. Reed didn't prove immune, either. The sound caught at his senses, twining around them and tugging. Damn. He hadn't felt this disturbed by a woman since his early teens. Not even Emily had caused such an intense reaction. Furious with himself for not simply ignoring her and continuing on to his office, Reed folded his arms across his chest and waited for her response.

"Why, that's very kind of you," the siren said, her deep brandy-wine voice a perfect match for her laugh. "But I don't need any help. At least, not yet." With a brilliant smile, she kept walking—coming straight for him.

His mouth twisted. No. Whoever this was, she didn't need help from anyone—a fact that challenged him to try and change her mind. Driven by some elemental force he'd sooner not analyze, he stepped into the middle of the hall and blocked her path. "Is there something *I* can do for you?"

She shrugged, long wayward curls playing hide-and-seek with her fine-boned shoulders. "It's not what you can do for me, Reed Harding. It's what I can do for you." With that intriguing comment, she brushed past him and crossed to his office, the dalmatian following along behind.

His eyes narrowed in assessment. So… She knew him. And she knew her way to his office. What sort of game was this?

She paused at the doorway, sending a teasing look from huge, fantasy-blue eyes. "Well… Are you coming?"

"Oh, definitely," he assured with a short, cynical laugh. "I wouldn't miss this for anything."

He followed her into his office and slammed the door closed. "Okay, sweetheart. Let's cut to the chase, shall we? Who are you and what do you want?"

"I'm Angie Makepeace."

With that pronouncement, she examined his office with interest. The dog followed suit, snuffling around the room for a few seconds before noticing the leather couch. With a yelp of what could only be described as sheer joy, he hurdled across the room.

"Oh, no, you don't," Reed began, grabbing for the animal's collar. He was a millisecond too late. Halfway to the couch, the dog leaped into the air and landed with pinpoint accuracy in the precise center of the cushions. "Hey! Get off of there, you mangy mutt."

The dalmatian ignored him. Turning in circles, he finally settled, chuffing in contentment. He regarded Reed for an instant before settling his muzzle on polka-dot paws and closing his eyes.

"He doesn't listen very well, does he?"

"He can't hear you," Angie explained, crossing to the couch. "Not with his eyes closed."

She didn't make a bit of sense. No surprise there. "Okay, I'll bite. Why can't he hear when his eyes are closed?"

"He's deaf."

"A deaf dalmatian."

"Right. The breed is prone to it. Almost twenty-five percent of the puppies suffer from either a unilateral or bilateral impairment."

"Come again?"

"Deaf in either one or both ears. Scratch is a bi. Can't hear a blessed thing."

"Fascinating, but—"

"So, whenever Scratch doesn't want to listen, he just shuts his eyes."

"Why?" Reed asked, momentarily distracted despite the inanity of their conversation. "So he won't *see* what we're saying?"

"Exactly. Not being able to hear, he can't be distracted by what people say. Instead, he listens with his heart." She spared a quick look toward the polka-dot puddle occupying the couch, then leaned closer to Reed, her mouth tilted at an angle that brought it to within inches of his. "This time, he's ignoring us deliberately, I'm sorry to say."

Her already low voice had dropped a further notch, sending another powerful ripple of awareness slamming through his body. It fired an image of sultry, humid nights, of slipping along a sensuous path of discovery over sweet, moist female skin. Her mouth was painted as wicked a red as her dress and Reed wondered what she'd do if he devoured the lipstick from those lush lips. She swayed out of reach before he could act, her movement as graceful and supple as a field of sun-drenched poppies caressed by a summer breeze. Her perfume lingered, teasing him with the scent of temptation.

"What the hell—" he muttered beneath his breath, shaking his head to clear it.

"Scratch has a leather fetish. Not exactly a sin, but far from angelic behavior. Don't you think?"

"Oh, absolutely." It was his turn to close the distance between them. "Sweetheart?"

"Yes?"

"Get your damn dog off my couch and get the hell out of my office." He wanted her out of his life before he succumbed to overwhelming lust and gave her a personal demonstration of his own particular fetishes. How could he have thought he preferred a more earthy woman? This one was as earthy as they came.

She slanted him a glance from her outrageously blue eyes—eyes brimming with sunny laughter. "Let's compromise. I'll get Scratch off your couch, but then you hear me out. Agreed?"

He refused to relent in the face of such blatant feminine appeal. He'd walked that particular path a time or two and knew the inherent dangers. Folding his arms across his chest, he held his ground, fixing her with a gimlet stare.

"That's a yes, right?" she dared to tease.

Turning to the dog, she crouched beside him, running a hand along his muzzle. The fire engine red dress clung lovingly to the length of her spine before molding to her pertly rounded bottom. Reed fought to ignore such an irresistible lure. What he wouldn't give to feel those hands stroking him with as much sweet attention as she gave her dog. And what he wouldn't give to do some stroking of his own.

Hell, it would be heaven on earth to explore the ripe curves barely contained within that scrap of a dress. Reed closed his eyes, his control nearly shot. Maybe if he didn't look, he wouldn't want what he absolutely couldn't possess.

Maybe.

She persevered, whispering quietly to the dog. Not that it did much good. Scratch simply whined a complaint before burrowing deeper into the leather. Just as Reed decided to haul the mutt off his couch and be done with it, the animal opened his eyes—eyes every bit as spectacular a blue as his owner's, the left one ringed by a large black patch. Reed released a silent sigh. Great. His life had turned into a Disney flick.

"About time you paid attention. Now, get down," she ordered.

Scratch barked sharply in response before lunging forward and flicking her cheek with his tongue. Then he turned his head away as though that ended the discussion.

She persisted, catching his muzzle in her hands again and poking her elegant nose to within inches of the dog's speckled snout. "That's not good enough. Kisses don't make up for bad behavior."

Reed considered arguing with that, but thought better of it. His goal these days was to avoid woman-trouble, not embrace it—no matter how delectable the armful.

"You'll jeopardize our mission if you don't stop," she continued.

Mission? Reed's eyes narrowed. "What mission?" he demanded.

Tension radiated down the length of her spine at his question, but she kept her attention focused on the dog. "Get down, Scratch."

With a surprisingly human-like grumble, the dog slinked off the couch before sitting obediently beside her red spiked heels. Angie turned to Reed. "Happy now?" she had the nerve to ask.

"Not even close." He glanced toward the stack of papers awaiting him and frowned. "Can we get on with this? As you can see I have a ton of work to do."

"Which is precisely why I'm here. You see, I'm your new secretary." With that pronouncement, she took the chair opposite his desk.

"You've got to be kidding."

"Not at all." She crossed her legs and his mouth went dry. "Now what did I do with the manual they gave me? Oh, I remember."

She opened the postage-stamp-size purse she'd strung over her shoulder and pulled out a small, rather battered book and an eyeglass case. How the items had fit, he couldn't quite figure. But apparently, they had. She removed a dainty pair of gold-rimmed spectacles and perched them on the tip of her nose. Then she flipped through the leather-bound book, eventually finding what must have been the appropriate page.

"First confirm identity," she muttered beneath her breath. "Oh, right. You'd think I'd remember that one by now." A tiny frown line appeared between her winged brows. "You *are* Reed Harding? I haven't messed that part up, have I?"

"I'm Reed. Look, lady, I don't know what the hell—"

"Second… Explain presence." She nodded in satisfaction. "Check that one off. I've already explained I'm your secretary. Third… Assess situation."

"Excellent suggestion. Assess the fact that I've had all I'm gonna take. Feel free to return to whatever agency sent you and tell them it didn't work out. I need an experienced secretary."

She swung her foot back and forth. The bright red shoe slipped off her heel and dangled from her toes, swaying rhythmically. Why such an innocent act should bother him, he couldn't quite figure. But it proved downright hypnotic, not to mention sexy as hell.

"How do you know I'm not experienced?" she asked.

He forced his gaze from toe to ankle to knee. And then, in an amazing demonstration of sheer willpower, he skipped the brevity of red between thigh and shoulder and focused instead on her face. This woman was supposed to be his secretary? Not a chance. How did she expect him to work when all he could think about was showing her in every conceivable way why he'd been made a man and she a woman? He had to get rid of her—find a legitimate excuse for refusing her services. Something that wouldn't land him in legal hot water.

Reed took a seat behind his desk. "I'll make this easy for you. How many construction or architectural design firms have you worked for?"

"None."

"See how easy that was? Thanks, but no thanks. Be sure to close the door on your way out."

"I don't think you really want me to leave. It says here you've gone through a dozen secretaries in the past six months." She checked her book again and frowned. "Or is that six secretaries in the past twelve months?"

"What can I say? I'm a demanding employer. I expect exceptional service. What's wrong with that?"

She shrugged, peering at him over the top of her wire rims. "Nothing. But since you demand exceptional service, you need an exceptional secretary to take care of your office."

"Exactly. I requested someone who could take dictation, not… Not…"

The laughter from her eyes spilled into her voice. "Not what? I'm fully qualified, I assure you."

"I don't doubt that. The question is… Qualified for what?"

Her inner flame dimmed ever so slightly and she thrust her glasses from the bridge of her nose to the crown of her head. She focused on him, her gaze more intense without the softening effect of the lenses. "To run your office. I'm very good at managing people. And I'm quite helpful."

"Not in my office, you're not."

"I'm afraid you don't have any choice."

Laughter broke free. "Sure I do. You're not qualified to work here. Which means, it only takes two words to send you on your way. 'You're fired.' See how easy that was?"

"You can't fire me."

"I just did."

A loud knock bounced off the door. Without waiting for a response, the person on the other side swatted the heavy oak panel inward. Six foot six inches of sheer muscle strode into the room. He held in tow a thin youngster who bore an amazing resemblance to Reed. "Sorry to interrupt, boss," the man said. He gave the boy a nudge which launched him into the center of the room.

"Hey, Tiger. You don't have to be so rough," the youth complained.

Reed swore beneath his breath. "Not again."

"Caught 'em on the Wellsby job site." Tiger folded his arms across his chest, the thick muscles gleaming like finely polished mahogany. "Third day this week. We're gonna start falling behind if I have to fetch the kid home every time he gets a notion to play carpenter."

Angie stood and smiled at the boy. "You must be Joel." She offered a hand. "I'm Angie Makepeace, your brother's new secretary."

"She is *not* my new secretary. And how the hell did you know my brother's name?"

Joel stared in fascination. "Well, whatever she is… Can I have one?"

"Dammit, Joel!"

Tiger smothered a laugh and Angie glanced his way, grinning. "You're Mr. Harding's foreman?" she asked, offering her hand again.

"Yes, ma'am."

"I've heard good things about you. You're quite highly thought of among the people I know."

"Funny. I've never heard of you at all." He slanted a humor-filled look toward his boss. "Wonder why."

Reed's mouth tightened. "Thanks for handling the situation, Tiger. I'll take it from here."

With a nod, the foreman let himself out. Reed focused his attention on his brother, struggling to conceal his anger. "Why do we have to keep having this conversation, Joel?"

The boy shifted restlessly. "Beats me. Why?"

"Because you're not listening. You can't hang around the construction sites. You're too young and it's too dangerous."

"I'm sixteen next month. You were sixteen when you started working. Besides, I'd think you'd be glad I want a job instead of ragging me about it. There's worse places I could be, you know."

"And you've been in a few of them already, haven't you?"

Joel's expression closed down and Reed released his breath in a gusty sigh. "That wasn't fair. I'm sorry. If you'd like a job, I'll get you one. But not on-site. End of discussion."

"What discussion?" Joel complained bitterly. "We never discuss anything. You just make the rules and expect me to go along."

"Welcome to the real world, kid."

The dog whined at that point and Angie opened her purse again, extracting a leash. "Joel? Would you mind taking Scratch for a walk?"

For the first time the boy's gaze lighted on the dog. "Hey, I didn't notice you before." He crouched beside the animal. "Where'd you come from, fella?"

"He's with me," Angie explained. "Let me warn you... He's deaf. So if you need to give instructions, make sure he's looking at you."

"Does he read lips?"

"Yes."

"No!" Reed glared. "Don't fill the kid's head with all that nonsense. Dogs don't read lips."

"Scratch does. He's...special. I told you. He hears with his heart."

"Whatever," Joel said with a shrug. He snapped the leash onto the dog's collar. "Catch you guys later." Not giving Reed a chance to protest, Joel and the dog darted through the door.

"Dammit all! I wasn't finished with him."

"You'll have an opportunity later. And by that time you'll both have cooled off enough to conduct a rational conversation."

"An expert, are you?"

"Let's just say I understand the yearnings hidden in a young man's heart."

"I'll bet you do."

He saw it again—the slight dimming of her inner flame. That incandescent spark surprised him. He'd never seen it so clearly displayed before. Nor had he ever seen the wound caused by a few thoughtless words. But with Angie Makepeace, he found the injury painfully visible, a dark cut slashing through the ethereal lightness of her spirit. Not only did he witness her reaction but, on some uncomfortable level, he felt it, as well.

"I'm sorry, Angie. That was uncalled for."

Her smile of acceptance was more generous than he deserved. "You're protective of your brother. I can understand that. But haven't you noticed? He wants to be like you, Reed. It doesn't take any special talent or training to see that."

"Now there you're wrong. Joel's been in a state of rebellion since age ten—ever since his father died. He's been in trouble with the law more times than I can count. Nothing major, but it would have escalated to that if someone hadn't taken him in hand."

"And that someone was you?"

He shrugged. "There wasn't anyone else. My mother tried, but with Joel's father gone..." He broke off, his silence speaking volumes. "When she couldn't control Joel any longer, she asked me to take over."

"He lives with you now?"

"For the past two years." A darkness settled over Reed's face, as though his memories were particularly painful. "I've done my best. I've tried to be mother, father and brother to him, but he's determined to make his own path through life."

"Most of us are," Angie observed.

"True. Unfortunately, Joel takes it to excess. If I suggest he take the left road, he'll choose the right just to be difficult. That's why I have such strict rules.''

"Rules?'' A hint of dismay tinged the word. "I don't suppose you limit your rules to Joel?''

"They cover my professional, as well as my personal life.''

Angie released a tiny sigh. "I was afraid you were going to say that. I'll bet Goodenkind is getting quite a laugh over this one.''

"Goodenkind?''

"My supervisor. He's aware I have this slight... aversion...to rules. He probably hopes you'll correct that.''

Reed shook his head. "Not a chance. I suspect getting you to follow rules is a full-time job, one I don't have the patience or inclination to take on. Now where were we?''

"We were discussing the terms of my employment.''

"No. We were discussing terms of your *un*employment. I believe I'd just fired you.''

"Oh, right. And I'd just said you can't.''

"And I explained that I can.''

She grinned. "Which means it's my turn.''

"I don't have time for this. I have a construction firm to run.''

"And a brother to care for,'' she inserted gently.

"That's none of your business.''

"Still, you need help.'' She picked up the small book she'd been consulting earlier. "Which brings me to number four....'' She slipped her glasses from the top of her head and returned them to their former perch on the tip of her nose. Sliding her finger along the page, she hesitated about halfway down. "Uh-oh."

He rested a hip on the edge of his desk, resigned to playing out her little farce. "Uh-oh?"

She cleared her throat in what appeared to be a suspiciously nervous gesture. "I think we'll come back to that one later. I was told to use my discretion regarding how much to reveal to you during our first day together."

"I see." It didn't take a mental giant to figure out what number four in her little black book concerned. He'd been right about her lack of experience. "Ms. Makepeace, have you ever worked as a secretary before?"

"Of course." She opened her impossibly small purse again and removed an impossibly large steno pad and pen. "See? I come fully equipped."

"Clever trick."

"Would you like to try me out?"

He couldn't resist. "On the desk or do you have a leather fetish, too? Now that Scratch is gone, the couch is available."

Her laugh curled around and through him. To his amazement, she didn't take exception to his remark. If anything, *she* appeared apologetic. "Perhaps I should rephrase that."

What little patience he'd started the day with, finally ran out. He wanted a secretary, dammit, not a sultry angel too sexy for his peace of mind. "Don't bother. The game's over. I don't know who sent you, but I don't have time for this sort of nonsense. Go on. Take off."

She sighed. "I'm afraid I can't do that."

"Sure you can. Try balancing yourself on top of those three-inch heels and wiggle that red dress over to the door. Then walk, shimmy, or whatever you call that cute little hip action. Just get yourself out of my office and out of my life. And take that polka-dot couch potato with—" He grimaced, belatedly recalling where the couch potato had gone.

"What will you do about a secretary?"

"I'll order another. A real one."

Only this time he'd specify a woman in her sixties with a grandmotherly figure and a no-nonsense attitude who liked rules as much as he did. In response to his comment, Angie settled more firmly into the chair as though she feared he'd physically eject her. Yeah, right. He didn't dare lay a finger on her. Not the way he reacted whenever she came within touching distance.

"Since we have to wait for Joel's return anyway, go ahead."

"Come again?"

"Order yourself up a new secretary."

"Order—"

"Do whatever's necessary to obtain another secretary. I'll just wait. If you find someone, I'll leave. If you don't, you'll give me the job."

"I'm not giving you the job, no matter what."

"Why?"

"You're not qualified. And to be blunt... You'd be

a disruptive influence. With you around, no one would get an ounce of work done.''

She shrugged. ''If any of that causes problems on the job, then you can fire me. But I don't understand why you won't give me a trial run. Doesn't everyone deserve a chance?''

He stiffened. ''Where did you hear that?''

''Isn't that your motto?'' she questioned. ''I understood you'd founded your construction company on that premise, that you have an open door policy toward ex-cons and welfare moms and people in trouble. Or are they just words meant to win awards and impress politicians?''

He clenched his teeth. ''They're not just words.''

''But they don't apply to me. Is that it?''

A pit of his own making yawned before him. Dammit! Why hadn't he seen this coming? He should have. He sure as hell should have. ''I—''

Her expression didn't reveal an ounce of triumph. Instead he caught a glimpse of sympathy. ''Yes?'' She had him and knew it.

''A two week trial period,'' he forced through gritted teeth. ''One screwup and you're out the door. Understood?''

Her smile glowed once more—a smile as beautiful as it was dangerous. ''I understand.''

''Don't look so pleased. We haven't discussed my rules, yet.'' He took a perverse pleasure in watching her smile slip. ''You know how to use that notepad and pen you're waving around?''

''Of course.''

''Then start writing. Since you detest rules so

much, I'll limit myself to three for now. I also have a list of duties."

She brightened. "Oh, you're a list person? I'm one, too. They're so helpful, don't you think? Much better than rules."

He eyed her suspiciously. Was she mocking him? Not that it mattered. She wouldn't last two days of her two week trial period. He'd see to that. "Rule number one. I'm the boss. What I say goes. No discussion. No argument. I win. Clear?"

She scribbled away at her pad of paper. "That's fine."

"Rule number two. No interoffice relationships. Find your dates outside the workplace."

More scribbles. "I can live with that," she said with a nod.

"And rule number three. No dogs."

This time the pen hovered over the notepad. She glanced at him, a small frown gathering between her brows. "Scratch has a mind of his own, I'm afraid. I'll tell him he can't come, though I doubt he'll listen."

"Try leaving him in the house and locking the door."

She started to reply, then hesitated, glancing down at what she'd written. "It's difficult to explain," she said cautiously. "Especially since you're the boss and I wouldn't dream of arguing. But leaving Scratch home won't work. He's very devious about getting his own way."

"A deaf *devious* dalmatian."

"*Very* devious."

"With a leather fetish and the ability to read lips."

"Well… He reads them when he chooses to. Which is much too infrequently as far as I'm concerned. He doesn't want to get distracted from his true purpose."

"Right."

"You don't believe me?"

"Not a word."

To his surprise a hint of anger intensified the brilliance of her eyes. "Let's get something straight, Mr. Harding. I may have my fair share of flaws. Perhaps more than my fair share. But I don't lie. Not ever."

He inclined his head. "My apologies. But you have to admit—"

"In fact, I tend to be too honest. And blunt," she confessed. "I can't help myself. And this might be a good time to tell you that I have a temper. A bad one. It's gotten me in trouble once or twice."

Reed's expression eased and a hint of a smile tilted his mouth. "I'll bet."

"Now that we have that straightened out… Do you have any more rules for me?"

"Probably. I'll let you know as the situation arises."

"Okay."

She examined her steno pad for a final time, then tucked it away in her purse along with her leather-bound book and pen. Once again, the mechanics of how she managed to fit so many items in such a tiny space defeated him. Must be a woman thing, he finally decided.

"What about my duties?" Angie asked. "You said something about a list."

"Right here." He opened a desk drawer and withdrew a sheet of paper. "After so many secretaries, I found it easier to write everything down."

"Very smart," she approved. "If you don't mind my asking, why have you lost all those secretaries?"

He leaned back in his chair and grinned. "I have something of a temper, too. And as I mentioned earlier, I'm very demanding."

A glimmer of an answering smile appeared before she turned her attention to his list. "All my duties recorded *and* numbered," she murmured. "Very thorough."

"Do you have any questions?"

"Let's see... Filing, phones, typing... Oh. I'm supposed to attend business meetings and conferences with you?"

"Is that a problem? There's one next month in Chicago. We'll leave early on a Friday and return sometime Sunday."

"I look forward to attending."

"You'll also have to go to various job sites with me if the need arises."

"That sounds interesting." She returned her attention to the paper. "Organize schedule, update computer, deal with clients..."

She'd reached the last item on his list and he stood. "Are you ready to get started? Casey Radcliff fills in when I'm between secretaries. She can answer any questions you might have."

Angie stood, as well, still reviewing her duties. "I

shouldn't have any problems. It all looks pretty routine,'' she said. Snagging her purse, she headed for the door, pausing to glance at him over her shoulder. ''Well... Except for that last item. That might prove a bit of a challenge.''

He frowned. ''What last item?''

''The one about finding you a wife.'' With another of her glittering smiles, she sauntered out of his office and closed the door.

Three inches of solid oak did little to muffle his roar of outrage.

CHAPTER TWO

ANGIE had just taken a seat at her desk when Reed ripped open the door separating them. He appeared angry. Very angry. She wasn't surprised. She'd hoped to mention that final item on his list so casually he wouldn't even notice. Apparently, she'd failed. One glance at six foot four inches of powerfully built infuriated male animal told her that much.

"Ms. Makepeace!" As though aware of the interest he'd generated among the nearby office staff, he reduced his roar to a more reasonable shout. "In my office. Now!"

Oh, dear. She hadn't seen an expression like that since Supervisor Goodenkind had discovered she'd slipped Napoleon through the Pearly Gates for a quick peek around the place. Reed looked even angrier. He hadn't been kidding about having a temper. It caught deep within his hazel eyes, inflaming the gold and shadowing the green. His roughly hewn features were stretched taut, emphasizing the square jaw and sharp cheekbones. And his lips—lips she'd noted as deliciously full and sensuous—had compressed into a tight line. How incredibly intimidating.

"Certainly, Mr. Harding," she replied with amazing calm. Picking up her steno pad and a pen, she stepped into his office ahead of him. The door slammed, underlining his fury, and she turned to face him. "Is there a problem?"

"You might say that."

He blocked the door, as though to prevent her from bolting. His body, hardened by years of working construction, appeared more than adequate for the job. Angie suppressed a sigh. As though running were an option. She couldn't leave until she'd completed her mission. And that had begun to look far more difficult than she'd initially anticipated. She tapped her steno pad against her thigh. What an impossible male this Reed Harding had turned out to be. Considering how much trouble he'd given her over working as his secretary, finding him a wife would no doubt be impossible.

"Am I supposed to guess what the problem is?" she asked with angelic sweetness—the sort that usually earned her a stern reprimand from her supervisor.

"What the hell do you mean you're here to find me a wife?"

"Oh. That."

"Yes, that."

She shrugged. "It was on your list."

"The hell it was."

"Shall I show you?"

"That would prove interesting since I wrote that list myself. And I didn't put anything about finding a wife on there."

Angie lifted an eyebrow. "Are you going to move so I can go get it, or am I supposed to fight my way past you?"

The grimness in his gaze ebbed and the mouth she

found so fascinating tilted to one side. "That's the most tempting offer I've had all day. Would you like to try?"

She eyed the breadth of shoulder and endless ridges of muscle his blue chambray shirt did little to conceal. She didn't stand a chance of budging him which almost prompted her to try. The urge to indulge in a wrestling match with such a gorgeous example of manhood proved an almost irresistible allure. Almost. She caught herself in time, remembering that her mission was to find him a wife, not gratify her earthly desires.

He must have read the refusal in her expression, because he inclined his head in acknowledgment, the spotlights above him catching in the bronze strands striping his dark brown hair. Stepping to one side, he allowed her access to the door. Unfortunately, he must have also seen how close she'd come to agreeing, for his hand fastened over hers as she reached for the knob.

"You see why our working together won't succeed?" Reed asked quietly. "You feel it, too, don't you?"

She couldn't deny it, any more than she could deny the bittersweet rush of sensation his work-roughened hand aroused. It had been so long since she'd felt the touch of a man, since she'd experienced the initial surge of desire, followed by that heady flush of need. Slowly, she lifted her gaze to his. "Once I find you a wife you can love, it won't bother you anymore. I promise. I'm a momentary distraction. But the feeling won't last."

"It won't last because *you* won't last." He spoke more urgently. "I have connections. I'll find you a job elsewhere. You must realize this road we're traveling is pure trouble."

"I'm afraid it's the only road I know," she admitted wryly. And that, more than anything she'd told him since they'd met, was heaven's own truth.

She turned the knob, wondering if he'd stop her. For a nerve-racking instant his hand tightened, while the harsh release of his breath rushed past her check. Then she heard an odd sound winging through her head, a whispered desire too faint for her to catch. With a muttered exclamation, Reed released her and moved toward his desk.

"Get the list," he snapped.

For the first time in her life—or since her death—Angie found it difficult to balance atop her three-inch spikes. She focused on planting one foot in front of the other. Reaching the desk, she picked up the list. Then she took a precious few seconds to gather her composure.

Reed Harding was just a man, she reminded herself, and she'd successfully dealt with men from the minute she'd escaped her cradle. She'd never been flustered by one before, never been bewitched or bewildered by the falseness of what most called "love."

Oh, sure, she'd experienced some of the more pleasurable aspects of that particular emotion. She'd known the giddy rush of passion that struck early on in a relationship and the pure sensual pleasure of physical desire. But she'd never allowed those feelings to rule her heart, let alone her head. She could handle this situation. It only called for ignoring her baser instincts while she sorted through the available women in Reed's life. There must be someone compatible for such a hard-a— *Hard case!*

Taking a deep breath, she returned to the office and closed the door. Crossing to his desk, she dropped the list on top of the stacks of clutter. "Last line. It says 'Find me a wife.'"

He snatched up the piece of paper, his brows snapping together as he read. "What sort of game are you playing?" he asked in a dangerously soft voice.

It wasn't a question she could answer. Not quite yet. Taking a seat, she flipped open her notebook and glanced at him, her pen poised above the page. "Shall we discuss what sort of woman you'd like?"

"No!" His shout almost knocked her out of the chair. "Tell me how that item got on my list."

"Didn't you put it there?"

"No way." He held her with eyes gone totally black. "Did you?"

"No." But she could guess who had. Guardian Angels could be pretty tricky when they chose.

He tossed the paper aside and studied her. "Honesty is vital to me. In fact, it's number one on my list of virtues."

She brightened. "Another list?"

"Ms. Makepeace!"

"All right, all right." She met his eyes so he couldn't doubt her sincerity. "I believe we've already addressed the subject of honesty. I don't lie, remember?"

"So you said."

"Now that we have that settled, shall we get down to business? If you'd tell me what you'd like in a wife, I'll take care of it. I promise to keep it strictly confidential. No problem."

"Wrong, sweetheart. It's a big problem. I hired you to be my secretary. That's it. Handle the responsibility for that position, and we'll get along fine. But I better not hear another word about finding me a wife. I'm not in the market. Is that clear?"

She sighed. "Is this rule number four?"

"I think rule number one covers it. I'm the boss, remember? What I say goes. No discussion. No argument. I win."

"I'm beginning to realize that particular rule's going to be a royal pain in the a— *Acorns!*"

He suppressed a smile. "I can live with that."

Maybe so, but she couldn't. She couldn't be certain how long she had to accomplish her mission, but it wouldn't be more than a month. If she hadn't achieved results within that time... Determination filled her. "Could you at least tell me what qualities you'd like in a wife?" she asked, praying her desperation didn't show. "Then we won't have to discuss it again."

"You don't give up, do you?"

"I can't." Not if she hoped to remain on the proper side of the Pearly Gates.

"Let me make it easy for you. My mother is the current matchmaker in my life. She's decided it's her duty to see me married and works quite hard at it."

"That sounds ominous."

"It's more inconvenient than anything else. At

least once a month she makes dinner reservations with the latest sacrificial lamb she's discovered and informs me of them at the last minute.''

"Awkward."

"To say the least."

Curiosity stirred. "Why don't you refuse to go?"

"That would hardly be fair to the woman involved. She's usually on the way to the restaurant by the time the call comes through. As for my mother… Let's just say I have my reasons for agreeing to her requests.'' Another subject off limits, it would seem. "So you see why I don't need your help finding a wife. I'm sure tonight's sacrifice has all the necessary qualities and virtues I could want in a woman.''

"Really?" Angie smiled in delight.

"Really."

She flipped closed her steno pad. "Tell me about tonight's date. What's she like?"

"You're not listening, are you?"

"I most certainly am," she informed him with a touch of indignation. "I've heard—and can repeat— every word you've said since we first met. And trust me, you've had quite a lot to say."

"Really? How tedious for you." His eyes glinted dangerously. "Would you care to repeat my exact comments in regards to discussing my personal life?"

"'I hired you to be my secretary,'" she quoted. "'That's it. Handle the responsibility for that position, and we'll get along fine. But I better not hear another word about finding me a wife. I'm not in the market. Is that clear?'"

"Impressive. Did you understand my instructions?'' he questioned softly. ''Was there any part that confused you?''

''You're not going to tell me about her, are you?''

''No.'' He thrust back his chair and stood. ''And now I suggest you memorize my next comment. Then you might want to type it up and keep it where you can refer to it on a regular basis. Are you ready?''

''I'm not going to like this, am I?''

''I seriously doubt it.'' He leaned across the desk toward her. ''You're stuck here for a two week trial period as we agreed. At which point I'll take great delight in firing your sweet backside and having you out of my life once and for all.''

A small whine from the far side of the room interrupted them.

''Gee,'' Joel announced cheerfully. ''I think we walked in at the wrong minute. What do you think, Scratch?''

''It's not my fault,'' Angie insisted. ''Reed Harding is impossible. Don't you give me that look. I am so trying. And get off his couch. If he finds any more dog hair on those cushions he won't bother waiting two weeks to fire us. We'll be out first thing in the morning.''

Scratch barked energetically before burrowing deeper into the leather nest he'd made.

''For your information, I do have a plan. In case you hadn't noticed, this is Reed's appointment book.'' She'd found it under the mounds of files and papers littering his desk. ''And tonight he happens to have a date with someone named Pamela at

Sarducci's.'' She brightened. ''Remember that restaurant? That was a fun assignment, wasn't it?''

The dog buried his muzzle in his paws and growled.

''I'm sure they've forgotten about that. Anyway…'' She dismissed his concern with a wave of her hand. ''You and I are going to Sarducci's tonight to observe their relationship. With a bit of luck Pamela will be perfect for Reed and it'll only take a gentle nudge to get them married and living happily-ever-after.''

She couldn't quite keep a cynical note from seeping into her voice, a fact Scratch noted with a reprimanding woof. But what did he expect? In all her days on earth, she'd never seen such a condition. Not the sort of love that lasted. She fought a sense of despair as she curled up on the couch next to the dog. Maybe Reed and Perfect Pamela would prove her wrong. She certainly hoped so. Because if they didn't…

Angie shuddered. She'd spent every one of the twenty-eight years of her earthly existence living on the ''outside.'' The thought of doing that for the rest of eternity was too horrible to contemplate. Just once she wanted to belong somewhere. And to have a home. A real home, where she was accepted and lo— Realizing where her thoughts had almost led, she laughed. Love. Did she really still yearn for such an impossible dream? Wrapping her arms around Scratch's neck, she laughed until she wept—which struck her as quite odd.

She'd never realized angels could cry.

*   *   *

To Angie's secret amusement, she arrived at Sarducci's at the exact same instant as Reed and Pamela. Reed looked far less amused by the "coincidence." Clearly, a sense of humor wasn't part of his nature, which made it all the more imperative that his future wife possess one. Angie studied his date, her pale brows drawing together. If this woman had a sense of humor, she kept it well hidden.

"What are you doing here?" Reed demanded in a rough undertone.

"I'm having dinner. What are you doing?"

"I have reservations, as I'm sure you're aware."

"Oh. Are reservations required?"

At long last he showed a spark of genuine amusement. "They're not just required. They're imperative." His attention shifted to Scratch. "You brought the dog?"

"I couldn't very well come without him."

"They'll never let him in. There must be health ordinances against animals in a restaurant."

"Really? I've never had a problem before."

She glanced at his date. Pamela was tall and attractive, if a bit quiet and controlled. She'd dressed in a conservative pearl gray dress, her hair restrained with an ivory clip. A set of fine brown eyes returned Angie's regard.

"Aren't you going to introduce us?" Pamela prompted politely.

His reluctance was palpable. "This is my secretary, Ms. Makepeace. Angie, Pamela James."

The two women shook hands. "Have you known each other long?" Angie asked.

Reed shot her a look that had her falling back a quick step. "Don't start or you'll be looking for a new job tomorrow."

"My goodness, Reed," Pamela interrupted. "What in the world did she say wrong? She simply asked how long we'd known each other."

Annoyance smoldered in his gaze. "That's not what she meant."

"It isn't?"

"It's just a friendly question, Reed," Angie interrupted.

His mouth tightened, not that it intimidated her. Progress couldn't be made without movement—and she fully intended to move this mountain of a man, no matter how hard she had to push. Though, by the look of him, she'd have to push da— *dang* hard.

"You already know the answer to that question, so why ask?"

"Apparently she doesn't or she wouldn't," Pamela retorted before addressing Angie. "We've only just met."

"Excellent."

"What the hell do you mean by that?" Reed demanded.

Pamela frowned. "For heaven's sake, it's just social chitchat."

"There's more to it. Count on it."

"I just meant first dates are so special," Angie explained. "The initial glimpse you catch of each other. The sudden, stunning physical awareness that follows. Then you start anticipating his first touch, anxious to determine if he feels as delicious as he looks."

Pamela appeared startled. "I never thought of it quite that way."

"Ms. Makepeace—"

"Really?" Angie frowned at Reed's date. "I always found the first few dates an exciting time. The hot and heavy passion that blinds each partner to certain painful truths." The dog pawed at her skirt, distracting her. "Stop it, Scratch. I'm talking about the fun stuff. When emotion causes you to ignore the flaws. The love rush."

Pamela folded her arms across her chest. "Flaws? What flaws?"

"Well... Let me think." It didn't take long to come up with a few. She only had to remember her day with Reed. "Like having a nasty temper. Or a blatant tendency toward stubbornness. Oh! And always wanting your own way about everything. Those sorts of flaws." Scratch gave a soft whine and Angie glared at him. "I remember what Goodenkind said. True love. Happily-ever-after. Yada, yada, yada. Well, love's love. Flaws and all." She turned her glare in Reed's direction. "Right?"

"I'll have to take your word for it. I wouldn't know. Are you quite through now?"

"I hope not," Pamela said. "I'd like someone to explain what she's talking about."

"No problem," Angie hastened to reply. "You see, you two haven't been together long enough to have seen the bad as well as the good. Reality hasn't set in. Or boredom. With any luck that won't happen until you're safely m—"

"Ms. Makepeace?" Reed interrupted gently.

"What?"

"I strongly recommend you don't finish that sentence."

"Perhaps we should have kept to meaningless social chitchat," Pamela commented.

Reed smiled without humor. "See? I told you her remarks weren't innocent. If you knew her as well as I do, you'd have realized that."

Pamela lifted an eyebrow. "Perhaps I should have been the one asking how long you two have known each other."

Angie grinned. "We just met today."

A pregnant silence followed her announcement, a silence Reed finally chose to break.

"Ms. Makepeace? In case you didn't realize, I'm not very happy with you."

She gave a tiny shrug, a wry smile tilting her mouth. "I'm used to it. I appear to have a knack for doing or saying the wrong thing. But if it makes you feel any better, if I fail this assignment, I won't be inflicted on anyone else. And my supervisor will send Chuck or Dotty to straighten out the mess. You won't be made to suffer. I promise."

The maître d' interrupted then. "Miss Makepeace! What a great delight to see you again."

Angie turned around and smiled with genuine pleasure. "Hello, Rollo. How's Beatrice?"

"Much recovered, thank you." He gestured expansively. "How do you like what we've done with the place?"

"It's beautiful. Why I can't even tell where the fire was."

"We covered it up very fine, yes?"

"You sure did. I'm sorry about the mess, by the way."

"Pfft. As you see, the mustache grew back, no problem."

He fingered the waxed tips and smiled broadly. "You have come for dinner?"

"Can you fit me in?"

"Of course. We always have room for you, Ms. Makepeace." He glanced at Scratch and frowned. "But, er, you know the rules."

"Told you," Reed murmured close to her ear.

With a tiny sigh, Angie opened her purse and removed a scrap of red elastic. She slipped it over Scratch's head, centering the snazzy red bow beneath his muzzle. "There? Satisfied?"

"You know our tie policy is strictly enforced," Rollo scolded gently. "Even for such honored guests."

"I understand completely." She almost laughed out loud at Reed's astonished expression. Tossing him a cheerful grin, she followed Rollo into the dining room. "Well, that went well, don't you think?" she said to Scratch.

"Am I the only one who finds it strange to be eating at a five star restaurant with a dalmatian?"

"You're not eating *with* a dalmatian," Pamela answered with what Reed had begun to realize was typical pigheaded logic.

So much for experiencing the "love rush" before noticing the flaws. Not that he minded. After Emily and the torment of the past two years, he didn't want to have anything more to do with love.

"There's no difference," he retorted.

"Yes, there is. You're dining in the same restaurant *as* a dalmatian, not *with* him," Pamela instantly corrected.

"And you don't find anything strange about that?"

She sent him a quizzical glance. "Should I?"

To hell with tact. "Yes, you should." He looked around the restaurant. "I can't believe no one's complaining. It's as though they don't even notice. There's a deaf dalmatian sitting at a table wearing a bow tie and a smirk and everyone's acting like it's an everyday occurrence."

"Well, it's not as though he's eating with his paws or slurping his soup or barking too loudly." Pamela returned her attention to the menu. "The sole looks good, doesn't it?"

Reed started to respond, then gave it up for a lost cause. He flipped open the menu, furious when his brand new secretary managed to snag his attention for the twentieth time in the past ten minutes.

Not that she did it deliberately. She hadn't waved or smiled or raised any further ruckus. She didn't need to.

Hell, no. All she had to do was sit there and every few minutes he found his gaze straying in that direction.

She occupied the centermost table, her bright red dress and pale blond hair seeming to catch and magnify the subdued lighting. Not only was she the most beautiful woman in the room, but she also appeared perfectly at ease having a dog for a "date." Not many women could pull that off with such flair. She wore her wire-rimmed glasses again, perching them precariously on the tip of her nose. His mouth twitched into a reluctant smile. How did she keep them from falling into her minestrone? As he watched, she pulled out that damned steno pad and busily scribbled another notation.

He winced, imagining what sort of comments she was recording. By the tiny frown centered on her brow, it couldn't be good. What had he done to deserve such a nutcase for a secretary? It must have been one hell of a sin.

"Have you decided what you're ordering?" Pamela asked.

"What? Oh. Sole."

She nodded in satisfaction. "Perfect. That's what I planned to order, too. It would seem we have a lot in common."

Reed released his breath in a silent sigh. Yeah, right. They shared a common interest in a dead fish. Undoubtedly a match made in heaven. "I'm sure Ms. Makepeace will be thrilled."

"Stop arguing, Scratch. A list is vital. He's a list person. I'm a list person. Now stop complaining and tell me what I should put on it. He rates honesty as the highest virtue of all, so that's number one." Angie peered at Reed's table over the top of her wire rims. "Now, how am I supposed to tell if Pamela's honest? It's not like she's wearing a sign or anything. I don't suppose Good's told you anything helpful?"

Scratch released a gusty sigh.

"That figures." She glanced at the list of virtues she'd started recording. "Let's see. What's next? Sense of humor. That's my choice, not Reed's. With a temper like his, having a mate who can turn his anger into laughter is imperative. Unfortunately, I haven't seen either of them so much as crack a smile." She added another notation. "And strong-willed. It wouldn't do to match him with a doormat. He'd be bored senseless before the week's out."

Scratch barked sharply.

"Why do you keep bringing that up? I'm aware that he's supposed to love her. But the man doesn't believe in love."

She removed her glasses and tossed them to the ivory tablecloth, thoroughly disheartened. The rims glittered like gold beneath the lights, though they were actually made of titanium. It didn't bother her. She'd learned long ago that dross often masqueraded as gold.

"Explain something to me, if you can. How am I supposed to convince Reed to believe in love, when I know da— *darn* well it isn't real? The man values honesty above all else. And yet I'm supposed to convince him to buy into a lie."

Scratch wrinkled his muzzle, the pity reflected in his intense blue eyes almost more than she could bear.

"How's your sole?" Pamela questioned.

"It's always perfect."

"Mine is a shade on the dry side."

"You took it without sauce."

''It's dry.''

''Fine. It's dry.'' Reed reached for the salt which allowed him a surreptitious glance at his watch. Damn. At least another forty-five minutes before he could safely escape.

''Salt is bad for your health, you know.''

He lifted an eyebrow, thoroughly out of sorts with the woman. ''Really?'' He bared his teeth. ''Want some?''

''I don't like this. They're both having sole.'' Angie swirled her fork in the fettuccine marinara. ''And they both look so...''

Scratch growled.

''Yeah. Bored. Where's the fire? I don't even see any sparks. Not so much as a wisp of smoke. He hasn't held her hand. Hasn't whispered sweet nothings in her ear. He hasn't even made her laugh.'' She glared at the dalmatian. ''How's he supposed to form a forever type relationship when they practically put each other to sleep?''

Rollo appeared at her elbow. ''How is your dinner, Ms. Makepeace?''

''Wonderful. You've changed your sauce, haven't you?''

The maître d' beamed. ''You could tell?''

''You've added anchovies. And you've switched to Greek olive oil. Shame on you, Rollo.''

''*Please,* Ms. Makepeace! Not so loud. You'll give away all our secrets.''

''Oh, sorry.'' She glanced toward Reed's table again and snagged Rollo's shirt. He bent low in order to hear her whispered question. "How often does he come here?"

"Mr. Harding? Twice a month like clockwork."

"Always with a different woman?"

Rollo shrugged. "Once in a great while the lady will last more than a single date. Not often."

She released him and considered the problem. Then she caught his sleeve and tugged until he bent close again. "The ones that last... Does he steal the occasional kiss?"

"I am sorry to say, no."

Uh-oh. "Does he ever touch his dates?"

The maître d's brow wrinkled for an instant before he smiled in triumph. "Once. He helped her up. The young lady had sprained the ankle."

Sh—*shoot!* She released Rollo's arm and he straightened. "Does he ever argue with his dates?"

"Never."

"Share secrets?"

He chuckled. "Not him."

"Laugh?" she asked weakly. "Smile at his women?"

The maître d' gave a distinctly Latin shrug—a shrug that spoke volumes.

She drummed the table with her fingernails, then snagged Rollo and yanked him downward. "Has he ever left with a woman before they'd finished eating?"

"Ah... The love rush." Reluctantly he shook his head. "He has never done this. Apparently, none of his dates has roused the urge to hurry a meal. My guess is that he always enjoys dessert at the table, more is the pity.''

Instead of in bed. Da— *Dang!* ''Thank you, Rollo.''

Scratch released a rumbly sigh as the maître d' scurried away.

''Yeah, that's what I thought.'' Angie fixed her stubborn boss with a determined gaze. ''It seems that in addition to secretarial duties I'm going to have to give Mr. Harding some lessons on romance.'' She shook her head. ''The things we angels have to do.''

CHAPTER THREE

A WEEK later, Angie had just finished sorting the last pile on Reed's desk when Scratch lifted his head and released an excited whine. Leaping from the couch, he sprinted toward the closed door leading to the outer reception area and glanced at her, shivering in undisguised pleasure.

"Joel's here?" she asked, lifting a pale eyebrow. She checked her watch. "It's only six. Rather early for him, isn't it?"

She crossed to the door and silently opened it a crack. Sure enough, Joel stood in front of a bank of file cabinets, fumbling through the folders overflowing one of the drawers. He hadn't turned on any lights. Instead he squinted in an effort to see with only the dusky dawn light to aid him. A lock of bronze-streaked hair curled across his brow above a straight, well-defined nose. A slight frown slashed sharp creases from his cheekbones to the side of his mouth, reminding her vividly of Reed.

"The site files aren't there anymore. I moved them," Angie announced, stepping into the outer office area.

Joel leaped in surprise, twisting to face her in an impressive, catlike move. "Holy sh—"

Scratch barked sharply—a clear reprimand.

Angie fought to hide a smile. "He doesn't approve of swearing, I'm afraid. He reads lips, remember?"

"Oh." Joel scuffed a sneaker-clad foot into the beige carpet. "Sorry. You scared me and it sorta slipped out."

"He also doesn't approve of burglars or thieves." Angie folded her arms across her chest. "Nor do I."

"I'm not stealing anything. I was—"

"Looking for another construction site to visit?"

He shrugged, flashing her an engaging grin. "Yeah. I have my own set of keys and—"

Scratch cut him off with a growl.

"Hey, I didn't swear."

"No. But lying doesn't go down well with him, either."

Joel sighed in exasperation. "Damn! Shoot! I mean…*darn!*"

Angie chuckled. "Don't worry. I slip up a lot, too. But I'm improving. I hardly goof at all anymore."

"With the lying or the swearing?"

"Swearing. I never lie."

Joel nodded toward the dog. "And he can tell if somebody fibs?" he asked curiously.

"Every time."

"How?"

"Scratch has this built-in lie detector," Angie confided. "It can be really annoying."

"Da— *Dang.* Sure am glad Reed doesn't have one of those."

It was said with such heartfelt sincerity that Angie couldn't help but laugh. "I'll bet. Now would you like to try again with the keys?"

"I...uh...borrowed—" He winced as Scratch released an infuriated howl and held up his hands. "Okay, okay! I lifted Reed's keys one day and made a duplicate set. Then whenever I want to find a construction site I haven't visited recently, I sneak in here and look 'em up. Since most people wouldn't peg me for a fifteen-year-old, I can usually hire on as a temporary without too much trouble."

"Until one of Reed's regular crew spots you."

"Somethin' like that." He cocked his head to one side and fixed her with familiar hazel eyes. "You gonna rat me out?"

"I haven't decided yet," Angie replied.

"It's not like I got what I came for." His grin flashed again. "It'd take a few more midnight raids before I find where you hid everything."

"May I make a suggestion?"

He exhaled gustily. "If you have to."

"Why don't you work with me for a few weeks?"

Joel reared back. "Hey! I'm not some sorta dumb secretary."

"Gee, thanks."

He blushed painfully at her dry tone. "I didn't mean it like that." Stepping away from the bank of file cabinets, he began to pace, his movements filled with restless energy. "Nobody understands. I want to be outside. I want to build something from start to finish with my own hands. I want to be part of the action, not trapped at school or inside some boring office for my whole life."

"You want to be like Reed." She waited for him to deny it. When he didn't, she added, "You've chosen to work construction sites because that's what your brother did at your age. Is that it?''

''Yeah. He could, so why can't I?''

''Will you also return to school the way your brother did? Are you going to get your college degree?''

''Maybe,'' he muttered.

''Reed worked hard to build this company. It took a lot of work and intelligence, as well as ambition. And it took schooling.''

Joel confronted her, his face settling into a fierce expression—the mantle of approaching adulthood hardening the boyish contours. ''I'm not afraid of hard work. And I'm ambitious, too.''

Angie studied him, aware she'd have to tread carefully if she hoped to avoid antagonizing him. He was so close to becoming a man, his body straight and tall, his shoulders straining to an impressive fullness, his coltish legs hinting at the muscular strength soon to come. He'd begun to shave, too, the downy darkness scraped from his upper lip, but too fine to remove from his cheeks and chin.

More than anything, she wished she had the power to reach out and slow him down, to halt his desperate, headlong rush toward maturity. Unfortunately, a boy like Joel wouldn't be slowed. Like an eagle fledging from its nest, he'd discovered his wings, had spread them wide and thrilled to his first exhilarating flight of freedom. He wouldn't be coaxed back into that nest ever again, not when he could ride the wild wind of adventure.

"No one is saying you can't work on the construction sites."

"Just not now," he cut in bitterly.

"Just not now," she concurred. "Think about something for a minute.... What would happen if you were injured on a Harding job? Reed would never forgive himself. But he'd shoulder the blame, anyway. That's a terrible burden to put on anyone. And your mother? What would it do to her?"

Joel shoved his hands into his pockets, hunching his shoulders. "She isn't too good in a crisis."

"Reed would have his hands full, wouldn't he?"

"And it would be my fault. Again," he muttered.

"Again?"

He shrugged without answering. After a few minutes' thought, he glanced up. "If nobody'll let me work the sites, what am I supposed to do? How can I prove that I'm capable?"

"First, you need to convince Reed that your interest is sincere."

"Yeah?" She heard the edge of impatience. "How do I do that?"

At least he was listening. "Which construction project is your favorite?"

"The Wellsby site," he answered without a moment's hesitation.

"The one Tiger oversees?"

"He's the best foreman Reed has. And it's a really cool building, too." Enthusiasm lit his angled features and rippled through his voice. "Not as large as some of the others, but complicated. They're starting to frame it this week. That's why I wanted to be there."

"What about working it from this end?"

His eyes narrowed in suspicion. "What do you mean?"

"I mean… What about dealing with some of the paperwork? You could work as Tiger's assistant— order supplies and organize the subcontracting."

"But I wanted to help build it."

"Okay… How about this? What if you constructed a working model of the building. While Tiger's crew constructs the framing, you do the same. You can use copies of their blueprints. And it would be a challenge because you'd have to reconfigure the measurements to scale."

She'd caught his interest. A hint of excitement burned in his gaze. "Do you think Reed would let me?"

"I'd have to check with him first. But I think I can get his agreement. Fair warning, though. You can't be on site unless supervised by Tiger or Reed. Still, you'd be learning the nitty-gritty aspects of the business from the best. What do you think?"

"I…I could try," he allowed cautiously.

Angie held out her hand and grinned. "Deal?"

"Deal with one addition."

It was her turn for suspicion. "What's that?"

Laughter sparked in Joel's eyes as he seized her hand, swallowing it in a man-size grip. "I get to be there when you explain it all to my brother."

"You agreed to *what?*"

Angie spared Joel a quick, reassuring glance before confronting Reed once more. He wasn't an easy man to challenge, his height alone put her at a distinct disadvantage. Combine that with a dose of blistering anger and it took every ounce of poise to stand up to him. "What didn't you understand?" she asked calmly. "You offered Joel a job, if you'll remember, and I—"

"No," he interrupted, planting his hands on his hips. "I do *not* remember."

"Well, you did on my first day here. You said— and I quote— 'If you want a job, I'll get you one. But not on-site. End of discussion.' And then Joel said—"

"'What discussion?'" Joel piped up.

Reed turned his wrath in his brother's direction. "*That* I remember. Now haul your carcass off my couch and get that damned dog off, too."

"Hey, watch it!" Joel reached down and covered up Scratch's eyes. "He doesn't like it when people swear."

"He doesn't like—" Reed slammed his hands onto the desk and glared at Angie. "This is all your fault."

She sighed. "Yes, I know. It usually is."

"Come with me for a minute. I want to show you something."

Giving Joel an encouraging smile that faded the moment she turned her back, Angie obediently trailed Reed to the office door. He yanked it open and pointed toward a cluster of desks at the far end of the massive room. Employees busily milled to and fro.

"Look at that."

She peeked around his shoulder, startled at the casual way he dropped an arm around her and drew her forward. Why did she overreact every time he touched her? She'd never had that problem before. It shouldn't happen, not when her job was to find him a bride. She set her chin. A *woman* for a bride, she reminded herself, not an *angel*.

"What precisely am I supposed to be looking at?" she asked lightly.

"Let's start with Mary Kressler."

"Pretty dress."

"It's red."

Angie smiled in delight. "No wonder I like it."

"She's never worn red before in her life. And check Doris."

"Which one is she?"

"The platinum blonde."

"Pretty."

"Yesterday she was a brunette."

Angie nodded sagely. "It's nice to see her admit her mistake and correct it."

"And see that?"

"Casey waved at us."

"She has…*things* attached to the end of her fingers."

"Um, Reed? They're called fingernails. Most people have them."

"Not like those," he retorted caustically. "They're three inches long and bright red. The first time she waved at me, I almost called 911. I thought she'd cut herself."

"I'm sure you were relieved to discover that wasn't the case."

"No, I wasn't. She can't even pick up a pencil

anymore. She's a damned bookkeeper! What good is she if she can't use her hands?''

''She'll get used to them,'' Angie soothed.

''You don't get it, do you?'' He scowled. ''You've only been here a week and already they're copying you!''

''Really?'' She was flattered by the suggestion. ''Now, isn't that sweet.''

''No! It's like… Like…*Invasion of the Body Snatchers* or *The Stepford Wives*.''

''Don't be ridiculous. Mary's gorgeous in red. It brings out the highlights in her hair. And have you noticed how much she's smiling? Did she used to smile that much?''

''I don't remember.''

''Probably no one else noticed, either. But they will now. And Doris hasn't only bleached her hair, she's also wearing makeup. And see? That nice man from accounting is talking to her.''

''If that nice man from accounting is talking to her, he's not working. I pay him to work, not fraternize with my employees.''

''Oh.'' Angie lifted an eyebrow in question. ''Would you like me to speak to them about it?''

He released his breath in a rough sigh and shot a quick look over his shoulder. ''No. It's just… Now Joel's fallen under your spell, too.''

She turned to face him, catching the sleeve of his shirt. Didn't he understand? ''I'm only trying to help. You want your brother away from the job sites, right? Well, this will do it. It'll give him a chance to learn more about the business. Isn't that your goal?''

"Yes, but—"

"I also had the feeling that he regarded this as an opportunity to prove himself. It's almost as if…" She frowned as she thought about it. "As if he had to make up for something. Is that possible?"

Reed closed his eyes, his mouth compressing into a grim line. "Yeah, it's possible." After a moment, he focused on her, his eyes as bleak as his voice. "He blames himself for an incident that happened a couple years back."

"*Was* it his fault?"

"Partially."

She glanced toward the office, relieved to see Joel engaged in a wrestling match with Scratch. "Then let him make amends. We all need an opportunity to atone for our mistakes."

He tilted his head to one side, studying her with open curiosity. "Are you speaking from experience?"

Why did it never get any easier? she wondered in despair. Slowly she lifted her gaze to his, knowing her pain couldn't be totally concealed from someone as discerning as Reed. "I'm speaking from a wealth of experience. Give Joel this chance. You won't regret it, I promise."

He took a minute to consider, before slowly nodding. "I'll have to get Tiger's agreement. But if he's willing to go along with it, so am I."

"I know reconciling Joel and Reed isn't part of my mission," Angie said in exasperation. "I don't need you to remind me."

Scratch whined as he shuffled in a circle on the couch cushion.

"Don't be ridiculous! Getting their relationship straightened out shouldn't be difficult at all. Besides, what could possibly go wrong?" She centered Reed's appointment book on his now-spotless desk. "It might even help. Keep in mind that if I'm to find Reed's 'true love,' I'll need Joel's cooperation."

"Do you always talk to yourself?" a husky voice interrupted from the doorway.

Angie whirled around to face Joel, then spared Scratch a reproving glance. "You're supposed to warn me when we have visitors." To her extreme annoyance, Scratch bared his teeth in half-grin, half-snarl. Da— *Darn,* but Guardian Angels were uppity creatures. She turned back to their visitor and smiled as casually as she could manage. Not that she fooled him. He was as irritatingly perceptive as his brother. "Oh, hi, Joel. I didn't see you."

"So, I figured." He glanced curiously from Angie to Scratch. "What's all this about finding Reed a true love?"

Angie edged her hip on the corner of the desk. "It's supposed to be a secret," she confessed.

She'd intrigued him with that one. "Really? I won't tell."

"You won't, huh?" She eyed him with open calculation. "Does that mean you'll help?"

"Find someone for Reed to love?" His eyes dimmed. "Maybe."

Less than the enthusiastic response she'd hoped for.

How unfortunate. "Don't you think he should get married? To have children?"

He bowed his head and shrugged, his attention focused on a ragged hole at the tip of his right sneaker. "Yeah. I guess. If that's what he wants."

Something felt out of kilter, but she couldn't quite put her finger on it. "What's wrong, Joel?" she asked gently.

"Nothin'."

Something was. And whatever the problem, it sounded serious. "You don't have to be involved, if you'd rather not. I can take care of this myself."

He slanted her a quick, belligerent look. "Tell me why you're doing it. What's it to you?"

"It's a job I've been assigned."

"By Reed?"

"Good heavens, no!" She hesitated. "Let's just say it's been requested by a higher authority."

"Oh." He nodded in complete understanding. "My mom must have sent you. She's been trying to get Reed married off ever since—" His words dried up and he returned to contemplating the hole in his sneaker. He poked his big toe into the gaping tear. "This woman you choose... Would—would you let me meet her? Let me get to know her before you marry her off to Reed?"

"Well, sure. Since you live with your brother, I think that's an excellent suggestion."

His lean frame tensed. "Promise?"

"Absolutely," she assured gravely. "Although, we're getting a little ahead of ourselves." She frowned as she thought about the multitude of problems she faced with this particular assignment. "First, I have to give him a little date training."

That grabbed Joel's attention. His chin jerked up. "Date training? Reed?"

Angie slid the rest of the way onto Reed's desk and jiggled a high-heeled shoe with the tips of her toes. "I know. It surprised me, too. But when I watched him at Sarducci's with Perfect Pamela he didn't quite have the hang of it."

"Oh." Joel made a face. "That must have been one of Mom's blind dates. She's the world's worst matchmaker. No wonder she brought in a specialist."

"She didn't exactly bring me in," Angie clarified uncomfortably. "Our missions happened to coincide. Will you trust me to do a better job than she's done so far?"

"He— *Heck!*" He spared Scratch a sheepish grin. "*I* could do better."

"Great. Then you'll help?"

The shadows invaded his expression again. "Only if you'll let me check her out first."

"I won't break the promise I made," Angie said gently. "I won't marry Reed off to anyone without your approval. You have my word on it."

"Thanks." The tension dissipated from his body and he glanced at her curiously. "So how are you going to date train him?"

"It'll be tricky. But I have a plan."

"Something sneaky, devious and underhanded?"

She grinned. "Absolutely."

Enthusiasm caught fire, blazing in Joel's hazel eyes. "In that case, count me in."

*   *   *

Reed strode into Sarducci's, silently fuming. This was the last time. Tonight would be the last damn time he allowed his mother to set him up on another blind date. He'd been patient with her obsession to see him married after that fiasco with Emily. More than patient. But enough was enough.

"Why, Mr. Harding. How good to see you again so soon."

"Hello, Rollo. I wish I could say the same."

The maître d' rubbed his hands together and grinned. "Ah, but you will. Trust me. You will be most pleased by the end of the evening. Your guest has already arrived. Shall I show you to your table?"

"Please."

He'd only taken three steps into the restaurant when he spotted his secretary. Angie Makepeace occupied the centermost table again. And as she had since they'd first met, she wore red. This particular dress strained every man's self-control to the absolute limit. Held on by two fragile spaghetti straps, the low-cut, golden-red silk molded a path from her generous chest to her minuscule waist, the shimmering color gradually deepening in hue as it lapped downward over her body. It reminded him of a fire, the color lighter at the edges, the red tinged with yellows and oranges. But the wide, handkerchief skirt captured the raging hot core of the inferno, flaring outward in streams of deep burned-red.

Great. How the hell was he expected to pay attention to his date when temptation beckoned. He'd have to make certain his chair faced away from—

Rollo stopped at Angie's table. "Here we are, Mr. Harding."

Reed's brows drew together. "Excuse me? What do you mean, 'here we are'?"

The maître d' cleared his throat, glancing apprehensively from one to the other. "Your date for the evening. It's Ms. Makepeace."

"Thank you, Rollo," Angie interrupted. "I'll take over now."

"What's going on?" Reed demanded in an undertone as the maître d' scurried away.

She offered one of those smiles guaranteed to ignite dangerous fantasies. With one twist of her full-lipped mouth she burned a searing path straight through to his gut, rousing every raw, primitively male instinct he possessed. He clenched his hands so he wouldn't be tempted to snatch her from her chair and brand her as his own. Why the hell had Seduction's handmaiden been foisted on him? And how the devil did he get rid of her?

"Would you like to sit down while I explain?" she suggested.

"What I'd like to do is walk out of here."

She inclined her head. "It's your choice. I won't try and stop you."

"Wise decision." He debated leaving, knowing full well it would be his smartest move. But then... When had he ever made the smart moves in life? Swearing beneath his breath, he snatched out a chair and planted himself in it. "Okay, Makepeace. Spill it. What the hell's going on?"

"It's a long story."

"In that case, I suggest you get started."

She selected a bread stick and snapped it in half, smiling at the pattern of crumbs that scattered far and wide across the crisp white tablecloth. "Do you know... I actually met someone who read bread crumbs the way some people read tea leaves. We used to do it for fun. They form the most interesting patterns. Have you ever noticed?"

"No."

"Try it."

"Ms. Makepeace—"

"Angie, remember?"

"Angie—"

"Please? Break a bread stick for me."

She was insane. There couldn't be any other explanation. Snatching a bread stick from the basket, he broke it in two. Crumbs pelted the table. "Satisfied?"

Fumbling for her purse, she removed her glasses. "It's so annoying. I can't see up close without these." Settling the wire rims onto the bridge of her nose, she slipped from her chair and crossed to his side. She crouched down until their shoulders bumped.

He could smell her perfume. The tantalizing scent held a crisp floral freshness, chaste and sweet. And yet for some reason it stirred an image of hot sultry nights and desperate lovemaking. He shook his head, trying to dispel the impression. How the hell could one odor combine such innocence with such decadence? Whoever had marketed it must have been a genius.

She leaned nearer and he noticed that she'd worn her hair piled on top of her head instead of loose. For some reason, that drove him crazy, too. Fine, silky curls clung to her temple and the pale nape of her neck, swirling hypnotically with her every movement. All he could think about was satin skin on top of satin sheets.

"This is interesting," she murmured.

He forced himself to focus. "What is?"

"The pattern your bread crumbs have made."

"This little game of yours is ridiculous, not interesting."

She laughed, the sound low and intimate, as though they shared a private joke. "Shall I see if I can remember how this works? It's been a while since I've played this game."

If it kept her this close, he'd agree to almost anything. "Sure. Be my guest."

She reached for the shaker filled with Parmesan cheese. Capturing his hand in hers, she dumped a small amount in his palm. Blowing gently, she sent the grated cheese scattering in among the bread crumbs.

"What did you do that for?" he questioned.

"Supposedly, the bread crumbs are our actions and the decisions we make. The cheese represents our emotions."

He stifled a laugh. "Of course. Makes perfect sense," he lied without compunction. "So what does it say?"

"Well... First of all, you're an innie."

"Come again?"

"You snap your stick inward, so it stays contained in one small area. That makes you an innie."

"You're an outie, aren't you?"

Her mouth tilted in a wry smile. "Oh, yes." She gestured toward her side of the table. "See? My crumbs go everywhere. It means I'm exuberant about life."

"Somehow that doesn't surprise me."

Her glasses slid to the tip of her nose and she fixed him with pure blue eyes. They were soft and pale, ringed on the outer edge in indigo. He'd never seen such unfettered warmth reflected in a woman's eyes before. And the promises he discovered there—promises of love and laughter and joy—stirred a craving he'd long ago suppressed. It had been years since someone had regarded him with such unconditional acceptance.

"What does it mean?" He held her gaze as he gestured toward the crumbs on his side of the table. "What characterizes an innie?"

"Innies like to control their life and those in it."

"That doesn't come as any surprise."

"It also means you're precise and careful." With a small sigh of regret, she shifted her attention to the tablecloth. A frown crept across her brow. "Even your crumbs are organized. Except—"

"Except what?"

"See on the edges, how some have scattered off in little tangents?"

"It's straight physics, sweetheart. You drop something from a specific height and it forms a similar pattern over and over."

"Similar, but not the same. That's where the art of reading bread crumbs comes in. Let's see what I still remember...." She tapped the aberrant crumb trail with a long red fingernail. "These tangents are your future. The way they've fallen means you're looking for something."

"And what is it I'm looking for?" Cynicism had drifted into his voice. "You?"

"No. Not me." She turned again and her lips were so close to his, he could feel her words brush by, like butterfly wings flitting lazily across his skin. "You're looking for a woman. The one woman you can love for the rest of your life."

Reed's mouth twisted into a parody of a smile. He should have seen it coming. He'd been a fool not to. Reaching out, he swept the crumbs from the table. "Wrong, sweetheart. That's the last thing I need in my life."

He caught her elbow in an iron grip, fighting to ignore the softness of her skin, fighting to resist the urge to feather his calloused hands over the sensitive curve of her inner arm. He wanted her. Wanted to explore the pale, sweet swell of her breasts and the vulnerable length of her neck. To lose himself in the moist lushness of her mouth until her desire matched his.

He gathered his control, refusing to be sidetracked. He wasn't about to let another woman screw up his life. Not again. Not ever again. "Now tell me what the hell you're doing here," he demanded. "And it had better be good."

"Okay." She offered a tentative smile. "You see... I'm your practice date."

CHAPTER FOUR

IT TOOK Reed a full minute to assimilate Angie's words. "Practice date?" he repeated.

"Right. Consider it a dress rehearsal. We go out and I show you how to treat a woman on a date." Ever so gently she tugged at the arm he held. "For instance, you don't grab a woman with such force. You might leave a bruise."

He unclamped his hand and allowed her to slip free. In a graceful swirl of silk, she rose and returned to her side of the table. "Thanks for the advice," he ground out. "I'll try and remember. Mind if I give you a dating tip in return?"

She tucked her eyeglasses into the pale curls crowning her head. "Not at all."

He leaned across the table. "Don't set up your boss. It could lead to a serious case of unemployment."

She sighed. "I suspected you wouldn't take this well."

"Then why do it?"

For a moment her amusement dimmed and her smile had a bittersweet quality. It tempted him to enclose her in his arms until the laughter returned to her eyes. But he didn't dare betray those feelings. She stirred in him a dangerous hunger, one he could never sate—a craving that wouldn't ease over time or with familiarity. No. If he ever cut loose enough to enjoy Ms. Makepeace's charms, one taste wouldn't satisfy him. Better to stay angry. At least anger enabled him to hold her at a safe distance.

She leaned an elbow on the table and cupped her chin in her palm. Candlelight licked across her cheekbones and silvered the pale blue of her eyes. "I watched you with Pamela the other night."

Watched *and* had taken notes. Were they still in that minuscule purse of hers, listed and numbered on that damned steno pad? "My personal life isn't any of your business."

"You made it my business when you requested my help finding a wife."

He leaned back in his seat with an audible groan. "Don't start that again."

"Don't you want to marry and have a family?"

His mouth thinned, her reference to a family more painful than he cared to admit. "When I'm ready and not a minute sooner."

"If you're not ready, why go along with all these dates your mother sets up?"

"Because it costs little to humor her and it eases her conscience over a past incident."

"Eases her conscience?" Angie paused to consider his comment. "A 'past incident' suggests that you were once involved in a serious relationship." He didn't respond, totally unwilling to explain about Emily and the circumstances under which she'd left. Not that his silence deterred her. "I gather your mother interfered in some way that she now regrets?"

"I don't want to discuss it. You're my secretary,

in case you've forgotten. I don't know why my family saw fit to involve you in any of this, but I'd appreciate it if you'd stay out.''

"The list—"

"Must have been someone's idea of a joke," he interrupted. "I don't need a wife. Should I change my mind sometime in the future, I'll take care of it myself, without the help of my mother, my brother or my secretary. Are we clear about this?''

She inclined her head. "Absolutely." Laughter returned to her expression, like the sun emerging from a bank of clouds after a summer shower. It brightened her features, caught in her eyes and teased at the corners of her lips. "But since we're here—"

"I should take advantage of your offer for a practice date?''

"Definitely." She reached for her purse and removed the infamous steno pad. Untangling her glasses from the curls on top of her head, she propped the gold wire rims on her nose once more. "I've made a list of suggestions that might help you.''

His mouth twisted. "Big surprise."

"Would you like to hear them?''

"Can I stop you?''

Her smile flashed again. "Doubtful."

"Then get it over with."

"Okay. Broken down into consumable pieces we have the following...." She ran her finger slowly down the length of the page. "The initial meeting. That's vital, of course, since first impressions are the most important. Second is the preliminary conversation, which is the best chance you'll have to pique her interest. That's followed by discussing the dinner order." She peered at him over the top of her wire rims. "I noticed you and Pamela didn't do much discussing the other night."

"You're quite right." He strove to appear suitably apologetic. "We were both so overcome by the urge to consume the sole, the conversation sort of dried up at that point."

She wrinkled her nose. "Why anyone would order sole at an Italian restaurant is quite beyond me."

He shrugged. "Sorry. I guess we both lost our heads."

"Humph. Perhaps if you *had* lost your heads a little, we wouldn't be having a practice date." She went back to perusing her list. "After the order you carefully enter into more serious conversation, find some common ground and learn more about each other. Next comes eating and the fine art of flirtation, followed by glances, a few brief touches and coffee."

"Touches *and* coffee? Aren't you rushing things a bit?" he asked mildly.

"No. Touching is vital. It cements the connection. Finally we have dessert or *dessert*. Also known as the love rush."

"What the hell is that?"

She lifted an eyebrow. "You've never experienced the love rush?"

He'd be damned if he'd admit to any such thing. "I didn't say that. I merely asked what it was."

"It's when the passion between the two of you is so strong, you don't bother wading all the way through the meal. Other, more important matters are on your mind.''

''Oh. You mean her apartment or yours.''

''I most certainly do not.'' She tossed her glasses to the table and glared at him. ''Only a man would phrase it so crudely. I'm talking about romance. I'm talking about that irresistible attraction that flares between a man and a woman. An attraction that's so strong, food is meaningless. The urge for privacy becomes paramount.''

Privacy, huh? He leaned forward. ''It's called sex, Ms. Makepeace.''

She leaned forward, as well. ''It's called love, Mr. Harding!''

''*Women* call it making love. *Men* call it getting—''

''Oh!'' She straightened abruptly. ''No wonder you need dating lessons!''

That stopped him. ''My apologies, Angie. Perhaps you're right. I guess I could use a few dating tips.''

She eyed him suspiciously. ''Are you serious?''

''It can't hurt.'' And it would be interesting to see how far she intended to take the evening. ''Let's start from the top, shall we? We've just arrived at the restaurant and we're meeting for the first time. What would make the best sort of first impression?''

''A smile.''

''That's it?''

''It's a great start.'' She tilted her head to one side. ''Do you realize you didn't smile once at Pamela?''

''There's a reason for that. Pamela didn't make me want to smile.'' When she started to interrupt, he held up his hands in mock surrender. "Okay, I'll smile. Do we touch at that point?"

"If you'd like to shake her hand, that's acceptable. A kiss on the cheek strikes me as too practiced, so I'd avoid that. And whatever you do, don't kiss her hand. Unless you're European it'll seem fake." She regarded him with a wistful expression. "I don't suppose you're European?"

"Born and bred in the good ol' U.S. of A. Why?"

She shrugged. "I've never had a man kiss my hand before. I thought it might be a new experience." Before he could think of a response, she buried her face in her steno pad again.

Plucking her glasses from the center of the table, he perched them on the tip of her nose. "Here. Try these."

"Oh, thanks." She adjusted them slightly, the crystal lenses appearing to wink at him. "That's much better. Okay, after the initial meeting, there's the preliminary conversation. You know, that initial break-the-ice chitchat."

"I've never been very good at that."

"Try asking how she met your mother."

"Excellent suggestion. How *did* you meet my mother?"

He'd caught her totally flat-footed. She stared at him, her eyes wide and startled. "I—I didn't."

Reed's regard turned sharkish. "Really? She called and arranged tonight. How could she have done that if she doesn't know you?"

She'd really stepped in it this time. "That's not important—"

Fury gathered in his eyes as he slowly put the pieces of the puzzle together. "You arranged this with her, didn't you? Perhaps with Joel's assistance?"

Angie watched him apprehensively. "You're beginning to look angry again. That's not a very good idea for a first date."

"Did the three of you put your heads together and decide that I needed dating lessons? Are you all in on it?"

She couldn't lie. Nor did she want to answer with the truth. Silence truly seemed the best option. Not that he'd let her get away with it.

Any remaining hint of humor vanished from his expression. "You set me up."

"You're not smiling anymore."

A dangerous glint appeared in his eyes. "It would seem everyone knows what's best for me. And they know it better than I do."

"That's not quite—"

"You'd like to teach me how to be a good date?" he interrupted.

"If it means another change of subject, I'd *love* to teach you how to be a good date."

"Then get on with it, Ms. Makepeace. It may be the last job you have at Harding's."

Actually, it *was* her last job opportunity. Not that she could explain that to him. "You're supposed to smile, remember?"

"Oh, right." He bared his teeth. "How's that."

"I guess it'll do."

"Next we're supposed to exchange general chit-chat."

"Perhaps we should skip that part," she muttered. "It seems to bring out the worst in you."

"Only when I discover I've been deceived."

"I haven't lied to you. Not once. You may not care for my methods, but I've answered every question you've ever asked with the truth."

"Then answer this one. Do you really think I'm in need of your services, Angie? That I don't know how to treat a date?"

He asked the question ever so softly, the words a blatant challenge. She studied him in open curiosity. Did he need help? She wouldn't have thought so.

Reed was a striking man, large and yet carrying himself with assurance and grace. She'd had over a week to watch him at work, to take note of his intelligence and patience. Sure, he had a temper, but he balanced it with justice. She suppressed her amusement. If he hadn't, she'd have been fired on her very first day. And what woman could resist the warmth in his eyes, the hint of molten gold that accented the autumnal greens and browns? If she'd still been a woman, instead of an angel—

The sharp pain of loss caught her totally off guard. What had she been thinking? This man wasn't for her. No man was. She'd been sent to provide him with an earthbound woman. One who would love him all his days and who would bear his children. A woman who'd greet the kiss of morning trapped snug within his arms. A wife who'd fill the night's passage with the music of her sleep-laden breath and the scented heat of her body. Someone he could grow old with, someone to delight in all the special memories they'd experience together and share the burden of their joint sorrows.

And that someone wasn't her.

"What is it, Angie? What's wrong?"

The urgent timbre of his voice banished her thoughts, forcing her to focus on the task she'd been set. "I was thinking about your future—"

"They didn't look like happy thoughts."

"They were," she insisted. *For you.*

"And you don't lie."

"I can't. Although there are times when I'd like to."

"Is this one of those times?"

"No. Actually, it isn't." She lifted her gaze to his, willing him to believe. "It's not always comfortable telling you the truth. It seems to irritate you."

"Nicely put."

"Thanks. But I'd still rather be frank."

"And you really think that as long as we're here, we should go ahead with our practice date?"

"I watched you with Pamela," she reminded. "Trust me. A little practice wouldn't hurt."

"Okay." She didn't like the way his eyes glittered. He looked like Scratch at the dog's most mischievous. "I'll practice my dating skills on you. I trust you'll warn me if I make a mistake?"

She regarded Reed with acute suspicion. How was it possible that this man could fill her with such uncertainty? No man had been able to do that, not in all her years on earth or all the time she'd spent within heaven's gates. And why now? Reed represented her very last chance to prove herself worthy. Just great.

Her last chance and Goodenkind had stuck her with a man capable of muddling her thinking and arousing desires totally inappropriate in an angel.

"Well? Is it a deal?" he asked.

Angie nodded. After all, what choice did she have? "It's a deal."

"And once you've taught me everything you know, you'll drop this nonsense about finding me a wife?"

She couldn't resist a little teasing of her own. "Teaching you all I know might take a while."

"Really?" His tone roughened. "I look forward to the education."

Their waiter appeared and Reed ordered wine and an appetizer. "Did I do that right?" he questioned the moment the waiter left. "Should I have asked your preference?"

Was he mocking her? She couldn't tell. Deciding to take him seriously, she said, "A woman doesn't mind if a man takes charge on occasion. *If* he knows what he's doing." She reached for another bread stick and snapped it, sending crumbs flying in every direction. "In this case, I've had the '85 *Verrazzano* and it's excellent. So is the *Braseola.*"

"Does that mean we're through with meaningless chitchat?"

"I certainly hope so."

"What's next on your list? Oh, that's right. It's time for a more serious conversation." He teased her with a slow smile. "Why don't you examine your bread crumbs and tell me what you see. Didn't you say you could read the future in them?"

She moistened her lips, not liking the direction he'd

chosen for their discussion. "The past and present, as well as the future," she admitted reluctantly. "Or so my friend claimed."

"Tell me what yours say."

She didn't want to look. After all, what could she possibly learn that she didn't know already? That she didn't belong here with him? That she had no future? Or worse... Perhaps she'd learn that her mission would fail and she'd be put outside the Pearly Gates. "I'd rather not," she whispered.

"Why?"

A deep sadness gripped her. "I'd rather not know."

He stared in wonder. "You're afraid."

She managed a smile. "A little."

"What in the world could *you* be afraid of?"

Nothing of *this* world. Heaven was another matter altogether. "You don't understand."

"Then explain it."

"The bread crumbs can't tell my future." She didn't have a future. At least not here.

"You can see mine, but not your own?"

"Not exactly." She fought her frustration. "It wouldn't apply. Not to me. Besides, it's nothing more than a game."

The cynicism stormed back into his expression. "Read what it says, anyway. Oh, and don't forget the cheese."

Reluctantly, she dropped her gaze to the tabletop. Toasted crumbs dusted the fine white linen. Upending the Parmesan shaker into her palm, she gently blew the grated cheese onto the tablecloth. It scattered among the crumbs. "Reed—"

"Start with the past."

She didn't need to look. She already knew what it revealed. Sure enough an arc stretched across the table in a thin, cut-off rainbow of Parmesan and crumbs. "It says…" She cleared her throat and tried again, forcing a hint of lightness into the husky tones. "It shows someone who lived life with enthusiasm. Someone who burned hot and bright. Someone who made a lot of mistakes, but never slowed her desperate rush through life."

"There's a lot of chunks in that section of crumbs."

She fought to conceal the pain that must be reflected in her eyes. "Those were my stumbling blocks."

"You had a lot of them."

"It happens."

His voice had gentled. "And the present?"

She tapped a long, red-tipped fingernail toward a small circle that had formed in the middle of the table. "It's here."

"It's so small."

"So's the present. Small. Brief. A mere moment."

"And what does it say?"

It said precisely what she expected. "That even though my time here is short, it, too, will have stumbling blocks."

"A tough past *and* a tough present? That doesn't seem fair."

She managed to look at him. "Who ever said life was fair?"

"What about your future?"

Only cheese lay in that area. She indicated it with a sweep of her hand. "See? No crumbs. It appears to be easy sailing." Either that...or no future. She couldn't quite remember what she'd been told. But she couldn't very well admit as much to him.

Fortunately the waiter arrived with their wine and appetizer. It brought a fast end to an uncomfortable topic. Reed must have felt the same way. The minute they'd placed their dinner orders and were left alone, he apologized.

"I didn't mean to upset you." He offered a repentant smile. "I guess I really do need dating lessons."

"Fair enough."

"Let's see... What other topics can we discuss?" He snapped his fingers, the sound as sharp as a gunshot. "I know. Tell me how you came to be my secretary."

She cupped her chin in her palm and released a gusty sigh. Why had the expression "out of the frying pan and into the fire" taken on a whole new meaning? "I was assigned to you by my supervisor."

"Mr. Goodenkind, wasn't it?"

"That's him."

"And what does he have against me?"

His comment hit so close to her own thoughts that Angie couldn't help it. She laughed. "I've been asking myself that same question."

"And what answer have you come up with?"

"I suspect we deserve each other," she replied promptly.

He grinned. "You're probably right." Taking a sip of wine, he studied her curiously. "So, tell me where else you worked before landing on my doorstep."

She found his phrasing amusing. Landed, indeed. If he only knew. "I've had quite a variety of jobs. I've been a hotel manager, worked for a law firm as a paralegal, done a bit of wrangling on a dude ranch, helped out at a computer firm and spent time as a dock worker. I've even been a chef."

"A chef?" Suspicion caught in his gaze. "Where?"

She cleared her throat. "Here."

"Here." His eyes narrowed. "Didn't Rollo mention something about a fire?"

She could feel a hint of warmth creep into her cheeks. "Not one of my finer hours, I must admit."

"And have all your jobs been equally successful?"

"'Fraid so," she confessed. "But don't worry. There's not much damage I can do at Harding Construction. I'm actually an excellent secretary. Some of those other jobs were...aberrations."

"Aberrations."

"Oh, don't let that worry you. I've had an excellent working relationship with each and every one of my employers."

"And the jobs themselves?"

Discretion seemed wise at this juncture. "Goodenkind is hoping I'll succeed with this one."

"And if you don't?"

"You won't suffer, I promise," she hastened to

say. "They'll send in someone who'll correct any mistakes I make."

"And what will happen to you?"

She shrugged, giving him a reassuring smile. "If it makes you feel any better, I won't be inflicted on anyone else."

Reed's brows knit together. "This is your last chance?"

"Lucky thirteen."

"They'll fire you if you fail again?"

Time for another change of subject. "You're doing really well, Reed. You're showing the perfect mix of interest and concern. There isn't a woman anywhere who could resist a man who does that."

"The hell with the dating lesson. I'm serious. What will you do if you're fired from this job?"

She attempted to ease his concern with a cheerful look. "Don't worry about it. I'll be out on my own, but I'm used to that." When he didn't appear convinced, she insisted, "Really. It's not like—" She swallowed hard. "It's not like the world will come to an end. And as I said. You won't be made to suffer. Good will see to it. He'll send in a cleanup crew and—"

"A *cleanup* crew!"

She waved her hand in airy dismissal. "That's just what I call them. It's an expression. Nothing more. There's rarely anything for them to clean up."

"Except the occasional fire?"

"Rollo's mustache grew back," she retorted defensively.

"I'm tempted to ask about those other jobs."

"I'd rather you didn't."

"I'll bet."

"Oh, look. Here comes dinner."

"Lucky escape."

"Or heavenly intervention," she murmured beneath her breath.

To her relief, he let it go, instead discussing various construction projects currently under development. And as he talked, she gradually relaxed, fascinated by his enthusiasm and knowledge of the industry. She suspected he'd deliberately set out to keep her entertained, to help ease the tension between them—which brought home the fact that this man didn't need dating lessons from anyone. He managed quite well on his own.

All too well.

It wasn't until halfway through the meal that he shoved his plate to one side and fixed her with a cool, determined gaze. "So tell me, Ms. Makepeace. Are you ready to admit the truth now?"

She froze, a forkful of *frenette nere* halfway to her mouth. "Excuse me?"

"I keep waiting for you to explain what we're doing here, but so far you haven't cooperated."

Carefully returning her fork to her plate, she scrambled for a reply. "Haven't we discussed this already?"

"We've danced around the subject any number of times." He leaned forward. "The question I want answered is…why? Why are you so interested in my love life? What the hell business is it of yours?"

"You don't understand."

"Then explain it to me."

"It's…it's complicated."

He reached out, capturing her hand in his. "You promised to always tell the truth."

"Please don't ask me this particular question."

"Why?" His index finger stroked the back of her hand, tracing a leisurely path upward. "Won't I like your answer?"

She fought to suppress an involuntary shiver. "Reed—"

"Tell me why we're really here, Angie."

"What do you mean?"

"You didn't arrange this evening because you thought I needed dating lessons."

She stared at him, startled. "Yes! Yes, I did."

"Then why are you looking at me like that?"

"Like what?"

"Like you're starving. Like you've been adrift for most of your life and just now found home port."

"I'm doing no such thing."

"You said you never lie. Yet, I'm looking into the most beautiful eyes I've ever seen and it's all right there. The hunger. The irresistible attraction. The invitation."

"Stop it, Reed."

"Relax, sweetheart. I feel the same way. I wanted you the first minute I saw you, too. You were trouble in a red dress, but I didn't have the willpower to send you away."

"You're not supposed to say these things to me."

"Isn't that why we're here?" His eyes darkened,

the dark browns and greens eclipsing the gold. "Isn't that why we're playing out this charade?"

She had the terrible suspicion that she'd screwed up another mission. Badly. "What do you mean?"

"You want me, Angie, every bit as much as I want you. Isn't that why you arranged tonight?"

"No! You've totally misunderstood. I arranged tonight in order to teach you how to date."

"Bull. You didn't come tonight to *teach* me how to date. You came to *date* me."

There was a horrible logic to his accusation. A logic she shied away from pursuing. "You've made a mistake," she insisted tightly.

"Come off it, Angie. Why don't you use some of that honesty you value so highly and admit the truth. Let's finish this. We've talked. We've exchanged glances. We've even touched, though not nearly enough. To hell with coffee. To hell with dessert. Call it a love rush. Rationalize the attraction any damn way you want. But be honest about your feelings and come home with me."

She stared at him, wide-eyed. Slowly she shook her head. "No. No, you've got it all wrong. You *have* to be wrong."

Abruptly, she thrust back her chair and snatched up her purse. And then she walked as quickly as she could toward the exit, moving faster and faster until she looked like a finger of fire racing across the restaurant. She heard Reed call to her, but ignored him, ignored everything except the urgent need to escape. She flew past Rollo and entered the revolving doors.

She felt Reed right behind, crowding her into the tiny cubicle, his heat branding her spine.

"Ah, the love rush," Rollo called after them, raising his fingers to his lips and blowing them a kiss. "At last."

The doors took forever to turn. Finally they opened onto the street, allowing her to escape. She didn't linger, instead hurrying down the sidewalk away from Sarducci's.

"Angie, wait." Reed caught her arm before she'd gone more than half a dozen steps.

"No!" She turned to confront him. Distant thunder rumbled through the city, echoing off steel and concrete. "You don't understand. You have it wrong. All wrong."

A flash of lightning lit the nighttime sky, throwing the taut planes of Reed's face into sharp relief and flashing eerily in the golden-green depths of his eyes. "Then explain it to me."

"I'm not here for you. This…this *thing* between us… It's impossible."

"Is it?" He caught her in his arms, pulled her firmly against him. She could feel his raw power, could sense the tight rein he kept on his desire. "You swore you wouldn't lie to me, Angie. But that's precisely what you're doing."

"There's nothing between us, Reed. There can't be."

"I can prove there is." He cupped her head, his hand sinking into the knot of curls. "It would be all too easy. All I'd have to do is this…."

CHAPTER FIVE

REED bent his head to steal a kiss, then hesitated, arrested by the expression on Angie's face.

Tears gathered in her eyes, giving mute testimony to the fact that this wasn't a game. Not for her. He'd never known anyone with as much self-possession as this woman, someone as comfortable with herself or with the unmistakable frailty she found in others. And yet, holding her in his arms, gazing into her sea-swept eyes, he saw the painful depth of her vulnerability. She stood before him, unshielded and assailable. In the far distance, lightning clawed apart the sky again, silvering her face in its unearthly glow, illuminating what she strove so hard to disguise.

She was afraid, he realized in shock. It radiated from her with stunning force.

"What is it?" he demanded. "What are you afraid of?"

She started to turn away and he didn't think she'd answer. Then she lifted her chin, anger vying for supremacy over her fear. "Da— *Darn* it all! I can't believe this is happening. You want an answer?" The words spilled from her in an emotional torrent. "Fine, I'll give you one. I'm afraid our relationship will get out of hand. I'm afraid I'll fail at my job. I'm afraid of the future. But most of all, I'm afraid of what I—"

Her voice broke painfully and she pulled against his hold.

He refused to release her. "Finish it. What are you most afraid of?"

"Of what I *feel*. There, are you satisfied now?"

"It's a simple kiss, Angie," he soothed. "It's nothing to fear."

After all, what could one kiss hurt?

He bent his head, waiting for a refusal that never came. Her silence gave him all the permission he needed. His mouth closed over hers and ever so gently he tasted the moist softness, allowing her to taste him, as well. It was a cautious give-and-take, slow and careful and considerate, the passion held firmly in check. It offered them a sampling of pleasures to come, a mere sip of wine-sweet anticipation.

"See?" he murmured, pulling back slightly. "Nothing to fear."

She made no move to escape. Instead she seemed to drink in the moment, intoxicated by the pure simplicity of their kiss. Her lashes fluttered and she looked at him. The sheer joy reflected in her dream-laden eyes stunned him as much as the intensity of her yearning roused his curiosity. Perhaps she'd had a bad experience recently. Perhaps she'd been holding men at a distance. Or perhaps she just needed the warmth of human touch. Not that it mattered. Her reaction drew him, invited him to magnify that joy.

He sealed her mouth once again and this time there was nothing tentative about his kiss. He didn't sample. He took. He didn't lightly linger, but explored with rapacious curiosity. He melded them with lips

and teeth and tongue. Her response came with a fe-
rocious power identical to the storm bearing down
around them.

It was her turn to take, her turn to explore, her turn
to brand him with her unique taste and touch. Thunder
reverberated beneath their feet, shuddering through
them, quickening the bone-deep longing and stirring
a primitive mating urge that was eons old. Her lips
parted and her breath became his. She tasted like raw
hunger, anticipation scenting her with the fragrance
of irresistible temptation.

Physical desire slammed through his body. He
wasn't alone. Reed could see the budded tips of
Angie's breasts pressing through the thin silk of her
dress, hear the harsh catch in her throat as he molded
her close, feel the urgent tripping of her heartbeat. He
wanted her. He wanted her in his bed, stripped of all
artifice, her vulnerability transposed into strength, her
passion equaled only by his own. The storm broke,
pelted them with stinging spears of chilly rain.
Reluctantly, Reed pulled back.

"You see?" he repeated. "There's nothing to
fear."

Raindrops clung to Angie's hair and lashes, glittering beneath the streetlights like liquid diamonds.
"And I told you this was impossible!"

He framed her face with his hands, laughing as the
skies finally opened and a cold, invigorating down-
pour drenched them. "Impossible? Wet, perhaps. But
not impossible."

"Yes, it is!" She could hardly hear her own words.
They were drowned out by all the sounds around

them—the muted roar of the traffic, the hiss of tires on rain-slick pavement, the distant rumble of thunder and the deadening thrumming of the summertime rain as it pelted the concrete-laden earth. She stepped back, forcing him to release her, forcing him to listen. "We can't do this!"

"Why?"

She shouted, lifting her voice so he'd hear across the great chasm that separated them—so that she'd hear, as well, and remember. "Because I'm not a woman. I'm an angel. And I was sent here to find you a wife. There. How's that for honesty?"

He laughed. "You're crazy, you know that? And I'm even crazier to stand here and listen, instead of getting us out of this."

As though in response to his comment, a cab pulled up to the curb, disgorging a load of passengers beneath Sarducci's canopy.

Reed grabbed her hand and ran to catch it, pulling her into the dry confines. After giving the driver the address to his office building, he settled back against the seat and wrapped her within the secure warmth of his arms. The cab pulled away from the curb—but not before Angie saw Scratch.

He sat on the curb, a splash of black and white on the puddled sidewalk, his red bow tie drooping beneath the relentless torrent. And in his pale eyes, she caught a wealth of sadness.

"Why are we going to the office?" she asked after a few minutes of silence.

"To dry off. I converted a section of the building into a small apartment. I use it the nights I work late.

We can shower and then I'll find you something to wear home.''

"You and Joel don't live there, though?"

"No. We share a house out of the city. A house-keeper stays with Joel when I can't be there."

"And it wouldn't do to bring your secretary home to dry off." Cynicism edged her voice.

He didn't react to her baiting, but answered calmly. "No, it wouldn't. Especially since I left my car at the office and we wouldn't have transportation to work tomorrow morning."

"I see."

"You don't approve of the apartment?"

"It's not my place—"

"When has that ever stopped you?" He tucked a sodden lock of hair behind her ear. "I have Joel to consider. It wouldn't be appropriate to entertain overnight visitors at the house. I'd be giving him tacit permission to do the same thing and that would be wrong."

"So you keep your affairs at the office."

"Very amusing, Makepeace." The cab pulled up outside Harding Construction and Reed paid the driver. "Come on. Let's get dry."

Walking into the silent office building proved very strange. They met a security guard when they first arrived, but other than that, a tomblike silence permeated the atmosphere. They rode the elevator without speaking. At the door to his apartment, Reed punched in a security code before stepping to one side so she could enter.

Angie slipped off her damp shoes and left them on

a rug by the doorway. Inside, the furnishings were spartan, yet attractive. Carpet gave way to bleached oak flooring and the walls were a clean, crisp white, displaying black and white photographs of construction sites in various stages of development. A huge picture window offered a view of the brightly lit city and on the opposite end another bank of shadowed windows overlooked the nearby river.

She chose that side of the apartment, preferring the protective darkness it afforded. "The river flooded a few years back, didn't it?" she asked, finally breaking the silence. "I remember seeing it on the news."

"Yeah. It was pretty grim." The glass mirrored the apartment behind her, warning of his approach. He paused directly behind her. Without her heels, he seemed impossibly large and broad, leaving her feeling small and insignificant. Amazing the difference three tiny inches could make. "The water came so high, it even covered the streets along the riverfront."

"It must have been a terrible summer."

"I gather you didn't live here then?"

"No."

"Which of your various jobs were you working that year?" he asked curiously. "Wrangling? The docks, perhaps?"

"None of them. I was living my own life. It was…before." She flicked her red-tipped fingernails toward the ceiling. "You know."

"Before you became an angel."

She heard the thread of amusement in his voice and shivered. "Right, before then. I haven't been one all that long. Just for a year."

"You're cold."

Surprised to discover she was shivering, she wrapped her arms around her waist. "Actually, it feels good. Each of the different senses feels good. I hadn't realized how much I missed them until—" She ground to a halt, afraid if she kept talking, she'd do something incredibly foolish. Like cry.

"Would you like a shower?" he asked. "I think I can dig up some sweats you could wear home."

"You don't believe me, do you?"

"About being an angel? No. I don't." He cupped her shoulders, running his hands down her back, his touch a painfully delicious caress. "I don't suppose you'd care to show me your wings."

"I have no control over who sees them and who doesn't. Sometimes they're visible. Other times..." She shrugged.

"And the halo?" He feathered his fingers through her damp hair.

"Not there, either?"

"Nope."

"Maybe it's because I'm not feeling terribly angelic." A bittersweet smile crept across her mouth and she bowed her head. "After tonight, I wonder if I'll still deserve one."

"Angie." He spoke her name in a soft whisper, concern clear in the husky tones. "What's going on?"

She gathered her strength. This was always the most difficult part. Some believed her when she told them. Some didn't. Some she told of her mission and others she chose not to. It depended on the individual. But in Reed's case, her mission had begun to go horribly wrong. She made a face. At some point, they *all* went horribly wrong. Still, he had to understand that she couldn't be a real woman for him. She had a vital job to accomplish—one that would affect the rest of his life. A job she didn't dare fail. She gathered her strength and turned to confront him.

Reed caught his breath at her anguished expression. The rain had washed away her makeup, leaving her even more beautiful, if that were possible. Except for the hint of color blossoming in her cheeks, her skin gleamed as though lit from within. Her hair had begun to dry, curling tightly in the humidity. Pale ringlets clung to her temple and brow, giving her an angelic appearance that lent credence to her celestial claims.

But it was her eyes that left him utterly speechless.

"Mirrors of the soul" didn't come close to describing them. In their soft blue depths he saw both devastation and great joy. He saw the tender buds of hope vying with the overwhelming weight of despair. He saw winter's frigid death and spring's warm rebirth. And he didn't doubt that if he looked long enough he could find all of eternity locked within her gaze.

What touched him most, though, was the brief, swiftly banked desire that burned there, the desperate need of a woman waiting for her lover's touch, yet afraid to grasp it.

"Angie. Don't look at me like that, sweetheart. It's killing me."

He reached for her then, pulling her into his arms. Her resistance was a fleeting thing, swiftly subdued beneath his urgent kiss. He was so damned ready for her, hot and full and straining. It had been ages since he'd made love to a woman. Hell. It had been ages since he'd wanted to. Emily had left him embittered, reluctant to trust intimacy. And yet he had too much self-respect to take a woman to bed for nothing more than sheer physical satisfaction. One-night stands had palled long ago.

But with Angie....

This wouldn't be a brief fling. No way could he satisfy his need for this woman in the course of a single night. Learning her secret desires and satisfying them would take time. A lot of time. He wanted to know everything. The scent and taste of her.... Which particular points on her body sent her instantly over the edge.... How sensitive her breasts were to his touch.... Whether she liked to sleep in a tangle of arms and legs or if she preferred curling into tightly fitted spoons....

The questions were as endless as they were vital. He wasn't just curious, his urge to discover the answers had grown to an overwhelming obsession. He held a woman he could lose himself in. A woman to sink into, body and soul. A woman of depth and character and passion. He shook his head in silent amusement.

A woman who thought she was an angel.

He hooked his index fingers beneath the thin straps of her dress and tugged them down her arms. She inhaled sharply, but didn't try and stop him. Instead, her gaze locked with his, a plea darkening her eyes. Whether she silently asked for him to stop or to continue, he couldn't quite tell. All he knew was that he didn't want to stop. Not ever.

The damp silk clung lovingly to her breasts, outlining their generous fullness. Slowly, with exquisite care, he lowered the bodice of her dress. She held perfectly still. And so did he. It was almost as though time slowed to a crawl, the universe hesitating for an instant in order to give them this brief moment together. A hush fell between them, the only sound the harsh give and take of their breath. He could sense her fear, even as he caught the lush scent of her desire. A sheen of perspiration dewed her throat and the upper curves of her breasts, gleaming in the subdued light from the window.

He reached for her, scraping the calloused tips of his fingers along her rib cage. Her breasts lifted in response, the tips peaking in glorious enticement. He filled his hands with the silken weight and bent, taking her into his mouth.

She tasted as sweet as heaven's nectar, the flavor utterly unique and unforgettable. He slipped an arm around her back, urging her closer. Her soft moan rang in his ears, strumming along his senses. And then she touched him. Like the first hesitant stirrings of a downy nestling, her hands fluttered across his cheekbones in a delicate caress as she tentatively learned the shape and texture of his face.

"It's all right," he murmured. "You don't have to be afraid."

He warmed her damp skin with his breath and she shuddered, slipping her fingers into his hair and cradling him in a tender hold. "I want you so much," she whispered. "It doesn't seem to matter that it's wrong or impossible. Nothing seems to matter when you touch me."

"That's because it's not wrong. And it's certainly not impossible."

He closed his teeth over her nipple and tugged, reveling in her muffled cry. Her hands slid downward along the taut line of his neck to curl around his shoulders, clinging as though she might fall. And then her words slipped into the night, ripe with pain. "I wish… I wish with all my heart that was true, that we could have tonight without consequence."

He straightened, gathering her in his arms. "I'll make it true. You'll see." He captured her lips in a brief kiss, before sliding his mouth along the sweep of her jaw, trapping her earlobe between his teeth. Her breath caught and he smiled against the frantic pulse fluttering on the side of her neck. Seemed like he'd found another of those sensitive points. Interesting that her reaction sent him as close to the edge as it sent her. "Now tell me how an angel makes love. Anything I should know ahead of time?"

"Angels don't make love." He heard the strain in her voice and sympathized. Their foreplay had grown painful. If he didn't get her into a bed soon, they'd have their first experience together right up against the window. "At least, this one doesn't."

"Perhaps I can change your mind." He cupped her breasts once more, sliding his thumbs along the sensitive undersides before skimming the crowns. Her nipples were full and ripe and hot to the touch. Hell, she was full and ripe and hot to the touch. So why did she continue to resist? "Hang up your halo for the night, sweetheart,'' he urged. ''Heaven won't mind if you take one evening off.''

''You don't understand. I can't do this,'' she murmured. ''It's wrong.''

''It's not wrong. It can't be.''

''I'm not meant for you.''

''No? Maybe heaven knows better. Maybe that's precisely why you've been sent.''

To his alarm, tears gathered in her eyes. Ever so carefully she eased from his arms. ''That's not possible.''

He smiled in gentle amusement. Without her high heels, she seemed so small and vulnerable, her sophisticated facade as transparent as her angel wings. ''It's possible that you were sent to be my secretary, but not my lover? Is that what you're trying to say?''

A low, husky laugh escaped her. ''I wasn't sent to be your secretary, either. At least, not exactly.'' To his extreme disappointment, she pulled the bodice of her dress back in place. Apparently the straps defeated her, for she left them dangling, tempting him to test her resolve with a gentle tug. ''Though as long as I'm here, I'll be happy to take care of your secretarial problems.''

''Just out of curiosity... How do I rate an angel?'' Reed asked.

Laughter glittered in her eyes along with the tears, giving her more of a mischievous look than an angelic one. He shook his head. An angel. Jeez. He'd had a great-aunt who claimed to be psychic and would often sit and chat with ''spirits.'' He'd also had a distant cousin had made a living ''divining'' water. One of his previous secretaries—number seven, he thought, the secretary from hell—had claimed to be a reincarnation of Cleopatra and was deathly afraid of snakes. But this was the first time he'd ever run across an angel.

"I'm on a mission. I told you that from the beginning. Remember?"

"A mission, huh?" He eyed her suspiciously. "What sort of mission?"

"I told you that, too, Reed. I'm here to find you a wife."

With another of her gut-wrenching, tear-filled smiles, she circled him and padded barefoot across the living room. Her movements were as graceful as he'd have expected from an angel, even one hampered by a damp skirt. Then she disappeared into his bathroom and closed the door, leaving him standing there in confounded silence.

Great.

No question this time, his luck continued to run true to form. He had an angel in his bathroom—one of the sultriest, sexiest, most kissable angels imaginable. And why had she come? To spread joy, peace and happiness? To offer good tidings? To take him to bed and make long, passionate love until his brain turned to mush? Hell, no. She'd come to give him the one thing on earth he least wanted. A wife. He shook his head at the irony. How damned fortunate could one man get?

The next morning, Angie found getting from the front door of Harding's to her desk took longer than ever.

Between her preoccupation with the events of the previous evening and all the various employees who suddenly needed to speak to her, her progress through the office building slowed to a crawl. It invariably happened on each of her missions and she'd come to expect it. She seemed to attract people. She'd always assumed that on some unconscious level they "sensed" who or what she was and were drawn to her.

This mission proved no different.

She couldn't pass a single co-worker without being stopped so they could share an interesting piece of news or some fascinating change in their lifestyle. Red had become the "in" color she noticed in amusement as she paused to congratulate the accounting supervisor on her new granddaughter. Everything from a pale pinkish shade to burnt orange to deep purple-red, the stunning range of hue brightened the entire office. Angie also couldn't help but notice the two new bottle-blondes that had appeared since the previous day. They looked good, she decided. Very perky.

Joel snagged her before she reached her desk. "Guess what? My order arrived."

Her brow wrinkled in confusion. "I'm sorry, Joel. You've lost me. What order?"

"Whaddaya mean, what order?" He shook his head in disgust. "Don't you remember? Da— *Dang,* Angie! You went toe-to-toe, nose-to-nose with Reed over it. I'd have thought that would leave a small impression."

A glimmer of understanding dawned. "You mean the model?"

"Right. The one I'm building for the Wellsby project." Enthusiasm lit his expression. "You can't believe all the stuff that came in!"

That didn't sound good. "Stuff?"

"Loads of it. Next I have to buy some tools and start converting the blueprints—"

"Uh, Joel? Just out of curiosity… Where did you put all the…*stuff*?"

"Didn't know where else to put it, so I had them dump it in—"

"Ms. Makepeace!"

Angie cringed. "Not in Reed's office?"

"It had the most space," Joel retorted defensively.

"Okay, don't worry. I'll handle it."

He shot her a cocky grin. "Oh, I wasn't worried."

With a tiny sigh, she made her way toward Reed's office. He stood in the half-open doorway, glaring at her. "Good morning, Mr. Harding," she said in a cheerful voice.

"It's *not* a good morning, Ms. Makepeace. In fact it's a *rotten* morning. Would you care to guess why it's a rotten morning?"

Because they hadn't made love the previous night? She thrust the thought from her mind. If Reed felt any regrets, he kept them well hidden. "I assume this has something to do with Joel's project?"

"Brilliant deduction."

"I realize he shouldn't have had the supplies stored in your office. Why don't I get them moved out of your way?"

For an instant she thought she caught a glimpse of amusement in his gaze. Then he stepped to one side, allowing her access. "Be my guest."

Angie started to open the door—not that it got her very far. Except for a narrow twelve-inch gap, the door wouldn't budge. "Wait...wait a minute."

"Take your time. My meeting's not for another forty-five minutes. That should give you ample opportunity to get everything cleared out of the way."

She wriggled through the opening and stumbled to a halt, her mouth dropping open. Stacks of plywood had been upended against the walls. Boxes of electrical cable were perched precariously on top of cartons of nails. There were cords of shingles, timber of all shapes and sizes, Sheetrock, tubes and pipes. A rather disgruntled doggy face appeared from beneath a tepee of miniature girders surrounding the couch. Scratch whined a sour complaint.

"Damn," she muttered, blistering her tongue on the expletive.

Reed maneuvered his shoulders through the narrow opening. Several contortions later, he managed to squeeze into the room after her. "Now, now, Ms. Makepeace. Is that any way for an angel to talk?"

Joel peered through the doorway and grinned. "Neat, isn't it?"

"That depends. What is it?"

"Materials for the Wellsby model."

Angie shook her head. "No. No, it can't be. A model is little." She turned to face them, holding up her hands to show them "little." "A model fits on top of a table. The parts fit in a box. One box. One *small* box.''

"This model will be a little bigger than that," Joel announced proudly. "I'm gonna build it so everything works, just like the real thing. I was thinking we could display it in the front reception area."

"My meeting is now in forty minutes," Reed announced. "I suggest you start getting this stuff out of here, Ms. Makepeace."

She stared at him wide-eyed. "Where am I supposed to put it?"

"This was your brilliant idea. You figure it out."

Words failed her. She could only stand, swaying on top of her three-inch spikes.

Reed clamped his jaw together and turned away. "You might start with the stuff stacked behind the door," he suggested in a muffled voice. "Once that's shifted, you can open the door wide enough to haul everything out of here. Let's make tracks, Ms. Makepeace. You're down to thirty-eight minutes."

Joel snorted. "She can't get all this stuff moved in that amount of time. It'll take her at least four or five hours."

Her eyes rounded. "I— You— He—"

"What's that, Ms. Makepeace? Speak up."

"Aw, quit teasing her, Reed," Joel said. "You can have your meeting in the conference room and you know it. If you want the supplies moved, tell me where to put 'em and I'll go round up some help."

"Stick them in the apartment for now." Reed fixed his brother with a pointed look. "After that, I'll have Tiger discuss your ordering methods with you."

Joel made a face. "Well, jeez," he muttered. "I thought enthusiasm was a good thing."

"Sure it is. The only problem is, you bypassed enthusiasm several steps back and jumped straight to 'gone off the deep end.' Call down to maintenance and arrange for some help. You can move this stuff after lunch."

A cunning gleam appeared in Joel's eyes. "And after work you'll help me start putting it together?"

"As soon as you have a blueprint drawn to scale. Now go on. Get out of here." The minute Joel disappeared, Reed turned to Angie. "Red again?"

"Excuse me?"

"You're wearing red again. An interesting choice for an angel."

"Oh, that." She shifted a carton of screws off the chair in front of his desk and took a seat. "For some reason they don't use the color much in heaven. So I wear it whenever I get the chance." She dug through her purse for her steno pad and glasses. "Now. Is there anything you want me to do before your meeting?"

"I think we'd better talk about last night."

She snuck a quick peek at Scratch. "No, we'd better not. Instead, we should make up for the hours we'll lose getting Joel's project out of your office. I've typed all those letters you dictated yesterday and printed them. But I'll need your signature before I can mail—"

"Is it because I'm your boss? Is that why you won't sleep with me?"

She cringed, shooting another look in Scratch's direction.

Da— *Dang!* For the first time since their mission started, he was paying attention. A hint of color crept into her cheeks. Good grief! She hadn't been guilty of blushing since she was fourteen and got caught French kissing Hugh Dailey behind the chemistry lab.

Scowling, she adjusted her glasses and fixed her gaze on her latest list. "I've confirmed your speaking engagement in Chicago. I believe you said your previous secretary made the hotel reservations, but if you want me to double check, I'll be happy to take care of it."

"Do I have to remind you about rule number one?"

She grimaced. "I have to admit that your rules do cause a lot of trouble. Especially rule number one."

"Don't worry. After your trial period they won't trouble you at all. Perhaps your next employer won't be so difficult."

Her pen hovered over her notepad and she studied him pensively. "Reed… I didn't turn you down because you're my boss. I realize that if I'd said no and meant it, you'd have kept our relationship strictly business."

"But you didn't mean it."

Honesty forced her to agree. "No, I didn't. I'm attracted to you. I admit it. That's not why I'm here, though. My job is to find you a wife."

A hint of fire flashed within his hazel eyes. "Your *job* is to perform secretarial duties, not marry me off."

"The list said—"

"To hell with the list! Do I look like the sort of man who'd ask my secretary to find me a woman?" His tone grated, the words sounding raw and tight.

"Not really. You look…frustrated."

"How observant. You're right. I am frustrated. Would you care to guess why?"

She sighed. "I have a funny feeling it has something to do with me."

"Right again. It has everything to do with you. I don't care what that list said, I do not want you finding me love—true or otherwise. Stay out of my personal life unless you intend to follow through on last night."

She snapped her steno pad closed and whipped off her glasses. "What you don't seem to understand is that I don't have any choice, either. I can't follow through on last night. And I have to find you true love. It's my mission."

He shut his eyes and took a deep breath. When he looked at her again, she couldn't mistake the determination that burned in his gaze. "You do have a choice, Angie. And it's a very simple one. Either you drop this nonsense about being an angel sent to marry me off or you find a new job."

"Please don't do this."

"Which is it going to be?" He lifted an eyebrow. "You've claimed you don't lie. So tell me… Will you promise to forget about this other nonsense and focus on your secretarial duties?"

"Please, Reed. I can promise almost anything else. But I can't promise that. I've been sent—"

"Enough!" He thrust back his chair and stood. "Enough, Angie. It's a cute story. Very amusing. Almost as amusing as a deaf dalmatian and wearing red all the time. Unfortunately, I have a business to run. And I can't do that when you're allowing Joel to run wild or when my office is overflowing with building supplies or when my secretary is more interested in arranging my love life than my business appointments."

"I can handle it all."

"Maybe you can, but I can't." He massaged the nape of his neck. "Choose, Ms. Makepeace. The job—with the condition that you'll never mention this angel business or love or marriage again—or we bid each other a fond farewell."

She moistened her lips. "You don't understand. You're my last chance."

"You don't have to leave," he urged. "Just promise me—"

"I can't," she whispered. "It would be a lie."

His face hardened. "I see. In that case I have no alternative. It's been...interesting working with you."

Angie stood. "Reed, please reconsider."

"I'm sorry. You're fired, Ms. Makepeace. I'll have accounting draft you a severance check."

"Don't bother." She managed a smile, though she suspected it looked as wobbly as her knees felt. "Angels don't need money."

And with that she snagged her purse and left, a disapproving dalmatian trotting at her heels.

CHAPTER SIX

"ANGIE MAKEPEACE. Please report to your supervisor. Angie Makepeace to Supervisor Goodenkind."

She heard the whispers start the moment she stepped onto the gilded path. Lifting her chin, she kept walking. Some things never changed, it would seem. It shouldn't surprise her. And yet, it did. No matter what happened, no matter how bad her situation became, no matter how many missions she failed, she couldn't quite kill the tiny spark of hope that burned deep in her heart—the hope for a better tomorrow.

If she ever lost that, she'd probably lose her soul. Because she didn't think she could continue without hope to keep her going. Her jaw clenched. Unfortunately, a better tomorrow never came—at least not for her—and it had become increasingly difficult to sustain a dream that might not exist.

Goodenkind wasn't alone, Angie noticed the minute she stepped into his office. Scratch sat there, too—a smug expression on his otherwise angelic face. No doubt he'd already given his own version of events. She greeted her supervisor with a plucky grin. "Hello, Good. Miss me?"

"It's been amazingly quiet without you, Ms. Makepeace."

"I'll see what I can do about that."

He regarded her with a stern countenance. "Assuming you remain, that is, which is highly questionable at this point. Have a seat, Angie."

That didn't sound too good. Nevertheless, she rallied with a brilliant smile and sat down. "I admit, lucky thirteen didn't turn out to be too lucky." She shot the pesky dalmatian a look of undisguised irritation. "But I guess you already heard about that."

The dog bared his teeth.

"I received Scratch's report, yes." Goodenkind steepled his hands, as he fixed her with an unwavering stare. "Would you care to give me your version of events?"

If she'd been a kid, she'd be squirming in her chair. As it was, she couldn't quite sit still. She fluttered her feathers for a bit and adjusted her halo to a jauntier angle. "I'm not sure what more I can add." At the blatant evasion, a teeny spot of soot appeared on her spotless white robes and she hastily tucked the telltale blemish from sight. "Mr. Harding isn't interested in my finding him a wife. When push came to shove, he fired me."

"I believe you're leaving out a few details—details of a more personal nature."

For the second time, a burning heat scalded her cheeks. Who would have thought angels could blush? Especially an angel like her. She'd have sworn it was impossible. And yet, here she sat, her cheeks as red as the dresses she favored. "Oh, that."

"Yes, that. You kissed the man. You were tempted to make love to him."

"I resisted!"

"True. That fact, and that fact alone, has earned you a temporary reprieve."

She moistened her lips. "I'm not...not going to be put out?" Was that tiny, aching voice really hers? It must have been, because a wealth of compassion dawned in Goodenkind's eyes.

"No, my dear. You're not. You haven't finished your mission."

"But, I thought—"

"You'll have to return and convince Mr. Harding he's in serious need of your secretarial services again. And then you'll have one final chance to complete your assignment."

"You don't understand—"

For the first time since she'd met him, he looked as though the wisdom of the ages hung heavily upon his shoulders. "I understand far more than you think." He spoke so gently, tears pricked her eyes.

"He fired me."

Goodenkind shrugged. "You'll have to convince him to rehire you."

She tried again. "He's forbidden me to discuss finding him a wife."

"Then don't discuss it. Simply find him one."

"Just like that." She snapped her fingers. "I'm supposed to chose some woman out of thin air and convince him to marry her."

"I'm afraid it won't be that simple."

She shot to her feet. "No sh— *Shoot!* No... No... No *joke* it won't be that easy. I don't suppose you have any suggestions?"

"Certainly."

"Well, that's a relief," she muttered.

"I suggest you listen to your heart and to your conscience. And I suggest you stop kissing the man."

"Great advice, Good."

"I thought so." A glimmer of a smile touched his mouth, despite her sarcasm. "I'll also give you a gift that may aid your quest."

Considering he thought listening to her heart and conscience had been a helpful suggestion, she didn't hold out too much hope that his gift would be of much more use. She sighed in resignation. "What is it?"

"You may grant him his heart's desire. Only one, mind. A wish he wants more than anything else on earth."

She brightened. "Wait a sec… You mean, if I get him to wish for a wife, that'll fulfill my mission?"

"If it's his true heart's desire, yes. Your mission will be completed."

"And…and I'll get to stay in heaven?"

"Yes, my dear," he replied kindly. "You'll remain in heaven."

Gathering the shreds of her dignity, she inclined her head. "Then, I'd better get going."

"One last thing, Ms. Makepeace."

Of course. There was *always* one last thing. She sighed. "Yes?"

Goodenkind smiled. "Don't forget to take Scratch with you."

Reed glared at Tiger. "What do you mean they've changed the plans again?"

"Here, you look." The foreman shoved a roll of blueprints at Reed. "They've switched around that damned east wing for the third time this week. How are we supposed to build the thing when they keep changing the structure on us every other day?"

Reed unrolled the pale blue paper, frowning over the alterations Tiger indicated. "This is what I get for using someone else's designs. If it were an in-house job—"

"The owners would still be changing the structure every other day."

"Maybe. But I'd have an accurate set of plans."

Joel peered over his brother's shoulder. "Hey, don't complain. At least they got the supports right this time."

Tiger grinned at Reed. "Not bad. The kid has an eye for detail—"

"Heads up!"

At the hoarse shout, Reed spun around and discovered all hell breaking loose. At the far edge of the site, he caught a splash of red picking a path across the piles of dirt and debris. A loaded dump truck, beeper wailing as it reversed, roared straight for her. There was only one person he knew who dressed in so determined a shade of red and had a prancing dalmatian at her side. Angie had returned, and he didn't have a hope in hell of reaching her before the dump truck. All he could do was bellow a warning and pray she heard.

"Angie! Look out!"

She paused, the breeze catching in her hair and tossing it in a sunny halo about her head. Then she lifted her hand and waved. Just as she started forward, Scratch leaped playfully upward, his paws landing on her shoulders. She staggered slightly beneath the weight, her forward momentum halted for a vital split second. The dump truck plowed across her path inches in front of her. It actually brushed Scratch's tail.

The three men swore in unison.

The minute the driver saw how close he'd come to hitting her, he turned off the engine, tumbled out of the cab and sank to his knees in the dirt. Angie appeared totally oblivious.

Tiger groaned. "Aw, hell. She's still coming."

"The bulldozer, the bulldozer," Joel chanted, his voice a thin squeak. "It's gonna get 'er. Yup. Gonna get 'er."

Tiger nodded. "She's a goner."

Reed thought his heart had stopped. He was still too far to reach her in time. Once again he shouted at her. "*Angie!* Behind you, honey. Look—"

The bulldozer swung, its mammoth maw filled with dirt. This time Scratch dropped to his belly in the dirt and rubbed his snout on her leather high-heeled shoe. Angie shook her finger at him, then bent and slipped off the shoe, shaking out a pebble. At the same instant, the dozer's steel blade sliced the air above her head. Tiger went down as though he'd been the one struck. The driver did a double take, turned a pale shade of green and folded like wet cardboard over the steering sticks.

"I can't look," Joel said with a moan, covering his eyes with shaking hands.

Reed struggled to speak. Somehow, his tongue had become three sizes too large for his mouth, making it almost impossible to form the words. "She made it. The dozer missed her."

"Not the dozer. The cement truck. Can't look. Nope. Can't do it."

"Wh—" And then he saw it, too. A cement truck barreling along at a speed the driver had no business going. "Dammit, Angie! *Run!*"

She lifted a hand to her ear. "What?"

A smile flashed across her face and Reed fought the eerie feeling it would be the last image he'd have of her alive. *"Run, dammit!"* Oh, please. Don't let those be the last thing I say to her, he prayed silently.

At the last possible instant, the driver saw her. He hit his brakes and jerked the wheel to one side, but it was far, far too late. A horrible screech rent the air. Angie glanced over her shoulder, and in a move far quicker than his eye could follow, she danced to one side. The massive truck slid past sideways, one dirt-encrusted wheel actually brushing her bright red skirt. The breeze it generated tossed her hair into disarray and lifted the hem of her dress to reveal a stunning pair of legs and a mind-blowing glimpse of a lacy black garter.

With a muffled groan, Joel toppled over next to Tiger.

Silence reigned. The few workman remaining on their feet looked from Reed to Angie. Reed didn't wait. He set off at a flat run to intercept her before she could injure any more of his men.

She greeted him with a sunny smile. "Good morning."

He didn't bother with a response. Slowing long enough to drop his shoulder and hoist her over it, he set out toward the construction trailer parked a short distance away. Scratch trotted along behind and released a long, noisy sigh. If an animal could whine in relief, Reed would have sworn the dalmatian did just that.

"What are you doing?" Angie demanded, shoving against his back. "What's going on?"

"Don't say a word. Not one single word."

"Why? What's wrong? What did I do?"

She wriggled in his hold, her breasts burning a delicious path of fire along his back, while the softness of her silk-clad thighs thrashed between his hands. Both threatened his sanity. His physical reaction hit hard, and he could only hope it wasn't too readily apparent to the men watching.

"If you value your life, you won't say anything else until we get in the trailer. And you sure as hell better hold real still or I swear I'll give these construction workers a spectacle they'll remember to their dying day."

To his utter astonishment, she chuckled. "I'm tempted to take you up on your offer. But I'll resist." Then she relaxed against his back and wrapped her arms around his waist. "I'm under orders now. No more fun at all."

Hoots and cheers greeted him as he climbed the four short stairs to the trailer and shoved open the door. Scratch took up guard outside. Crossing the threshold, he dropped Angie to her feet and slammed the door closed, locking it.

The urge to kiss her senseless nearly overwhelmed him. The fact that she stood there, looking deliciously rumpled, didn't help. He funneled his desire into rage. "What the *hell* did you think you were doing out here?"

She actually had the temerity to smile at him. "I was coming to see you," she explained, pushing a tangle of blond curls from her eyes. "I wanted to ask for my job back."

He wondered if sheer, unadulterated fury truly could cause steam to pour from a person's ears. If so, it should be jetting out of his. "Hire you again? You're kidding, right? After that little stunt you pulled, you're lucky I don't have you arrested!"

She stared at him, her eyes huge and startled. "What stunt?"

"Let me see now... How about such minor infractions as trespassing.... Coming on-site without an escort. Without a hard hat. And without a clue!" He shoved his slightly battered nose against her more dainty one, not in the least appeased that her big baby blues went cross-eyed in an attempt to focus on him. "Do you realize you were almost killed?"

"Don't be silly, Reed. I can't be killed. I'm already—"

"*Don't!*" He cut her off with a slash of his hand. "Don't start that nonsense with me again. If you hadn't jumped out of the way so fast—"

She shrugged. "Then you and all the other construction workers would have had proof that I'm an angel.''

"You're absolutely right. If that truck had hit you, you'd have become an instant angel.''

"That's not what I meant.''

"I'm serious, Angie. What you did was unbelievably dangerous. Even worse, you've left a wake of bodies strewn in your path.''

"Bodies?" She darted for the door. Before he could stop her, she'd turned the lock and stepped outside. "What bodies?" she asked, shading her eyes as she inspected the site.

Reed joined her, grabbing her by the arm before she could wander back into harm's way. "Start where you first walked in and follow the path of destruction from there.''

Her brows drew together as she looked toward the entrance of the site. "Why is the dump truck driver on the ground?''

"I believe he's puking his guts out.''

"I'm serious." She glanced at Reed in concern. "What's wrong with him?''

"It's panic resulting from almost running you down.''

Her attention shifted further along the path she'd taken. "And the bulldozer operator? Is he sleeping?''

"No. My men rarely sleep on the job," he retorted dryly. "I believe he's unconscious. Either that or he's had a heart attack after almost decapitating you.''

"He almost—" She swallowed. "It's a good thing I'm not alive or that really would have hurt." Before he could respond to that bit of inanity, she pointed.

"And…and the cement truck? Is…is that *blood* on his face?"

"Probably. My guess is that Tiger just finished explaining the appropriate speed in a construction zone to the man. Not that he had to. The poor fellow looks like he lost about twenty years off his life."

Angie wrung her hands. "If it was my fault, I'm sure Good will restore them," she said in a contrite voice. For the first time she seemed to notice the deathly silence. She shrank a little closer to him. "Why is everyone standing around staring at us?" she whispered uneasily.

"They're not all staring. Only the ones able to stand are paying any attention. The dozer operator and cement truck driver are still unconscious. Though Tiger and Joel seem to be on their feet again."

"Tiger— Where…?" She let out her breath in a sigh of relief. "Oh, there he is. He and Joel are coming over."

"Do you want me to kill her?" Tiger asked the minute he got within shouting distance. He rolled up his sleeves as though preparing for battle.

Angie's eyes widened in alarm. "He's joking, right?"

Reed tilted his head to one side. "No. I believe he's serious. Are you serious, Tiger?"

"Dead serious. You want me to off her? Won't take but a second."

Reed took a full minute to consider. "No," he finally said with notable reluctance. "Instead, why don't you track down the security guard. The one who's supposed to stop people from wandering onto the site. And then I want you to break him into little pieces and drag his butt over here so I can break him into even smaller pieces.''

"You got it.'' With a brief glare at Angie, he stomped away.

"I—I guess I shouldn't have come here.''

"I can't believe you weren't run over,'' Joel croaked. "I thought you were a goner, fer sure.''

Contrition filled her eyes. "I'm so sorry, Joel. I didn't mean to frighten you. I really wasn't in any danger.''

"And why is that?'' Reed asked with unmistakable sarcasm. "Because you think you're an angel?''

"You might say that.'' She glanced at Scratch and smiled. "And because I had a guardian angel with me.''

"Get inside, Ms. Makepeace, before I have a riot on my hands.'' The words came out with such grated force that she could only stare. "And take the mutt with you.''

"Can I watch Scratch?'' Joel pleaded. "I've really missed him this past week. I'll make sure he stays out of trouble.''

"Fine.'' Reed jerked his head toward the trailer. "Inside, Ms. Makepeace.''

Without another word, she did as he requested.

"I'm sorry,'' she said as soon as he joined her. "I didn't realize I was doing anything wrong. No one stopped me and—''

"Why are you here?''

"I told you. I came to ask for my old job back.''

He folded his arms across his chest. "It's been a

whole week since I fired you. How do you know I haven't already hired a replacement?''

She peeked at him from beneath her lashes. ''Have you?''

''Yes.'' He waited a moment before adding, ''As a matter of fact, I've hired six replacements in the past week.''

A tiny smile snagged the corner of her mouth. ''Six?''

''I had three come and go in one day, alone.''

The smile grew. ''I think that must be a record.''

''So I've been told. The placement agency is refusing to send anyone else.''

''Then it's a good thing I'm back. Isn't it?''

''That depends.''

A gruffness shredded his voice—and she noticed, dammit. He could see it in the softening of her gaze and the gentling of her smile. He watched for any hint of triumph, for the sly knowledge that she'd won. But it never came. Instead he caught a trace of uncertainty, a whisper of vulnerability. It stole the remnants of his anger.

''It depends…on what?'' she asked.

''On whether you're willing to agree to my rules.''

''Okay. Why don't you tell me what they are.''

He grinned at that. ''Have you forgotten already?''

''Let's see…'' Amusement turned her eyes a sunny blue. ''As I recall, the first rule is that you're the boss.''

He nodded. ''That's right. What I say goes. No discussion. No argument. I win.''

Angie didn't bother to hide her relief. They were

on familiar ground now, back to their old footing. "And rule number two?"

"No interoffice relationships. Remember?"

It was an excellent rule. Perhaps if she'd obeyed it last time, she wouldn't be in her current situation. "That goes for the boss, too. Right?"

"Especially for the boss," he retorted grimly.

"And number three… No dogs. Wasn't that it?"

"I'm changing that one."

"Really?" She perked up at that. "Scratch is allowed at the office?"

Reed shook his head in disgust. "Since he's been at the office every damn day since you started, I don't see much point in trying to enforce that particular rule."

"So what's the new one?" She suspected that whatever it was, she wouldn't like it.

"No talk about angels or wives."

"Not a problem." She dismissed his concern with a wave of her hand. "I've been told that I don't have to mention it anymore."

"Oh, yeah? Does that mean you're done finding me a wife?"

"It means I'm not going to *talk* about marriage or true love or potential wives," she corrected carefully. "Is that a reasonable enough compromise?"

"I guess it'll have to do. What about this angel nonsense?"

She caught her lower lip between her teeth as she considered. "It's possible that we can ignore that aspect, too. But I need to tell you something first."

He folded his arms across his chest. "Go ahead."

"I spoke with my supervisor and he's given me one last chance to complete my assignment."

"What's your assignment this time?"

"Still you."

"Tough job."

"Very," she said with feeling. "Anyway, Good gave me a rather special gift for you."

"Generous man."

"Actually, he is. And compassionate. And just plain kindhearted."

Reed propped his shoulder against the wall of the trailer. His eyes were awash with shadows, the green and gold muted by the darker browns. "Lives up to his name, does he?"

"In every way. To be honest," she confessed. "I haven't met too many men like him."

"Is there a point to this conversation?"

She'd annoyed him, she realized in surprise. Irritation carved his face into harsh lines. What in the world had she said? All she'd done was compliment Good— Her eyes narrowed. She knew of only one emotion that stirred that sort of irrational anger. Jealousy. But in this case, that didn't seem likely. She frowned. Or did it? Once upon a time, she'd have known. With Reed, however, her instincts were sadly out of kilter.

An awkward moment of silence simmered between them. Angie cleared her throat. "The point is..." she tried again, "Goodenkind's given me a gift to pass on to you."

"Tell him thanks, but no thanks."

"But…" She stared in confusion. "You haven't heard what it is, yet."

"Anything I need, I'll get myself."

She scowled at him, thoroughly aggravated. "You said I can't discuss this angel business with you, any-more. That means, I have to tell you everything now, since I can't bother you with it later. How am I sup-posed to do that if I can't explain about the gift?"

He shrugged. "It's a dilemma."

"Reed!"

He shifted his stance, his sudden approach catching her by surprise. "Do you want your job back or not?"

"You know I do."

"Are you going to agree to my rules?" He towered above her. "Are you going to drop all this BS about angels and wives?"

"Do I have a choice?"

"No."

Perhaps she'd have an opportunity to tell him about his gift later. Perhaps after a few days he'd listen. She shot him a final, assessing glance. Pushing the issue now wouldn't work. A wise woman knew when to call a strategic retreat. She's tackle him later, when he had no other option but to listen. "Then, I agree."

"In that case, welcome back to work, Ms. Makepeace."

"Thank you, Mr. Harding." She tried a smile, hop-ing it might ease his irritation. "It's a pleasure to be back."

To her utter amazement, he slipped a hand around her neck and tugged her closer. "The pleasure is mine," he said.

And then he kissed her, a hard, fierce stamp of possession. She should have protested. She should have pulled free. It would have been the smart, angelic thing to do. At the very least, she should have stood there quietly and let him take what he so desperately wanted without responding. But she did none of those things.

Instead, she wound her arms around his neck and practically swallowed him whole. Heaven help her, she'd missed him. Missed his touch, his voice, his beautiful kisses. It didn't seem to matter how many times she told herself it was wrong. Without this man, she felt empty, alone and incomplete. She needed him more than she'd ever needed anyone.

At long last, he ended the kiss. Angie forced her eyes open, gradually focusing on Reed's face. She ran the tip of her tongue along the swollen line of her lips, watching in fascination as a blistering tension deepened the creases cut into the corners of his mouth.

His thumb traced the path her tongue had taken. "Don't do that or I swear I'll take you here and now."

"I can still taste you," she murmured.

"Does it taste good?" The question bit, as though it had ripped free against his will.

She didn't hesitate answering. "Really good."

"Good enough to try some more?"

She didn't want to spoil the moment. Nor did she want him to stop kissing her. Unfortunately, her wants weren't important. She had a mission, whether she liked it or not. She sighed. "As much as it kills me to mention this... We're breaking rule number two."

"That's the nice thing about rule number one. It allows me the luxury of breaking any damn rule I choose." But her reminder served its purpose. He set her gently from him. "Now get the hell off my site, Ms. Makepeace, before I'm tempted to break rule number two beyond repair."

She glanced toward the door of the trailer, deciding he'd made an excellent suggestion. She'd already blown one of Goodenkind's suggestions—that she stop kissing her earthbound boss. If she didn't want to further jeopardize her assignment, she'd better leave before temptation proved too much to resist. "Should I return the way I came?"

"No!" He took a deep breath. "No. Wait right here. I'll take care of it."

Crossing to a microphone dangling near the door, he flipped a switch. "Harding, here." His voice blasted from a nearby speaker, echoing across the construction site. "Tiger, report to the trailer and bring a hard hat. As for the rest of you... Turn off all engines and step away from your machinery. I'm bringing her out in five minutes. No one is to move until she's left."

"Was that really necessary?" Angie demanded the minute he released the button on the mike.

"Absolutely. And just so there's no question about it, you're to stay off of my construction sites unless I'm with you. Understood?"

"No problem. I'm not deliberately trying to cause trouble, you know."

"It just follows you naturally?"

She laughed wryly. "You could say that."

"Ready to go?"

"Is it safe or am I likely to get lynched?"

A flash of his earlier desire sparked in his gold-tinted eyes, coupled with an almost protective look. "Don't panic. I'll see you safely off the site."

"I don't doubt it."

He reached for the doorknob and then turned unexpectedly. Before she could draw away, he leaned down and kissed her again. This time the touch was light. Gentle. Hungry. Irresistible. His mouth conveyed all that was left unsaid between them and more. Finally, he released her.

"Welcome back, Ms. Makepeace."

"It's good to be back," she whispered the confession.

Far, far too good.

CHAPTER SEVEN

THE next few weeks passed with a speed that left Angie shaken. Every morning she set herself a goal to ignore her attraction for Reed and find him a bride. And every evening, she found that she'd spent the entire day secretly watching him and working harder than she'd ever thought possible to match her boss's breakneck pace. Neither helped her mission. If she were a suspicious person, she'd suspect Reed deliberately kept her too busy to meddle in his affairs. Not that he was conducting any affairs—at least none that she knew about.

Even his mother left him alone—not setting up so much as a single date at Sarducci's. Nor had Angie been able to tell him about the wish Goodenkind had granted. She frowned at the stack of correspondence overflowing her "in" basket. If she could just get him to describe the "perfect" woman, maybe she could convince him to wish her into existence. And then this torture would end. Because that's what her assignment had become—sheer torture.

She didn't want to *find* him the perfect woman, she realized with painful clarity. She wanted to *be* that woman. And the impossibility of that desire ate at her soul.

"I can't keep this up," she informed Scratch as she jiggled Casey Radcliff's eight-month-old grandson on her lap. "I have to get him a wife. And it had better be soon." She gazed broodingly around the office. "There must be someone out there that he'd be willing to marry."

Beside her, the dog growled a warning while Kip pumped his chubby limbs and gurgled an incoherent response.

"I know. I know. She has to be his true heart's desire." Angie smoothed the silky blond hair from the baby's forehead. "But how am I supposed to get him to desire her, if he won't even discuss it?"

"Talking to yourself, Ms. Makepeace?"

She glared at Scratch. "You could have warned me," she muttered before pasting a pleasant expression on her face. "Did you need something, Mr. Harding?"

"Yes. As a matter of fact, I need you." He teased her with a heart-stopping smile. "In my office, that is. And Scratch did warn you. He always growls when I stop by your desk."

She swiveled to face him. "He's still holding a grudge about your couch," she explained. "You shouldn't have covered it in plastic. He hates plastic."

"Gee. I'm crushed." His gaze fell on Kip and a frown descended like a bank of threatening storm clouds. "That's a baby."

She couldn't help it. She grinned. "How observant of you."

"Where did it come from?"

"It?" she repeated, lifting an eyebrow. "Kip is a boy, not an it. And *he* came from Casey. Well, her daughter to be exact. He's Casey's grandson."

Reed's mouth tightened. "What are you doing with him?"

"Baby-sitting while they're at lunch. And before you get upset with her, I volunteered." She lifted Kip to her shoulder, snuggling him close. He blew bubbles against her neck and she chuckled. "Slimy little critters, aren't they?"

A muscle in his jaw tensed and the storm broke, sweeping into his gaze with a ferocity that unnerved her. "Ms. Makepeace? In my office, please."

"With the baby?"

His mouth thinned. "Unless your dog is capable of baby-sitting."

"Actually, Guardian Angels make the very best baby-sitters," she admitted, standing. "But I'm not ready to give Kip up, yet." Grabbing her steno pad and glasses, she preceded him into the office, carrying the chattering baby.

Reed closed the door behind them. "Let me get that plastic out of your way and then you can sit on the couch."

"That's okay..." Before he realized what she intended, Angie dumped the baby into his arms and took care of it herself. Settling onto the leather cushion, she flipped open her steno pad. "So what's up?" She propped her glasses on the tip of her nose and peered at him over the wire rims.

Reed held Kip away from his body as though the baby had dynamite in his diapers. "Er, Ms. Makepeace?" When she didn't immediately reclaim his armload, his voice took on a more urgent tone. "Angie?"

"Would you mind?" she asked sweetly. "I have to take notes. Now... What precisely am I taking notes about?"

"I thought you didn't want to part with the kid."

"If you won't hold him, put him out with Scratch."

Her suggestion went over just as she'd predicted. He hesitated a further moment before reluctantly taking the chair opposite her and dangling Kip from one knee. "I wanted to discuss this weekend with you—make sure everything's arranged."

She tilted her head to one side. "Don't you like children?"

"I like them just fine. And don't change the subject."

"Then why don't you want to hold Kip?"

He didn't answer. But a myriad of emotions chased across his face, rousing her curiosity. Resistance was uppermost and an expression that could have been anguish. Most interesting of all, though, was the unmistakable yearning that betrayed him every time he looked at Kip's innocent face or cupped a large, protective hand around the baby's plump body.

Moved beyond words, she buried her nose in her steno pad. "It's the conference for the American Contractors Association, right?" she forced herself to ask. "The one in Chicago?"

"Yes. My previous secretary booked us two rooms. Check the file. There should be a confirmation from the hotel. If not, call them and make sure we have reservations."

"Which hotel is it?"

He turned Kip to face him. The baby grabbed a

fistful of chambray shirt, crumpling it in his damp hand. A faint smile creased Reed's face. "It's the Grand Majesty."

"Oh," she murmured faintly. "I didn't realize."

"Oh?" Reed lifted an eyebrow, momentarily distracted from the baby. "Why don't I like the sound of that?"

She busied herself taking notes. "Don't worry. I'm sure they've forgotten all about that other little incident."

"*What* other little incident?"

"The one that happened when I worked there."

She glanced up to see how he'd taken that tiny nugget of information. Not well, if his frown was anything to go by. He lifted the baby to his shoulder and Angie snatched her gaze from the sight of Reed's dark head tilted so close to Kip's pale curls. She fought to breathe, to hide the shaft of sorrow that pierced her.

She would never know the joy of motherhood. She'd never watch her husband smile at their child's sweet face the way Reed smiled at Kip. It had never bothered her so desperately before. Until now.

"You used to work at the Grand?" he asked.

She forced her attention to the matter at hand. "Briefly. Very briefly—fortunately for them. I believe my replacement corrected the situation, so they shouldn't be too mad anymore." Poor Chuck. She wondered how long it had taken him to repair all the damage. She risked another glance in Reed's direction, relieved to discover her sorrow had eased somewhat. "I'd tell you about it, except that rule number three prevents me from going into more detail."

Reed groaned. ''I thought we'd put a rest to that nonsense.''

''I agreed I wouldn't discuss it anymore.'' She widened her eyes in mock innocence. ''Unless you'd care to bring it up. Since you're the boss, you're at liberty to break any rule you want.''

''Thanks for the offer, but I'll pass,'' he retorted dryly. ''I assume you'll leave Scratch behind? That won't be a problem?''

''Well,'' she hedged. ''I'm not sure what his plans are for this weekend. I'll need to discuss it with him first.''

To her alarm, his jaw clenched, though he spoke calmly enough. ''I'd appreciate it if you'd convince him to remain behind. Perhaps he could stay with Joel.''

''I'll suggest it.''

''Thank you.''

Time to move the discussion to new ground. ''What sort of clothes will I need?''

''Business attire. A cocktail dress or two. Casual clothes for Saturday's picnic. And a bathing suit.'' To Reed's utter astonishment, the color drained from her face and he was grateful that he held the baby instead of Angie.

''A bathing suit?'' she repeated faintly.

''There's a lake where we picnic and—''

''I don't swim.''

He shrugged. ''Then don't go in the water. But you might bring along a suit in case you want to go wading.''

''I won't.'' She stood, clutching her notebook to

her chest in a white-knuckle grip. "Is that it? I have work to do."

He stood, as well. "Now why is an angel afraid of a little ol' lake?" he questioned softly. "I wouldn't think you'd be afraid of anything."

"You'd be amazed by what I feel. Fear of water is one." She eyed the baby. "Regret for roads not taken is another."

"Don't go there," he warned.

But she didn't listen. Hell. When did she ever? The passion vibrated from her like a chord pitched too high, threatening to shatter the fragile hold she kept on her emotions. "You don't know how lucky you are. Do you have any idea what I'd give to have a future? To have the choices still open to you?"

"Angie, please—"

But she didn't stop, couldn't in all likelihood. "You have a chance, Reed. A change to have it all— love, marriage, children. I'll never know that. Not ever. But you—" She lifted her gaze to his, her pain a living entity. The sunniness that normally filled her eyes had taken on the tint of twilight, gathering in the bruised shades of indigo that appeared just as dusk smothered the final rays of light. "You could have it all and instead—" Her voice broke and she darted forward, scooping Kip into her arms and burying her face against his powder-fresh neck.

"You don't understand," he managed to say, knowing full well he couldn't explain. Not about Emily, not about the torment that had plagued him for the past two years. Holding Kip was as much a torture for him as it was for her. He might have a child out there somewhere. A son like Kip or a daughter whose face remained a mystery.

A child without a father.

"You're right," she whispered. "I don't understand. And I never will."

Without another word, she stalked from the room and he watched her every step of the way. Her platinum curls continued to bounce provocatively about her shoulders. The sway of her hips still turned a simple red skirt into an emergency beacon. Somehow she managed to balance those endless legs on top of three-inch spikes while carrying a wriggling baby. But for the first time, he saw a crack in her breezy confidence.

And he was the cause.

"You sure they won't remember you?" Reed asked as they entered the lobby of the Grand Majesty Hotel.

Angie grinned. "Oh, they'll remember me, all right."

Stupid question. Who the hell could forget her? "I thought you said—"

She tucked her hand in the crook of his elbow and slanted those bewitching blue eyes in his direction. "I said they wouldn't hold it against me."

"Hold *what* against you?"

"Just a teeny little flood." She dismissed his concern with a flick of her fingers and continued toward the reception desk. "It's hardly worth mentioning."

"A *flood?*"

"A sprinkler malfunction." She sighed. "Who'd have thought."

Before he could ask any further questions, they reached the reception desk. The man standing behind the marble counter took one look at Angie and turned white. "Ms. Makepeace!"

"Why, hello, Tick. How's business?"

"Better, thank you. Much better." A muscle jerked in his cheek. "You're not staying here, are you?"

"'Fraid so," she admitted cheerfully. "But don't worry. I'll keep my hands off the plumbing."

The clerk's mouth relaxed into a tiny smile. "The owners will be so pleased to hear that."

She leaned across the counter toward him, dropping her voice confidentially. "I assume Chuck fixed everything?"

To Reed's amusement, Tick unbent slightly. "Mr. Cross did a remarkable job," he confided. "We only had to tear down a small section of the hotel."

"Well, then. That's good, right?"

"A miracle."

Angie nodded in total understanding. "Chuck excels at those."

Reed groaned silently. Aw, hell, not more angel talk. "Do you think we could register?" he interrupted.

Tick's eyes widened in alarm. "Of course, sir. Is the reservation in the name of Makepeace?"

"No," Reed corrected. "The reservation is in the name of Harding. Two rooms."

"I confirmed it yesterday," Angie added.

The clerk punched away at his computer. "Ah, yes. I have it right here. Hey, Angie!" He shot a guilty look toward Reed. "I mean...Ms. Makepeace.

You've been upgraded to a two-bedroom suite. No additional cost.''

"Why, thank you, Tick. That's very sweet of you."

"Mr. Jenson must still have a soft spot for you," the clerk whispered. "This is his authorization code."

Angie lowered her voice, as well. "I'll be sure to thank him."

Reed drummed his fingers on the marble counter. "Mr. Jenson? Who's he?"

"One of the owners," she volunteered. "He was my tenth—no, I take that back. He was my eleventh mission. An utter failure, but I can't blame him for that."

"Of course not." Reed swept up the envelope with their card keys and eyed Tick. "Have our luggage brought up as soon as possible."

"Right away, sir. And enjoy your visit. If there's anything we can do to make your stay more enjoyable, don't hesitate to ask."

"I'll do that." Picking up his briefcase and the bag containing his laptop computer, he glanced at Angie. "Ready?"

"All set." She smiled at the clerk. He proved as susceptible as every other male Reed had seen. He grinned back with all the fervor of a lovesick puppy. If he'd had a tail, he'd be wagging it clean off. "I'll talk to you later, Tick."

"Absolutely. Have a nice stay."

"So what were you supposed to do for Jenson?" Reed asked as they walked to the bank of elevators. "Find the poor guy a wife, too?"

She pushed the call button. "Are we officially breaking rule number three?"

"Apparently."

"Okay. Just checking." She faced him, folding her arms across her chest. "No, to answer your question. I wasn't assigned to find Mr. Jenson a wife. He already has one. Millie's a real darling, too, which made it all the more upsetting when I failed them."

The elevator doors parted and they entered the glass-paneled car. "So what was your mission?"

"To convince Mr. Jenson to let his grandson take over the management of the hotel. There was only one tiny problem. The more I tried to help, the worse trouble I caused poor Ralph."

"Heaven help him."

"They tried." She sighed. "Unfortunately, they sent me. And my execution proved a bit flawed."

"Ralph didn't make a good manager?"

"Don't misunderstand. He's an incredibly smart man. But he had a slight problem with authority."

"He didn't like taking orders?"

"No, not that." She darted him a quick, brittle smile. "He didn't like *giving* them."

"So how did you resolve the problem?"

A shadow drifted across her face, stealing the amusement from her expression. "I didn't." The doors opened and they stepped from the elevator. "Chuck had to take over when the hotel flooded."

Reed approached the door to their suite and inserted the card into the locking mechanism. "And why did the hotel flood? You never mentioned."

"I thought if there were an emergency situation, Ralph would be forced to give orders."

The lock released and Reed opened the door. "And instead?"

She sighed. "Instead, he panicked. Rather than getting the water turned off, he called for help. By the time the fire department arrived, the damage was done."

"And then?"

"And then Goodenkind removed me from the assignment and sent Charles CrosstoBear in my place."

Reed lifted an eyebrow in disbelief. "Crossto-Bear?"

"He's assigned to cleanup."

"Very amusing, Ms. Makepeace."

"It's true!"

"And you never lie."

"Never."

"Stretch the truth a little, perhaps?"

She set her chin at a stubborn angle. "Not at all. It's not acceptable."

Reed let it go and turned his attention to the suite. "Nice place. It must be convenient having friends in high places."

"Sometimes. Oh, and look!" She crossed to the sitting area. A large basket of fruit topped the coffee table. "I'll bet it's from Mr. Jenson."

"Generous of him."

She opened the card and shook her head. "Seems I'm wrong. They're from Ralph and— Good gracious. He married little Ruthie Evans, the concierge. That must have been Chuck's doing." She tapped the card with her fingernail. "Now why didn't I think of that? She'll make a perfect wife, too. She never gets ruffled in a crisis."

"There's that word again."

Angie looked up, startled. "What word?"

"Wife."

Comprehension dawned and she smiled. "Did you think that was a not-so-subtle way of bringing up the subject?"

He lifted an eyebrow. "Was it?"

"Not at all. I—"

"Good. Before you change your mind, I'm going to get ready for my first meeting." He checked his briefcase and pulled out a file, dropping it onto the coffee table next to the fruit basket. "Why don't you go ahead and set up my laptop and see about typing the notes in that file. I should return around five, six at the latest. There's a banquet tonight, so wear one of your formal dresses."

"Reed?"

He glanced at her, his hazel eyes filled with warning. "What?"

"I wasn't going to bring it up," she said seriously. "One of these days maybe you'll believe me when I tell you something. I don't lie. Remember?"

"Maybe I should write that down." Some of the tension eased from his expression. "I have to go."

"I'll be here when you get back," she promised.

An odd smile slanted across his mouth. "You know... I could get used to hearing that." Snapping closed his briefcase, he left.

But long after he'd gone, Angie still stood motionless in the middle of the room, forced to face the distressing realization. *She could get used to saying it, too.*

"Angie."

She drifted awake, pulled to consciousness against her will. "What? Who's there?"

"Your assignment, Ms. Makepeace. It's almost at an end."

"Good? Is that you?"

She sat up, amazed to discover that she'd nodded off at the sitting room table while typing up Reed's notes. She couldn't remember ever having slept before—at least, not since becoming an angel. A faint tremor disrupted the air nearby and she could just make out Goodenkind's outline materializing beside her. That fact alone unnerved her. He'd never visited in the course of an assignment before. She'd always been brought to him.

"Your time is almost through," he said.

"But—but I'm not finished."

"That doesn't matter, my dear. You've had ample opportunity to complete your mission. Dotty DoGooder can take over. Come home, now."

Sheer panic gripped her. "No! No, please. You have to give me a little longer. Reed needs me."

"He doesn't need you," Goodenkind corrected, his voice compassionate, yet unyielding. "He needs a wife. And he needs love. That's what you've been sent to give him, remember? That's what you've *failed* to give him. Or have you forgotten your purpose for being here?"

"I haven't forgotten. I'll take care of it. I will. Please—"

"Very well. I'll give you three more days. You have until Monday morning to complete your assignment and then you must come home." His outline faded, his final words drifting to her as though borne on the wings of a sweet summer breeze. "Remember the gift, Angie. Give him his gift."

And with that, he was gone.

As Reed dressed for dinner that night, he found himself wondering what shade of red Angie would choose for the evening and how outrageous her dress would be. Whatever she wore, she'd undoubtedly end up the center of attention. She possessed the innate ability to attract people. And once they came within her sphere of influence, she instantly enchanted them. He'd never met anyone with that much charm before.

Walking into the sitting room, he found her standing by the windows, waiting for him. As he'd anticipated, she wore red—rose-red, to be exact. The dress had a halter top that left her back bare to the base of her spine, the skirt flaring at her hips and falling to the floor in graceful folds. Her skin gleamed in the subdued lighting, as soft and creamy as an angel's should be. He shook his head, disgusted with himself. An angel. She said it with such sincerity she had him half-believing.

"How did your meetings go?" she asked without turning around.

"Very successful, thanks. I'm sorry I'm late. My final appointment ran longer than expected."

"That's all right. It gave me plenty of time to set up the laptop and type some preliminary notes."

She still hadn't turned around and he caught a glimpse of her reflection in the window. He could see the silvery gleam of her hair, the moist redness of her mouth and the glint from wistful blue eyes. She seemed so distant, so untouchable.

So angelic.

A chill swept through him. He'd never been a superstitious man. He'd always been pragmatic to the extreme. He believed in what he could touch and see and taste and build with his own two hands. But as he stood there, watching Angie, some sixth sense stirred to life. Something was wrong. He could feel it, like a living entity writhing in the air.

"Angie—"

"I called the office, by the way." She cut him off, as though she knew what he intended to ask. "I spoke to Casey."

"And?"

She shrugged, the movement causing her skirt to ripple in gentle waves. "There's been another change on the Wellsby project."

"No surprise there."

"She offered to fax the information to you."

"It'll keep until Monday."

"She also reported that Joel caused a minor uproar when he moved his project into the reception area. He claimed it had to be done now or the model would be too big to fit through the apartment door."

Reed shifted irritably. "I'll deal with it when we

return.'' He waited a moment, finally prompting, ''Is that everything Casey had to say?''

''Yes.''

''No other problems?''

''None.''

The hell there weren't. Something had upset her. If not at the office, then here at the hotel. Or perhaps in her personal life. The tension poured off her, simmering in the air between them. ''What going on, sweetheart? What's wrong?''

She lifted her hand to the window, her fingers splayed against the thick glass. ''I can feel the vibration of the traffic in my palm,'' she commented quietly. ''It rumbles like distant thunder. You know... I never noticed that before. I was always so busy, I never paid attention.''

He approached, standing directly behind her. Reaching out, he planted his hand next to hers. ''You're noticing now.''

She bowed her head, exposing the tender nape of her neck. ''It's too late now.''

''It's never too late.''

''It is for me.'' She turned, caught within his arms. To his alarm, tears glistened in her eyes. ''But it isn't too late for you.''

He didn't have to ask what she meant. ''I don't want a wife.''

''Don't you understand? I have to leave soon. I don't have much longer to accomplish my assignment.'' She caught the lapels of his suit coat, crumpling them in her fists. He doubted she even noticed.

"What do you want, Reed? Tell me and I'll give it to you."

He didn't hesitate. "Just this..." He closed his mouth over hers. She tasted like heaven. Sweet and moist and deliciously warm. He could get used to holding her, kissing her, loving her. It would be easy. So very easy. He wanted her, wanted her more than he had any other woman.

Even Emily.

She pulled back slightly, her lips hovering a scant inch beneath his. She inhaled deeply, blinking in confusion. "I'm sorry. What did you say?"

"I didn't say anything." He nuzzled her cheek, following the silken line of her jaw to beneath her ear—to the spot he knew would arouse her passion. Sure enough, her pulse beat frantically against his mouth.

"I thought I heard you ask for something," she insisted.

"I asked for a kiss."

"No. I mean, after that. I thought you asked for—"

"It was a kiss, not a request."

"I must have been hearing things."

"Do angels do that?" he teased.

She stilled, her eyes widening. "Sometimes." She searched his face, as though desperate for an answer to some vital question. "Sometimes wishes speak so loudly, angels hear. Especially when those wishes are your true heart's desire. What was your wish, Reed?"

He dropped his arms and stepped free of her embrace. "I don't believe in wishes any more than I believe in angels."

She stretched out a hand, then hesitated. "What if

I were to offer you the chance to have your heart's desire? One wish granted, free of charge—''

His mouth twisted. ''I'd say thanks, but no thanks. Wishes don't come true. And nothing in this life is free of charge. There's always a catch.''

''Are you so sure?''

''Have wishes ever come true for you?'' She started to turn away and he caught her chin, forcing her to look at him. ''You swore you'd never lie to me. So tell me, Angie. Have you ever had one of your dreams come true?''

Slowly she shook her head, compressing her lips to conceal an almost imperceptible tremor. ''No. Never.''

He felt the depth of her distress and understood how much their conversation hurt her. Not that it stopped him. ''And love,'' he demanded. ''Have you ever experienced any such emotion? I'm talking about the soul-shattering, forever-after sort of love.''

Again she shook her head, the intense pain in her eyes almost more than he could handle. ''But that doesn't mean it doesn't exist.''

He heard the desperate edge to her voice. Still he forced the issue, unable to help himself. ''No? And this wish you're so eager to grant. Name one wish anyone's ever given you. A wish with no strings attached. Yours for the taking.''

She stood before him—delicate, ethereal, heartbreakingly beautiful. And unflinchingly honest. ''No one's ever given me that, either.''

''You don't believe in dreams or true love or wishes. And yet, you expect me to?''

"Yes."

"I can't, Angie. I'm sorry."

"This wish…" She tried again. "It's Goodenkind's gift, not mine. I'm merely the messenger."

"And what if I'd rather have the messenger instead of the message?"

He could practically see her vulnerability, it surrounded her like a pale, shimmering aura—paper thin and painfully exposed. Just a few cutting words would slice through it. A sharp comment or two and he'd destroy her month-long pretence and settle this nonsense once and for all. He'd wait until the tears had passed, hear the painful story that had prompted her to invent her "angel guise," and then he'd take her to bed. They'd have a brief passionate affair before gradually drifting apart. Of course, they'd part friends, he'd see to that. Except for Emily, all his relationships had ended on good terms. It would be the same with Angie.

All he had to do was force the issue.

Just say the words.

"You look stunning tonight," he told her gently. "Shall we go down now? I don't know about you, but I'm starving."

A smile broke free, winning out over the anguish, a smile as beautiful and soul-shattering as any he'd ever seen. "Thank you. I'd like that."

She stepped forward and slipped her hand into the crook of his arm. But as they walked toward the door, he saw her lift a trembling finger and surreptitiously brush tears from the corner of her eyes. And that, more than anything that had gone before, filled him with remorse.

Dammit all. He'd made an angel cry.

CHAPTER EIGHT

THE next few hours were the most enchanting Angie had ever known. She and Reed ate in a huge dining room, sharing a table with three other couples attending the conference. Most of the participants had brought families and looked forward to the picnic the next day. To her surprise, she was the only secretary present—not that anyone believed she'd come in that capacity.

"If you all brought families, where are they?" Angie asked one of the wives.

"Oh, they have events organized for the younger children and sitters for the babies." She wrinkled her brow. "I think tonight's the pajama party. They'll have pizza, popcorn and a triple feature."

"Sounds like fun."

"It is. We attend every year." She winked at her husband. "We wouldn't miss it for the world, would we, Donald?"

"Not a chance."

"It's my only opportunity each year to go dancing," another of the wives commented. Everyone laughed at the long-suffering expression on her husband's face. "Oh, don't you believe him," she scoffed, giving him a loving pinch. "You watch. He'll be the first out on the floor and the last to leave." Sure enough, the minute they'd adjourned to the ballroom, the two headed straight for the dance floor.

"Shall we?" Reed murmured. Not waiting for an answer, he drew her into his arms.

"This is so wrong," Angie confessed with a sigh.

In fact, after Good's warning, it was downright foolhardy. She didn't dare waste a single second of her remaining days. And she wouldn't have, except for one tiny problem. The truth was, she didn't have a chance in a million of finding Reed a wife this weekend. Not unless he fell in love at first sight—and knowing him, that seemed highly unlikely. Nor could she simply pick the next eligible woman walking by and force him to fall in love.

No. The only chance she had of completing her mission was to get her reluctant boss to "wish" his future bride into existence. That gave her precisely two and a half days to work on him, to convince him that he wanted a wife with all his heart.

And what better way to get him in the mood, than a romantic evening of dancing? At least... That's what she told herself.

"So tell me, Ms. Makepeace." He rested his cheek against the top of her head, his breath stirring the pale curls. "Why is enjoying a simple dance wrong?" he asked, his tone indulgent.

"Because I'm neglecting my responsibilities."

"You're off duty tonight. I insist."

"I may be off duty as your secretary, but that doesn't let me off the hook as far as Goodenkind is concerned."

"You're my angel, which means you have to do

what I say," he insisted stubbornly. "And I say you're to forget everything except enjoying yourself."

She chuckled. "I'm not sure Good would agree with that, but I'm having too marvelous a time to argue. And since Scratch isn't around to debate the issue…" She snuggled into his embrace and sighed. "It's been so long since I last danced. How about you?"

He pulled her closer. "It's been a while."

"Do you miss it?"

"Yeah, I do."

She heard the surprise in his voice and smiled. It was a start. She'd planted a reminder of what he currently lacked in his life. Now she just had to convince him he missed it sufficiently to "wish" it into existence. Her smile faded. Whomever he ended up marrying would be a lucky woman. And though she should be happy for him, she couldn't quite ignore the pain that knowledge stirred.

Glancing up at the firm sweep of his jaw and the warmth in his gaze, the pain intensified. She closed her eyes to blot out the sight. Not that it helped. Instead she felt the hard strength of his body moving in rhythm with hers, the delicious friction of male on female. Tears burned against her lids. *Darn it all, Angie Makepeace!* Angels had no business feeling envy or desire or longing. Angels intent on maintaining their status in heaven needed to focus on their mission.

Determined to do just that, she threw herself into her plan, encouraging the various couples they sat with between dances to talk about their family life. She even asked how they'd met and decided to marry. Perhaps it was her imagination, but she could have sworn she caught a wistful gleam in Reed's eyes when the discussion turned to children. Not that it lasted long. In the middle of the conversation, he decided they should turn in. Still, it was enough to give her hope during the long silent ride in the elevator.

"Thank you for a lovely evening," she said the minute they entered the suite. "I enjoyed every minute."

He cupped her shoulders, turning her around. "It doesn't have to end. We could make it last all night."

Her breath caught in a small hitch. At the revealing sound his eyes glittered an intense gold. "That wouldn't be a good idea," she said unsteadily.

"I happen to think it's an excellent idea." He cupped her face and tilted it to accept his kiss, the touch light and gentle and frighteningly persuasive. "See how good that was?"

"It was wonderful," she admitted, catching his taste with the tip of her tongue. It made her hungry for more, so very hungry.

"Truthful to the end, Ms. Makepeace?"

She bowed her head. "I told you I'd always be honest."

"Then can you honestly say you want the evening to end?"

"I want it to last forever." The confession slipped out before she could prevent it. "But my wishes aren't important."

"Just mine are."

"Yes."

He snagged her chin, forcing her to look at him. "And what if I wished for this evening to last forever? What if I wished for you in my bed?"

"I don't know what would happen," she confessed. "I'm not sure that even heaven's powers can create a never-ending night. Nor do I think they'd willingly put an angel in your bed."

"So there are limits to my wish?"

"Only one that I'm aware of."

"And what's the one condition?"

"That the wish be your true heart's desire."

His mouth skated to the base of her throat, dipping into the shallow hollow he found there. "And how will you know if it's my true desire?"

"I won't need to." She could barely think, the words a confused jumble in her head. "Heaven will."

"Come to bed with me, Angie." His hand slipped around her neck, finding the closing to her halter top. He eased one button after another through the tiny eyelet fastenings. "Maybe we can find that desire together."

Tears gathered in her eyes. Why did this have to be so difficult? "I can't," she whispered. "As much as I want to, it would be wrong. I'm not meant for you and you're not meant for me. You have to find love, Reed. True love. And you have to find it with a living woman, not a shadow from the past."

"If that's all you are and this moment is all you have, don't you deserve to enjoy life for a night?"

He released the final button and the halter top drifted downward, baring her to his gaze. "Make love with me, Angie."

She swayed, a mere breath from surrender. Perhaps she would have followed him into his room, if his final words hadn't reverberated straight through to her soul. *Make love with me, Angie.*

Love.

Make love.

The pain nearly sent her to her knees. If she went with him, it wouldn't be love they shared, but lust. And she knew all about lust. She'd experienced it once during her years in the real world and that single instance had been more than enough. Slowly she pulled away, lifting the scarlet pieces of her bodice with trembling hands. For the first time in her angelic life, she saw the color as a brand. Shame filled her.

"I would make love with you, Reed—if that's what it was." She attempted a smile and failed miserably. "But we both know it's not."

"Angie—"

"Don't you understand, yet?" A tear escaped and she brushed it away. Not that it helped. Another came. And then another. "You want me to act out a lie. And I can't. I don't lie."

His eyes turned black. "Are you so sure it would be one?"

"For you? Yes." She lifted her chin and met his gaze with every ounce of remaining courage. "Which means it would be for me, too." There was nothing left to be said. Turning, she walked away from the one man she could have loved…if he'd been capable of such an emotion.

And if she hadn't been an angel on a mission.

"We're not taking the bus to the picnic with everyone else?" Angie asked the next morning. She kept her question light and impersonal, hoping he wouldn't mention what had passed between them the previous night. To her relief, he didn't.

"Nope. I don't feel like a bus ride, so I rented a car for the day." He led her out into the underground garage. "In fact, I rented one just for you."

That caught her by surprise. "Really?"

"Yup. They had quite a nice selection. I thought— now which would Ms. Makepeace pick, if were up to her?" He paused by a BMW. "The silver sedan?"

She couldn't resist his lighthearted game. "Too sedate," she said, shaking her head in mock reproof.

"My feelings exactly." He continued on, stopping next to a limo protectively guarded by a chauffeur. "The white Rolls?"

"Too elegant for a picnic," Angie decided.

"Then we'll keep looking. I know." He snapped his fingers. "How about the black Ferrari?"

She cocked her head to one side as she considered the low-slung piece of high-powered machinery. "Tempting…"

"And the perfect color for a sophisticated blonde, don't you think?" He winked and pointed to the car parked next to it. "Which is why I chose the red convertible."

She laughed, admiring the sporty Mercedes. "Perfect choice, Mr. Harding."

"Glad you approve." He opened the door on the driver's side. "Would you care to take it for a spin?"

"Are you…" Her voice caught and she tried again. "Are you serious?"

"When's the last time you drove?"

"Over a year ago," she confessed softly. "Really? May I drive?"

"You reminded me last night how important it is to enjoy the little things in life. And right now I can't think of anything more enjoyable than a beautiful blonde driving a flashy red convertible on a sunny Saturday morning." He lifted an eyebrow. "Can you?"

Her mouth trembled into a smile. "Just one thing more."

"And what's that?"

"Taking that drive with a good-looking man at my side."

His return smile came slow and easy, sliding across her like a warm caress. "I think I can arrange that. Do you have a license?"

"I could dig one up if I had to." Slipping into the driver's seat, Angie opened her purse and removed a pair of large-framed sunglasses and perched them on the end of her nose. Next she pulled out a wide gold clip and used it to anchor her hair at the nape of her neck.

"I've been meaning to ask you something," Reed asked as he climbed into the passenger seat. "How does all that stuff fit in such a tiny purse?"

She laughed. "What can I tell you? It's an angel thing." With that, she started the car, punched in the clutch and shifted into reverse. Tires screeching, she whipped out of the parking space. Freedom beckoned and she didn't want to miss a single minute.

Reed had given her an unexpected gift—a brief moment to escape back into life. And she treasured every second, savoring each sensation that came her way. Despite the clip, the wind tore at her hair, whipping the curls around her face before tossing them behind her in a long, silvery stream. The scent of summer filled the air, crisply floral and yet tasting of the sweet corn ripening beside the freeway. The sun kissed her pale skin, giving it a rosy bloom she hadn't known in over a year. The instant Reed noticed, he insisted they pull over so she could put on sunscreen. But she didn't even mind that, because he helped, rubbing the creamy lotion into her arms and neck, then swiping the excess from the tip of her nose before planting a kiss there.

It took an hour and a half to reach Pointer's Lake. The buses had arrived ahead of them and the families were busily unloading and marking their sites with beach towels and folding chairs.

"How about under the tree by the lake?" Reed suggested, pointing to a vacant spot.

"How about under the tree by the swings?"

"Ah, right. You don't swim." He cocked an eyebrow. "Does that also mean you don't like the water?"

She forced a lightness to her reply. "Only if it's in a bathtub covered up with lots of bubbles."

"Remind me when we get to the hotel and I'll see what I can do." He snagged a large blanket from the back seat of the car. "So what happened to cause such a strong dislike for water?"

"I had a bad experience once." She deliberately understated the case.

He gave her a sympathetic look. "Almost drowned?"

"Something like that."

"I could help, if you'd like. It seems a shame to cut yourself off from so many pleasures because of one unfortunate experience."

She released a silent sigh. "I died from that one unfortunate experience. And even though I can't actually be killed again, I'd rather not relive it."

He dropped the blanket and faced her. "You died."

"Well, how the he—*heck* did you think I became an angel? Dying happens to be a prerequisite, you know."

"We're back to that, are we?"

"We never really left it," she informed him regretfully. "We merely set it aside for a short time."

"Angie, this is getting ridiculous."

"You're right. Here I am allowing myself to play when I should be completing my assignment." She planted her hands on her hips and surveyed the crowd. "There must be someone here you can fall in love with. Or..." She turned and eyed him hopefully. "You can make a wish."

"Wish for what?"

"A wife, of course," she snapped. "True love. Haven't you been paying attention?"

He settled onto his back on the blanket and folded his arms behind his head. "Apparently not."

"Reed! *Wish,* darn it all!"

"Okay. I wish for true love. There. Satisfied?"

"No!" She dropped to her knees beside him. "That's not good enough. It has to be your heart's desire."

"Wishing for marriage isn't my heart's desire. I don't want to fall in love. Nor do I need a wife."

"Well, what *do* you need?" she demanded in exasperation.

His expression closed over. "Nothing you can give me."

"I—" She broke off, her brow wrinkling in confusion. A whisper brushed by, a faint longing too soft for her to catch. "There is something you want. What is it? I almost heard."

"Drop it, Angie." There was no mistaking the finality in his voice. "I've tried love. It didn't work out. End of subject. Hey, look. They're starting up a volleyball game." It was a clear effort to distract her attention. "Care to play?"

She glanced over her shoulder toward the lake. Sand had been dumped along the shoreline and a group had congregated there, forming into teams. "I— It's by the lake."

"That's okay." His voice gentled. "You don't have to go near the water. We'll play on the sand."

"I don't know," she murmured reluctantly.

"Tell you what. You don't have to play if you'd rather not." Ignoring her protests, he yanked off her bright red tennis shoes and helped her to her feet. "Just come over and watch from the grass."

Of course, that didn't last. Before long several of

the couples they'd met the previous evening coaxed her into joining the game. Soon she was so caught up in the action, she succeeded in ignoring the sinister threat of the water lapping at the sand nearby. For the next hour they pelted the ball back and forth, laughing at everyone's lack of skill. To Angie's amusement, the ball plummeted out of bounds more often than in.

"Heads up, Ms. Makepeace!" Reed called as the ball soared over her for the twentieth time.

With a quick laugh, she gave chase. It rolled toward the lake and she hesitated for a split second. *Please, not the lake!* she whispered beneath her breath. Gathering her courage, she raced full-tilt to the water's edge, intent on grabbing the ball and escaping before fear incapacitated her.

A husky youth from the opposite side of the net apparently had the same idea. Just as she reached for the ball, he careened into her, knocking her off her feet. It was destined, she realized then—she'd sensed it from the moment she'd arrived. She fell backward, straight into the lake. Her scream rent the air as the water closed over her head, washing into her nose and mouth. She was going to drown. And her last panicked thought was that perhaps angels could die twice.

The world tilted in that instant. She wasn't Angie Makepeace anymore, but a different Angie, in a different time and place. An Angie with far different memories.

The dark-haired woman walked along the dock, admiring the boats, her gurgling baby resting on one plump hip. The husky youth came out of nowhere, racing along the wooden planks, the slap of the worn boards beneath his feet echoing across the water. The woman took a single step toward the edge of the dock, drawing the baby's attention to something offshore. They were tiny details. Insignificant details. Details that would never have mattered or been remembered by Angie, if not for two unfortunate events.

The first was the large boat that passed the dock, creating a small wake as it entered the harbor.

The other was that the youth looked over his shoulder at his friends, shouting as he ran.

Angie realized the danger long before anyone else. It was as though time slowed to a crawl, allowing her to watch the incident unravel—giving her an opportunity to make a life-altering decision. Then it happened. The boy's shoulder clipped the woman square in the back just as the boat's wake hit the dock. Unprepared for the impact, off balance from the waves lifting the dock beneath her feet, the mother started to fall. The little girl practically flew from the woman's arms, arcing out over the water. The woman screamed, frantically pinwheeling for an instant in a desperate attempt to regain her balance. She failed, falling first against the motorboat anchored in the slip beside her, and then into the water.

Angie didn't wait to see any more. She was closer than anyone else. Leaping from the dock, she hit the water at almost the same instant as the baby. It was a foolish thing to do considering she couldn't swim. But her only thought was saving the child. Her fingers snagged in silky-fine hair and she tugged with all her strength, lifting the baby over her head toward the *surface. She could see hands reaching for the child. Others on the dock had finally arrived on the scene.*

And then Angie's hair caught in the heavy chain anchoring the motorboat, preventing her from clawing her way to the surface. She opened her mouth to scream, felt the sting of salt water washing into her nose and eyes, felt the burn in her lungs as she strained for oxygen. Her vision clouded over and in that timeless instant she'd known that her life was ending—that she'd never find love or happiness, never have a husband or children, never grow old with someone...

"Please," she'd cried silently. "Please, don't let me die without ever having known love!"

Strong hands grabbed her, yanking her to the surface. "Angie!"

"Reed! Oh, Reed!" She coughed, choking on water. "The baby! Is the baby all right?"

"What baby?"

"The infant. From the dock."

"There's no infant, sweetheart. And no dock. Just you. And you're safe."

"No dock?"

Then she remembered, remembered that the baby had been from a lifetime ago. A life she'd lived and left behind. Angie shuddered. She also remembered her death—and more to the point—remembered her heavenly mission and the consequences if she failed that mission. With a whimper of pain, she collapsed in Reed's arms, burying her face against his shoulder.

"Is she okay?" The youth who'd knocked her in

the water approached, regarding her apprehensively. "I'm really sorry. I didn't mean to hurt her."

"She'll be fine. It was a little scare." Reed raised his voice. "Go on with your game. We'll catch up later."

With that he lifted her into his arms and returned to their blanket. Wrapping her in it, he proceeded to rub away her fear-induced chill. "You scared me for a minute there, sweetheart. I thought you were actually going to drown in two feet of water."

Angie peered at him from beneath the plaid cotton and Reed buried a smile. She looked like a half-drowned kitten, all big blue eyes and wet, tufted hair. "Two feet?"

"You'd have had to work hard to drown in that."

She shivered. "It felt a lot deeper."

"Panic will do that to you—screw with your perception."

"Oh." She let the blanket fall and bent her knees, wrapping her arms around them. "I didn't mean to cause such an uproar."

"You mentioned a baby. What was that about?"

"It was my one redeeming grace, apparently," she muttered.

"Come again?"

"Da— *Dang!* Where did I put my purse?"

She tugged at the blanket until she found it. Digging around inside, she extracted a comb and started working the tangles from her hair. She also avoided his gaze, he noticed. That was a first.

"The baby?" he prompted patiently.

She didn't want to answer, but he continued to sit

and wait. Finally, she heaved a sigh of exasperation. "All right, fine. I'll tell you. Satisfied?"

"For the moment."

She glared her resentment. "There was a mother and a little girl. An infant. About Kip's age, I guess." Angie shrugged as though it didn't mean anything, but her careless attitude didn't quite ring true. It mattered. If he were any judge, it mattered a hell of a lot. "They were knocked into the water and I jumped in to try and help."

"I thought you said you couldn't swim."

"I can't."

"You still jumped in, anyway?" he asked incredulously. "Wasn't that a foolhardy?"

"As it turns out, it was downright stupid."

"What happened to the little girl?"

"She made it." Angie radiated tension. "I, unfortunately, didn't."

"And that's when you became an angel?" He tried to say it without inflection. From the anger flaring to life in her eyes, he suspected his skepticism showed.

"If I'd considered the consequences, I probably wouldn't have done it. Happy now?"

"But you did."

"Yeah. I did. And my one act of self-sacrifice gave me an opportunity for redemption. Not total redemption, you understand. At least, not yet. Just a shot at having a place inside the Pearly Gates. The downside is… If I don't succeed with you, I won't have to worry about being an angel anymore."

"Ah. That's right. I'm your last chance to earn your wings, aren't I?"

"This isn't a Jimmy Stewart movie," she snapped. "I've already earned my wings, thank you very much. What I haven't earned is a permanent place in heaven. That's where you come in." She tossed the comb to the blanket. "So, spill it, Harding. Why the he—*heck* are you so opposed to love and marriage? At least I have an excuse for my phobia. I'm afraid of water because I drowned. What's your excuse?"

"I'm not afraid. Just cautious."

"Why?" she demanded.

"I tried love once. It didn't work out."

"I gathered as much. What happened?" When he didn't reply, she pressed. "Come on, Reed. I answered your questions. Now answer mine."

It took him a full minute to reach a decision. He'd never spoken of his time with Emily to anyone. Not even his family. He ran a hand through his hair. Hell, especially not his family. But he wanted to tell Angie, to make her understand that his decision to remain single wasn't an irrational one. He glanced at her, watching the sun break through the boughs of the oak above them and kiss her hair with gold. A gentle breeze stirred the drying curls, defeating her efforts to tame them. Damn, but she was beautiful. Lively, intelligent... His mouth twitched. And only slightly insane.

"Okay, Ms. Makepeace. You want the whole story? Fine. You've got it." He plucked a long stem of grass and clamped it between his teeth. "Emily and I were planning to marry. We were living together at the time."

"When was this?"

"A little over two years ago. Everything seemed perfect. And then my mother asked me to take in Joel."

"Because she couldn't control him? Isn't that what you told me?"

Reed nodded. "Right. Mom thought he'd listen to me." He stared broodingly at the lake. "Hell, Angie. What could I say? He's my brother."

"I gather Emily expected you to say no."

"She sure did. She and Joel didn't get along at all. She'd never had brothers and what she referred to as his 'wildness' frightened her." He glanced her way. "He was being headstrong, same as I'd been at his age. But I couldn't convince her of that. So she issued an ultimatum."

Compassion crept into Angie's husky voice. "You had to choose between Emily and Joel?"

"Yup."

"And you chose your brother?"

He laughed without humor. "As a matter of fact, I never had to make that call. When I arrived home from work the next day, she'd cleared out."

"There's more, isn't there?"

He didn't answer immediately. He didn't want to answer at all. But she'd been honest with him from the start. It was the least he could offer in return. "I found a box in the trash. A home pregnancy test."

"She was *pregnant?*"

"I don't know," he admitted roughly. He tossed the blade of grass he'd been chewing to the ground. "That's the damnable part. I've spent over two years trying to find out. I've hired private detectives, spoken to all her friends and business associates. No one knows anything, or if they do, they're not saying. It's like she's disappeared off the face of the earth."

"You have no idea where she might have gone?"

"She has a mother. Somewhere. But I can't remember the woman's name or where she lives." He slammed his fist into the ground beside him, the soft earth absorbing the impact. "You wondered why I found holding Kip so difficult? It's driving me crazy, wondering if I have a son—a boy like Kip or a daughter."

"Have you told your mother any of this?"

He shook his head. "You're the only one who's heard the entire story, other than the detectives." He shot her a grim look. "I don't want anyone else informed, either. My mother and Joel already feel bad enough about Emily's leaving. If they knew she might have been pregnant—"

Understanding dawned. "But that's why your mother is so anxious to find you a wife."

Reed nodded. "She's guilty about the breakup. She figures that if she hadn't asked me to take Joel, Emily wouldn't have left. Mom's been trying to atone for it ever since."

"Which is why you tolerate her matchmaking."

"Yes. It's a small inconvenience and it helps ease her conscience."

"And poor Joel. He must be feeling guilty, too."

"I've talked to him about it. Explained that I don't hold him responsible. I think he believes me. At least, he hasn't said otherwise." He glanced at her, lifting an eyebrow in question. "Now do you understand why I'm not interested in marrying?"

"Not really. Granted, you've had one bad experience, but—"

"You don't get it, do you?" He surged to his feet, towering over her, his anger practically blistering the air. "One of these days I'm going to find Emily. And when I do, I'll know whether or not she had my baby. If she did, I plan on marrying her. I want my child, and I'll move heaven and earth to get him and keep him in my life. So unless you can produce my ex-fiancée and allow me to settle the issue of my paternity once and for all, I'm off the market."

And with that, he walked away.

"Angie?"

Reed pushed open the door between his bedroom and the sitting area, intent on offering the apology he'd resisted making all day. Unfortunately, she wasn't there. But he could hear her. She hummed softly, the unfamiliar tune strangely beguiling.

He followed the sound, pausing at the threshold of her bathroom. The door stood slightly ajar and he realized an instant too late that he never should have intruded this far. Though now that he had, no power on earth could stop him from looking.

Angie must have just gotten out of the shower. Steam filled the air, wheeling in lazy circles around the room. Thin tendrils of mist crept toward the open doorway, reaching for him like so many ghostly fingers. But they dissipated at the first taste of cooler air, falling short of their goal.

To his relief, Angie hadn't seen him. She stood in profile, one elegant foot resting on the edge of the tub as she bent at the waist, drying her leg. Her hair was a mass of pale ringlets, tumbling down her back and across her shoulder. Moisture sparkled on her flawless skin, as though someone had dusted her with gold glitter.

She bent lower and her breasts swayed ever so slightly, drawing his attention. They were full and round, the color of rich cream, with tightly furled rose buds tipping the crests. He could still remember the comfortable weight of them snug within his palms, while the honeyed taste filled his mouth. His gaze drifted lower. Her waist nipped in above neatly curved hips and her legs were long and toned and every bit as shapely as he'd anticipated.

The air current swirled around her, kissing her body in a loving caress. It circled her ankles and calves, dancing in delight between her thighs, before sweeping over her tightly muscled buttocks and along the arch in her back. The mist parted there, outlining something soft and downy that clung from her shoulders to the base of her spine. A gauzy silhouette formed in the shape of alabaster feathers—feathers aflutter, gently stirring the air. He shook his head in disbelief, fighting to deny what couldn't be denied.

Angie Makepeace had wings.

He must have made some sound because her chin jerked up and her damp towel slipped from nerveless fingers to the pink tile floor. Slowly she turned toward the door and he caught a glimpse of a thin band of gold shimmering over her head. For a long moment, neither of them moved. She stood before him in all her glory, without apology or artifice.

"You're an angel," he said at last.

"I told you I was."

"I don't want an angel in my life." The words slipped out of their own volition, unintentionally cruel, though starkly honesty.

A deep sadness welled into her heavenly blue eyes. "I know."

No, he didn't want an angel, he realized. He wanted Angie. He wanted her with every fibre of his being. He wanted her in his bed and in his life and by his side.

Heaven had given him an angel, but he wanted the woman.

CHAPTER NINE

"I THOUGHT you wanted to go for a drive," Angie said uneasily, watching as a familiar-looking farmhouse flashed by the car window. "Isn't this the way to the lake?"

"I decided to head out there again."

"But...why?"

"Let's just say we have some unfinished business to take care of."

"Unfinished business?" she repeated nervously. "At the lake?"

"Right." He spared her a quick glance, his serious expression increasing her apprehension. "We need to talk."

Her mouth went dry—always a bad sign. "I don't understand. What do we have to talk about?"

"Any number of topics, wouldn't you say?"

She fell into a concerned silence. Did he intend to continue their discussion about finding him a wife? Or did he have more to tell her about Emily? Somehow she doubted that was it. They could have held either of those conversations at the hotel. Perhaps it was her angel status he hoped to address. That seemed the most likely of all. But... Why at the lake?

He parked the car in the deserted lot and snagged the blanket from the back seat again. Bypassing the spot beneath the tree they'd occupied the day before, he cut across the volleyball field and continued straight on to the empty shoreline. Inches from the water's edge, he kicked off his shoes and spread the blanket across the sand.

"Come on, Angie. I thought we could sit here for a while and talk."

She stood at the border between grass and sand, unwilling to follow him to such a treacherous location. A pollen-drunk bumblebee wobbled by. At another time, in another place, she'd have taken a moment to savor the image, to store it away for a dark day when memories were all she had. Too bad anxiety held even that possible joy at bay. "Why can't we have our talk over here?"

He trudged back through the sand to her side. He didn't touch her, simply held her with a calm, reassuring gaze. "Will you trust me?"

Could she? Angie closed her eyes, hating the position he'd put her in. She did trust him. Totally. But her fear of the water refused to be so easily set aside. "Please, don't do this."

"Trust me, Angie," he said again. "Take my hand. I'll keep you safe."

Unable to refuse, she slipped her hand in his and walked with him toward the water, trembling so badly her legs threatened to buckle. Reaching the blanket, she collapsed to her knees, nausea riding her hard. He came down beside her and pulled her close. She practically crawled into his lap, wrapping her arms around his neck and burying her face in his shoulder.

"I'm scared," she confessed in a muffled voice.

"I know you are."

"Then why are you doing this?"

"Because angels shouldn't be afraid."

She lifted her chin slightly. "You really do believe I'm an angel?"

Ever so gently he feathered his hand from the crown of her head to the base of her spine as though he might feel what he could no longer see. "After last night, it would be a little difficult to deny."

"Are you shocked?"

"Yes."

"Because you don't believe in angels?"

"As far as I'm aware, they're not an everyday occurrence. At least, I've never run into one before."

"That you know of. There are more of us than you might think."

"Since you're the expert, I'll have to take your word for it." His hand tangled in her hair as he tucked her into the curve of his shoulder. "Now tell me why heaven thinks I should have a wife."

"They don't always offer an explanation," she admitted, relaxing against him. "I suspect it's because you need to set a good example for Joel. He follows your lead, copies everything you do. Perhaps heaven feels he should see true love work in your life, in order to find it himself someday."

Reed bowed his head, absorbing her comments as if they were a blow. "I'm sorry, Angie," he finally said. "I can't help you succeed at your mission."

"Because of Emily?"

"Yes."

She understood. She wished she didn't, but she did.

"You plan to marry her, if you find her." It wasn't a question.

"If she has my child, yes."

"Doesn't she have some say in this?" Angie asked carefully.

His hand fisted. "It's tearing me apart, wondering whether I have a child out there somewhere. Not a day goes by that I don't imagine what he'd look like, sound like, act like. I worry about his health, worry that he might be lost or in trouble. And when I think about him growing up, never knowing his father—" He broke off and his throat worked for a minute before he recovered his composure. "Isn't that good enough for heaven? Can't I find love through my child? Does it matter whether or not I love his mother?"

He'd confirmed the question she hadn't dared ask. "Then you don't love Emily?"

"I did love her. Once. At least I thought so." He stared across the water, despair in his gaze. "Perhaps I can again."

"You'll marry her, regardless, won't you?"

His mouth tightened. "Yes."

"Let me tell you something my uncle used to say. Maybe it'll help." She shot him a reprimanding look. "And no, it wasn't that sort of uncle. He was my mother's brother. He died when I was very young. But I still remember what he once told me."

"Life advice?"

"Advice on choosing a path through life, yes. He said that when you're traveling along the right path, mountains turn into molehills and are easily overcome. But when you're heading in the wrong direction, molehills become mountains and are impossible to scale."

"You think Emily is my mountain?"

"You've been searching for over two years without success. Perhaps you weren't meant to find her. Perhaps it's time to open yourself to other possibilities."

"Like love?"

He said it so caustically, she winced. "You can't fool me, Reed. I know the sort of person you are. I see the love you have for Joel and your mother—"

"Of course I love them. They're family."

"And me?" She stirred in his arms, tracing the protective width of his shoulders with a tender hand. "You're holding me with such warmth, with such concern. Why?"

"You know the answer to that."

"Because I'm afraid of the water."

"Yes."

"But don't you understand? That's my point. You care enough to try and help. You brought me here because you hoped to ease my fears, didn't you?"

"I told you. Angels shouldn't have fears. After you—" He clenched his teeth, a fierce denial forming in his eyes.

So she said the words for him. "After I died... Go on."

"Heaven should have taken the terror from you." His voice took on a raspy edge. "They should have taken those memories away, too."

"And since heaven didn't, you intend to?" She

gazed up at him, cupping the hard length of his jaw. "Whether you're willing to admit it or not, you have a huge capacity for love. And yet, you shut yourself off from it."

"I've told you," he insisted stubbornly. "I don't need love, just my kid."

"Let me tell you something, Reed. I spent a lifetime on the outside looking in, hoping to find what you could receive with one simple wish. I never found it and now I never will. It's too late for me, but you still have a chance. All you have to do is say the words and it's yours. Have you any idea what I'd give for that opportunity?"

"I can't, Angie. I can't do it." He caught her shoulders. "If you want to help, tell me where Emily is."

"I don't know where she is. Reed, she may not even have been pregnant."

"What if she was?"

"What if she gave the baby up for adoption?"

"No! I refuse to accept that."

"You might have to."

"This wish you promised me… Can I use it to find Emily?"

She was forced to tell the truth. "Yes."

"And what happens if I make that my wish?"

"I suspect that your detectives will miraculously locate her."

"And if she has my baby? If I marry her?"

She didn't pull her punches. "If you marry without love, my mission fails."

That stopped him. "What happens to angels who fail their missions?"

Angie shrugged. "It depends. Sometimes they send in another angel, one who won't fail. Like at Sarducci's or with Ralph at the Majesty." Or sometimes—when an angel had tarnished her halo beyond repair—she found herself on the wrong side of the Pearly Gates. Angie didn't trouble Reed with those details, though. How could she put such a burden on his shoulders?

"Another angel won't work in my case." It wasn't a question. "Chuck or Dotty won't be able to find me love, either. Will they?"

"Probably not. At least, not if you marry Emily."

She met his gaze, using every ounce of strength she possessed to bury her apprehension. Goodenkind had sent Reed a gift and, regardless of the personal consequences, she'd give it to him. She'd give him his request freely and with an open heart.

Because she loved him.

Her eyes widened in sheer wonder. Oh, God. *She loved him!*

How had that happened? When had it happened? It defied understanding. At least, her understanding. She smiled, smiled with utter joy as she gave mute thanks—smiled as she lifted her face to the warmth of the sun, tears of elation welling in her eyes. She'd lived a life barren of love. Empty and alone, dread and cynicism her constant companions. But today she'd been given the ultimate gift. For the first time in her entire existence, she knew a love that radiated to every portion of her body and soul. Never again would she stand on the outside looking in. Reed was part of her now. She wasn't alone.

"Thank you, Good," she whispered silently. "Thank you for that much." Even if she was put out of heaven, she'd have her love for Reed to carry with her, to help her through the dark times ahead. It gave her the strength she needed to ask the question she so dreaded. "Is that your wish, Reed? Is finding Emily your heart's desire?"

"I want to think about it a little longer before I decide."

Angie nodded, more relieved than she could say. Perhaps she'd have a chance to change his mind. "So what now?"

He tucked a lock of hair behind her ear, smiling as it curled possessively around his finger. "Now we address your problem."

"That's not necessary," she hastened to reply. "It's just one tiny fear."

"You've worked hard to grant my wish. I'd like to give you something in exchange."

Her mouth pulled to one side. "I'd be happier if it were something other than a swimming lesson. Besides, we're not dressed for this." It was a half-hearted argument, at best. And he knew it.

"We're wearing shorts. It won't matter if they get wet. What does matter is to try and free you from your phobia."

"Reed, I really appreciate what—"

"Trust me," he interrupted. "Can you do that much? I promise that if it doesn't work, I'll stop."

It was such a small request, although one that filled

her with dread. Slowly she nodded, fighting the panic that formed in the pit of her stomach. A bitter coldness seeped into her pores, creeping to her very bones. "Okay. But, please hurry and get it over with."

Two short steps brought them to the water's edge. Reed turned her so that she faced away from the lake, then eased her downward. Pulling her between his legs, he molded her back against his chest. The water was only inches deep here, lapping about their legs. Still, it terrified her.

"I won't bother to tell you to relax—"

"Good. Because I can't."

"But I do need you to close your eyes." As soon as she had, he asked, "Do you know what I thought the very first time I saw you?"

"Here comes trouble?" she managed to tease.

"Exactly. And the next minute I wondered how much trouble I could get in with you." He filled his hands with water and dribbled it along her arms. She shivered at the sensation—first in fright, and then in pleasure. "How's that?"

"Not bad," she admitted in surprise.

"Good. Now, just relax. I'm going a little deeper. No, don't stiffen up. Feel the water lift you? Carry you?"

Her eyes shot open. "Don't let go." She hated how panicked she sounded.

Instantly, his arms tightened around her. "I'll never let you go," he reassured. His legs tangled with hers, his hair-roughened calves tickling her smooth skin. "So, were you always trouble, even before you became an angel?"

"Every single day of my life," she confessed.

The water was to her waist now, seeping up her red blouse to lap beneath her breasts. The lake seemed so innocuous, the color a clear greenish-blue, the sun glittering in a carefree, golden dance across the wind-ruffled surface. Further down the shoreline she could see willows bending over the water, as though peeking at their reflection in the still depths. Long streaming switches of yellow-green leaves dangled above the water like braids of hair, whispering secrets to the curious breeze.

Reed eased Angie onto her belly, his hard body providing her with a secure raft. "And were you always so good with people?"

She clung to his shoulders, kicking with him, feeling the power of his thighs moving in tempo with hers. "I'm not good with people," she denied.

"Sure you are. Haven't you noticed? You attract them." He spread her hair in a carpet of curls across the water. "At first, I think it's your appearance that appeals to them. Men want you and women want to be like you. But then they stop looking at the surface and they see your spirit. It's like a bright golden flame that draws people to you."

"It's an angel thing. Like the purse."

He chuckled in genuine amusement. "No, sweetheart. It's you. It's the kindness in your eyes, the warmth of your smile, the gentleness of your touch and the zest for life that they hear in your voice."

"No, you're wrong." She felt a shaft of pain slip beneath her guard. "I told you. I was always on the outside looking in. I never belonged anywhere. Not really.''

''You never allowed yourself to belong.'' He eased the hair from her brow and cupped her face, his thumb stroking the curve of her cheek. ''They'd have let you in, love. All you had to do was ask.''

The truth hit her, devastating in its impact. She *had* held people at a distance. She'd been so afraid—afraid of being hurt, afraid of rejection. Afraid to reach for her dreams. And it had been a waste. A total waste of life and happiness. Dear heaven, what had she done to herself? Why had she so foolishly thrown it all away?

''You don't have to be afraid, Angie. Look, sweetheart. Look around you.''

She lifted her head, forcing herself to take note of their surroundings. They were far from shore, and yet, far from fear, too. She'd floated through the warm, silken water, so secure within Reed's arms that she'd never looked back. Never doubted. Never once been afraid.

The fear was gone. He'd taken it from her. A sudden storm of tears caught her by surprise and she burrowed into his shoulder and wept. She wept in relief that her terror was gone and wept in sorrow over her death. She wept at how much she'd missed in her brief lifetime and at how long it had taken her to find love. But most of all she wept because now that she'd found love, it was far, far too late.

Reed held her in his arms, allowing her time to cry through her grief. And even that was a memory she'd treasure when she left him—the beauty of today and his unstinting generosity. ''You don't have to be afraid,'' he repeated, slowly kicking toward shore. ''Not of the water and not of life. Neither can hurt you anymore.''

''I miss it, Reed,'' she whispered in anguish. ''I miss it so much.''

He helped her from the water. Once they'd settled onto the blanket, he lifted her hand to his mouth and kissed it. Then he turned her hand over, enclosing another kiss in her palm.

''Why did you do that?'' she asked gruffly.

''You once said that you'd never had a man kiss your hand. I don't want you to go back without having experienced it.''

''Oh, Reed.''

''I wish you hadn't died, Angie. That we could have met under different circumstances. You tried to find true love for me...'' His eyes turned a shade she'd never seen before—richer, more vibrant, charged with an emotion she couldn't name. ''Instead I found you. I know I shouldn't want to make love to an angel. That I shouldn't feel—''

She sealed his mouth with her fingers. ''Shh. Don't say it. What you want...what *I* want, isn't possible.'' But his yearning continued to ring in her head, echoing so loudly it threatened to deafen her. The impossibility of it all overwhelmed her and she covered her ears to shut out the silent cry.

''Let me make love to you,'' he urged, catching her hands in his. ''Just this one time. So we both have something to remember. It won't be lust. I promise it won't.''

She was tempted. So horribly tempted. But if she let him love her and allowed herself to love him in return, she'd cross a line that shouldn't be crossed. Even though it would give her an eternity's worth of memories—memories she could cherish when she lost her place in heaven, memories that would see her through the dark times to come—it would be wrong. She'd been sent to help Reed, not to steal the love he owed a more deserving woman. A courage she'd never possessed before filled her, an unassailable certainty that she had it within her to face whatever destiny had in store. But only if she did right.

"We can't," she said, disengaging herself. She didn't know where she found the strength. "I won't be able to stay much longer. Goodenkind will put an end to my mission soon."

"Angie—"

His whispered plea almost destroyed her. She couldn't meet his gaze, could only shake her head. "Would you like your wish now?"

He didn't answer immediately. When he did, his voice sounded impossibly cold, shattering the warmth and joy they'd shared. "Yes."

Oh, why did it hurt even to breathe? "Make it."

"I want you to find Emily for me. I want to know once and for all whether she had my baby. And if she did, I want to marry her."

"Is this your heart's desire?" she whispered.

He didn't answer and she forced herself to look at him. He stared across the water, his jaw set at a grim angle. He'd clenched his hands so tightly the muscles along his forearms stood out in thick cords. His eyes were shadowed, the gold totally eclipsed by a nut-hard brown.

"Reed? You don't have to do this," she urged. "You can still wish for true love. That doesn't mean you won't find Emily, that you won't be able to discover whether she had your baby."

"You're right. I want my child, if he exists. But there's something else I crave every bit as much." He faced her then, and the bleakness she read in his expression struck hard. "But it's a craving you can't satisfy."

"What do you mean?" she asked uneasily.

"You know."

"I don't."

"If I can't have heaven, I'll take hell. Give me my wish, Angie."

"Wish for love!"

"You heard my wish," he grated. "Are you going to grant it?"

"You want Emily? You want to know whether you have a child?"

"And I want marriage, if that child does exist."

"And this is your heart's desire?" she asked once more, her own heart breaking.

"It is."

He'd said it. Said it loud and clear, so there couldn't be any mistake. Tears filled Angie's eyes again. "So be it," she whispered.

He reached for her. His fingers brushed her cheek in a lingering caress. "It hurts, sweetheart." His words were low, torn from the deepest part of him.

"No matter what I wish, a piece of myself will always be missing. You know that, don't you?"

His pain echoed her own. That's how she'd feel when her time was up—like she'd left a vital part of herself behind. Angie closed her eyes, savoring Reed's touch, savoring each brief second she had with him, well aware this would be one of their final moments together.

"Yes. I do know."

Angie arrived at Reed's office early Monday morning, wanting to weep at the knowledge that her mission had come to an end. This would be the last time she'd watch a slow smile build across Reed's full, wide mouth, the last time she'd see the golden spark in his hazel eyes catch fire. The last time she'd feel his touch or breathe his scent or hear the rough timbre of his voice.

Praying for the strength she'd need to get through the next fleeting hour, she opened the door. Reed stood profiled by the windows overlooking the river. He hadn't heard her enter and she took a moment to study him unobserved. To her surprise, strain rode him hard and she frowned in concern. Knowing his wish would soon be granted should have eased his worries. Instead, deep crevices slashed a path from cheekbone to mouth, emphasizing the taut set of his jaw. His brows were furrowed as he stared out at the rain-streaked panorama.

"Reed?"

He turned, his greedy gaze feasting on her. "I thought you'd gone."

"I couldn't. Not yet." She'd miss him. Dear heaven, how she'd miss this man.

His lips pulled to the side in a half-smile, amusement easing the strain from his face. "I'm shocked, Angie. You're wearing white. That's quite a switch."

"My days of red are over, I'm afraid."

His tension was quick to return. "Over? Why are they over?"

"You know why. Because I have to leave soon. Before I do, there's one final chore to complete."

"If you're talking about finding me a wife—"

"I'm not," she hastened to say, holding up her hands. "I admit my mission to bring love into your life was an utter failure."

"No, it wasn't." An odd emotion raged in his eyes. "Sweetheart, I don't want you to leave."

"That's not your decision to make, any more than it's mine." She fought to be strong—for both their sakes. "Listen, Reed, I need to apologize."

"You have nothing to apologize for."

"Yes. I do." She risked approaching him, desperate to feel that momentary closeness one last time. If she were wise, she'd keep the length of the room between them. But then... When had she ever made wise choices? "I should have tried harder to find you a wife."

"I didn't want one."

"You deserve to have love. It does exist, Reed." The words burst from her, urgent in her need to convince him. "I know I told you I didn't believe in it. But, I was wrong."

"Don't go back," he whispered. "Stay with me."

He was breaking her heart—a heart she'd never truly believed she possessed. How wrong she'd been. How horribly, painfully wrong. "I don't belong here. Not anymore. I lived my life. Now you have to live yours."

The blaze that had started in his eyes grew, the gold burning hard and fierce, igniting the specks of green and brown. "I want you in that life."

Oh, please, Goodenkind! Don't make me go through this. It hurts so much. "That's not possible."

"Make it possible." He reached her in two short steps. "You'd like to find me a wife? Fine. Do it. I'll even cooperate. We can spend a lifetime together looking for the right woman. One practice date didn't cut it, Angie. It'll take months to get me in shape for my future wife. Years, maybe. And once you've decided I'm ready, we still have to locate her. It could take all of eternity to find the woman I should marry."

"Reed, please—" She couldn't continue and he snatched her into his arms, cradling her close.

"You can't leave me. I won't let you."

His mouth found hers, drinking with a thirst that wouldn't be sated. Resistance was impossible. How could she resist something that graced her soul with such peace and contentment? His breath gave her life. His voice filled her ears with music more beautiful than all the heavenly choirs combined. His touch completed her. He deepened the kiss, desperation lending a bittersweet quality to the moment. Locked in his arms she found love. A forever love, a blessing she'd treasure to the end of time and beyond.

I love you! Her soul sang the words even as she gently released him from their kiss. Her lips lingered on his for a final instant, savoring the shape and texture and unforgettable flavor, her final touch as fleeting as a dream.

He cupped her face, his eyes ablaze with savage determination. "I want you. I lo—"

She stopped his words with her hand. "No! Don't say it. Don't even think it. I didn't come for this. I came to fulfill your wish."

He stared blankly. "What wish?"

"The one Goodenkind gave you. The one by the lake, remember?"

A knock sounded behind them like a death knell.

"You found Emily?" He stared at the door, then shook his head. "Get rid of her. I've changed my mind. I can handle this on my own. I don't need your help."

"It's too late," Angie whispered, stepping away from him. "What's done is done."

CHAPTER TEN

THE door swung open and a woman stood there, a woman well into her fifties. She glanced nervously at Angie, before turning her attention to Reed. She clasped her hands together, clearly nervous. "Mr. Harding?"

"I'm Reed."

"I'm Lorraine Enders, Emily's mother." She stepped into the room, her fear palpable. "I wonder if I could speak with you for a minute?"

"Where's Emily?" he demanded.

"That's what I wanted to talk to you about."

"Please come in, Mrs. Enders," Angie interrupted. She gestured toward the couch. "Won't you have a seat?"

"Thank you." The woman perched on the edge of the leather cushions and studied Angie, a slight frown creasing her brow. "Don't I know you?"

"We've never actually met."

"You look so familiar. I feel I should recognize you."

"Mrs. Enders," Reed interrupted. "About Emily. Where is she?"

"I'm not sure how to tell you this." Tears welled into the woman's eyes. "Emily died a year ago. She was killed in an accident."

"Died!" It took a moment for Reed to absorb her

comments and subdue his shock. Then compassion took over. He crossed to Lorraine's side and sat next to her. "I'm so sorry. I hadn't heard. In fact, I've been looking for her ever since she left."

"I'm well aware of that, Mr. Harding."

"Make it Reed."

She inclined her head. "Thank you. Please call me Lorraine."

"I don't mean to add to your suffering... But could you tell me what happened to Emily after she left?"

"My daughter joined me in Delaware. I think you should know that she was quite frank about her reasons for leaving you. Emily told me about your brother's problems—how he'd been in and out of trouble for so many years. And she told me how nervous the idea of living with him made her. I thought she was wrong not to give young Joel a chance, but she was adamant because—" Lorraine broke off, twisting her hands together.

"Because she was pregnant?" Reed finished for her.

"Yes," Lorraine whispered.

"Did she have my baby?"

"She did. A little girl, named Becca. Rebecca Angeline."

"What happened to my daughter, Lorraine?" A sudden thought occurred and he paled. "Was she with Emily when—?"

"Yes. Though, Becca wasn't seriously injured." Lorraine bowed her head. "After Emily's death, I did a terrible thing. I kept the baby instead of getting in touch with you. It was wrong. I should have contacted you immediately after the accident, but—"

"*Why?* Why did you keep her from me?"

Angie crossed to his side, resting a restraining hand on his shoulder. "Easy, Reed. She's doing the right thing now."

He turned toward her, catching hold of her fingers and drawing them to his mouth. It was such a simple gesture, one of acknowledgment and acceptance. Yet, it meant the world to her. "I'm sorry if I seem anxious, Lorraine. It's just that I've spent over two years searching for the truth. Please go on."

"I knew I shouldn't have kept Becca from you—" Her mouth worked for a moment. Finally she gathered herself, her hands closing into fists. "It took a while, but I finally realized that I had to do right, no matter what. Even if it meant—" She broke off, fumbling in her purse for a tissue.

"Where's Becca?"

"She's here. I have one request before I bring her in, if you don't object." She dabbed the tears from her eyes, then lifted her chin and gave Reed a direct look. "Will you let me say goodbye to her before I leave?"

His eyes narrowed. "Say goodbye?"

"Please." Angie could tell the word came hard to her, that she wasn't a woman accustomed to begging. "I know I don't deserve your compassion, but I'm asking for it, nonetheless."

Reed shook his head in disbelief. "Is that why you kept her all this time?" He captured Lorraine's hand.

"Did you think I'd shut you out of Becca's life because of what Emily did?"

Her control broke. "I wouldn't blame you." Tears filled her eyes again, spilling uncontrollably to her cheeks. "You've lost eighteen months of fatherhood. How can you forgive either of us for that?"

"I forgive you because you gave me a daughter I never knew about." He hesitated, then admitted. "I'm angry that you didn't come to me sooner, I can't deny that. But Becca's still your granddaughter, Lorraine. She needs you. I'd never take her from you."

A small whine sounded at the door. Scratch waited there, a small girl beside him, clinging to his red collar. She had a head full of black ringlets pulled into a miniature ponytail and wore a bright yellow gingham dress with a yellow collar in the shape of sunflower petals. She was also one of the prettiest little girls Angie had ever seen. Reed stood and stared at his daughter, unable to utter a single word. Spotting her grandmother, the little girl raced across the room. Lorraine picked her up and hugged her close. Then she turned the child in Reed's direction.

"Becca, sweetness, this is your daddy. Can you say hello?"

Reed stooped so he'd be nearer to her level. "Hi, Becca," he said softly.

The little girl hesitated, clearly overcome with shyness. She curled her hands in her dress and lifted it to her mouth, revealing a frilly white petticoat beneath. Peeking over the hem she regarded her father with familiar hazel eyes, eyes glowing with bright golden lights. Finally, she offered an eight-tooth smile. "Daddy," she said.

Reed shut his eyes, his jaw tensing as he struggled with emotions he'd kept locked away for two full years. He held out his hand and waited, hope warring with apprehension. Becca didn't hesitate, she ran toward him, flinging herself into his arms. He lifted her over his head, chuckling at her squeals of laughter.

"I can see your face now," he announced in triumph. "I've been wondering for so long what you looked like. And now I know."

His daughter didn't understand his comment, but Angie did—as did Lorraine. She lifted her tissue again, overcome with grief. Angie slipped an arm around the woman and held her close, allowing angelic compassion to wash away some of the pain. "You're afraid you might lose Becca. But you won't. I promise."

Lorraine's voice caught on a sob. "I deserve to."

"We all make mistakes. We also all deserve second chances. I know Reed. He'll give you that second chance."

"I've already lost Emily. I couldn't bear to lose Becca, as well."

"It'll work out, you'll see. Reed wished it." Angie bowed her head, elation mingling with despair. "And even though I haven't been very good at granting wishes in the past," she confessed, "this time I'll succeed." It was a vow from the heart.

She looked at Reed then. He sat cross-legged on the floor, Becca perched on his lap facing him. She chattered a mile a minute, half her comments incomprehensible. Not that that bothered Reed. He simply sat, grinning. Every few minutes he'd reach out and touch his daughter—winding an ebony lock around his finger, feathering a thumb across her rosy cheeks, catching her dainty fingers in his massive hands. Angie touched Lorraine's shoulder.

"See the good you've done?" she asked. "You've given him a gift no one else could have. How could he not be grateful?"

Scratch approached, pawing at Angie's skirt. She understood his unspoken request. It was time to say goodbye. She'd been dreading this moment from the instant she'd arrived. Slowly she left the couch and joined Reed, kneeling beside him.

Becca took one look at Angie and immediately deserted her father's lap. She held out her arms in clear demand, her hazel eyes so like Reed's they were breathtaking. Unlike her father's, though, these eyes were unfettered by shadows. Instead they reflected the beauty of the child's soul and the sweetness of her nature. Utterly helpless beneath their joyous regard, Angie found herself falling in love all over again. Like father, like daughter, came the helpless thought as Angie took the little girl in her arms.

"Pretty!" Becca exclaimed.

It would seem her angel status was visible to Reed's daughter. She caught at Angie's wings, giggling as they fanned her, the downy feathers tickling the rounded chin and tumbling her tiny ponytail. She reached up, twining chubby fingers in platinum curls before swirling her hands through the halo's golden light, scattering it like stardust. Becca gasped in astonishment as the light danced around them in brilliant swirls.

All too soon she was through with her play. Turning back to her father, she launched herself toward him, already secure in the knowledge that his arms would always be there to catch her.

For an instant Angie's gaze locked with Reed's. He appeared so replete, so contented. Yet even as she took pleasure in his satisfaction it faded from his face as realization dawned. His happiness had come at her expense.

"Angie—"

"I just remembered where I've seen you," Lorraine suddenly interrupted. "But I thought you drowned with Emily."

Reed turned sharply. "What?"

"That's right. I never told you about the accident, did I?" Lorraine managed a brave smile. "Emily was knocked off a dock into the water while she was holding Becca. She hit her head on a boat when she fell, and drowned. A woman standing on the dock jumped in and managed to save Becca." Lorraine looked at Angie in confusion. "The newspaper said that you drowned, too. Obviously, you didn't."

"Lorraine, please take my daughter and wait for me in the outer office," Reed requested. "We'll only be a minute."

Without a word, Lorraine did as he'd asked, clearly sensing something amiss. The instant the door closed, Reed turned on Angie. "You saved my daughter's life? You *died* saving her?"

"I didn't die on purpose, you understand," Angie said with gentle irony.

"Why didn't you tell me?"

"I wasn't positive it was Becca I'd saved. Not until recently." She smiled, hoping to ease his distress. "I guess it's Goodenkind's way of helping me find completion. I can leave knowing that my death had a purpose. That it gave you your heart's desire."

"My heart's desire?" He gripped her shoulders, pulling her up against his warmth. "*You're* my heart's desire."

She carefully disengaged herself. "Not me, Reed. Becca is. She's your wish, remember?"

She'd never seen a man so tortured, so torn. His teeth clamped together and a wild light flamed in his eyes. "No. No, you're wrong. I didn't wish for Becca." His voice had taken on a fierce edge. "I wished for Emily. I wished to marry her if she had my child. *That* was what I asked."

"Emily died."

"Which means you didn't grant my wish," he bargained desperately. "Becca's mine regardless. But you didn't give me a wife. I'm short one bride."

If it wasn't so serious, she'd have laughed. "You didn't want a wife. You told me that right from the start. Now you have your true heart's desire—your child."

"No! We made a bargain. And—and since you didn't give me Emily, you have to fill in for her." He thrust his hand through his hair, his fury dying beneath the strength of his despair. "Angie, please. Stay and marry me."

"You know that's not possible." She took a step backward. And then another.

"No, dammit! If you don't stay, you won't have given me my heart's desire. Becca is my world, but you... You're my life."

Angie shivered, feeling the familiar tingle that seized her whenever she was being called home. "It's time for me to go."

He made a move toward her. "No, wait. You can't leave. Not yet!"

"Goodbye, Reed. Be happy." She heard the call grow louder, felt the irresistible pull. She reached for love, but it was too late. He was beyond her grasp. "I love you," she whispered.

"Angie! No!"

She heard his shout, heard the torment, heard the painful echo all the way to the gates of Heaven.

"Angie! No!"

He stood in the middle of the room and bellowed the denial. Not that it did him any good. She was gone, snatched from him before he could even respond to her whispered confession.

She loved him!

He closed his eyes, the pain threatening to rip him in two.

He hadn't been able to tell her... Tell her that he loved her, too. Loved her with all his heart and soul. The irony didn't escape him. He glared heavenward. "You sent her to me on a mission, a mission to find true love. Well, I finally found it. Only now you've taken her from me." His hands fisted. "You heard my wish—the one I made by the lake. And it wasn't what I told Angie. I didn't know Becca existed then, so I didn't wish for her. You know that! *You know it!*"

His voice caught, shattered into fragments. "You know what I asked," he whispered. "I asked for Angie."

"*Angie!* Angie! Angie..."

His call followed her all the way through heaven's gates, the final faint whisper chasing her down the hallowed halls, filling her ears and beating against her heart. She forced herself to ignore it, to pretend that the painful longing in his voice didn't cause her the most intense misery she'd ever experienced.

"Angie Makepeace. Please report to your supervisor. Angie Makepeace to Supervisor Goodenkind."

She stepped onto the gilded path, suddenly realizing that no one looked askance or muttered comments behind their hands. In fact, several angels smiled at her. How odd. Perhaps they were glad to be seeing the last of her. No sooner had the suspicion entered her head, then shame filled her. Such uncharitable thoughts were no longer acceptable. Taking a deep breath, she returned their smiles with a cheerful grin and continued on her way.

Goodenkind stood in the threshold of his office, waiting for her, his expression as solemn as always. "Ah, there you are. Finally. You've really made a mess of things this time, my dear young angel."

"I excel at it, as you're well aware."

"That's quite possibly the understatement of the century. Come in and sit down."

"Thank you for all your help, Good," she said, taking her usual seat. "I know you tried your best."

"I most certainly did."

"So what happens now? Am I..." She swallowed hard. "Am I out?"

"Yes."

Blunt and to the point. She appreciated his candor. "It's not like I really belonged," she said, hoping to ease his disappointment. "I just made it in by the tips of my fingernails, anyway."

"Oh, really?" Goodenkind tilted his head to one side, regarding her sternly. "And why do you think that, Ms. Makepeace?"

"You and I both know that I didn't live an exemplary life. I made more than my fair share of mistakes."

"Do you seriously believe that you only came into our care because you saved young Becca's life?"

"Didn't I?" she asked uncertainly.

"Far from it, my dear. It's not quite that easy. We expect more from our angels, even angels-in-training." He leaned forward, his words hitting with quiet force. "You have a capacity for love and acceptance that outstrips most angels of my acquaintance. You were always kind to others, forever cheerful and helpful."

"But I made mistakes—"

He dismissed that with a wave of his hand. "Everyone makes mistakes as you so rightly told Lorraine.

For instance, this wish business.'' He shook his head. ''You really turned that into an unmitigated disaster.''

''I—I gave Reed his wish.''

''No, my dear. You did not.''

''I don't understand,'' she said, thoroughly bewildered. ''I gave him his daughter.''

''You were supposed to give him true love.''

''He didn't wish for love. He wished for—''

She heard a whisper, a whisper of longing. "I know I shouldn't want to make love to an angel. That I shouldn't feel—" She'd sealed his mouth with her fingers, refusing to allow him to say the words. But his yearning continued to ring in her head, echoing so loudly it threatened to deafen her. The impossibility of it all overwhelmed her and she'd covered her ears to shut out the silent cry.

Tears filled her eyes. ''He—he wished for me,'' she murmured brokenly. ''At the lake that day. And I wouldn't listen.''

''Yes, my dear.'' It was so gently said that she wept. ''You've bungled your last mission, Ms. Makepeace, and now you must go. We've decided that the reason for such a wealth of failure is due to one unfortunate problem. You've never known true love. That's why his wish never reached your ears, even when it was shouted so loudly all of heaven heard the cry.''

''I do know true love,'' she protested through her tears. ''I didn't for a long time, but—''

''I'm sorry, my dear. You haven't learned it as well as you should. And until you've experienced love in all its guises, you won't be a successful angel. So, we're giving Mr. Harding his wish and when you return to us, perhaps you'll be more victorious in your missions.''

Understanding finally dawned. He wasn't just putting her outside the Pearly Gates, he was returning her to earth—sending her back to the one man she loved with all her heart and soul. She wept in earnest, spending the very last of her angel tears. "How can I thank you? How can I ever—''

The tingling started again, the unmistakable pull. "Love long and well, my dear," Goodenkind said. "That's all I ask of you. Love long and well. Heaven won't be the same without you."

Her tears turned to laughter, her joy too great to contain. "Don't get complacent, Good. I'll be back."

He smiled at her wavering image. "Of that, we have no doubt," he whispered. "Farewell, Ms. Makepeace."

Angie stood outside a large Victorian-style house, as beautiful a home as she'd ever seen. A white picket fence surrounded the property, the gate firmly shut. It was late evening, the shadows thick and heavy. She heard voices coming from the driveway to her right and watched as Joel, Reed and Becca progressed along the walkway from the garage to the front door.

Lorraine opened the door and called a greeting, bright, welcoming light streamed onto the covered porch. Becca and Joel stepped inside with Lorraine. But at the last minute, Reed hesitated. Slowly, he turned, searching the shadows.

He couldn't see her, she suddenly realized, merely

sensed her presence. So she stepped forward, into the light.

"Angie?" Her name sounded raw and harsh on his lips.

"Hello, Reed." *Hello, my love.*

He didn't move, simply stood and stared as though afraid she'd disappear if he came too close. "What are you doing here?"

For the first time a twinge of fear gripped her. "I've been put out of heaven."

"But what are you doing *here?*"

She moistened her lips. "Same thing I've always done. I'm standing on the outside—" She bowed her head, unable to finish.

He took a single step toward her. "Looking in?"

"Yes." She took a deep breath and forced herself to meet his gaze. "You once told me I didn't have to do that ever again. That I could find a way in."

His expression softened and a small smile played at the corners of his mouth. "You only have to do one small thing. It's always tough the first time you try, but I have confidence in you, sweetheart."

Ask, he'd told her on that special day by the lake. All she had to do was ask. Never had anything been so difficult—or so badly desired. "Please, Reed. I don't want to be on the outside anymore."

"Then come in." He took another step in her direction. "Joel needs a sister. Becca needs a mother. And I— Hell, sweetheart. I'm in desperate need of a wife."

Still she hesitated. "I can't come in. Not yet."

"Why not?"

She heard the underlying fear, but she'd given her word. And she wasn't about to go back on it now. "I promised Joel that he could approve your choice for a wife. So, I'm afraid I can't come in until he agrees."

Reed turned toward the open doorway. "Joel!" he shouted. "Come here. I need you."

Within seconds, Joel shot through the front door, skidding across the porch to stand beside Reed. "What? What's wrong?" He caught sight of Angie and grinned.

Becca came tottering onto the porch, too. One look at their visitor and she let out a shriek of sheer happiness. If Reed hadn't caught her up in his arms, she'd have chased down the sidewalk after Angie.

"Where the he— *heck* have you been?" Joel questioned.

"It's a long story."

"She says she made you a promise, little brother. She says she won't marry me unless you approve my choice."

"Oh, yeah. That's right." He winked at her. "Angels aren't allowed to break their promises, are they?"

Reed glared at his brother. "How did you know she was an angel?"

"Scratch told me."

Angie sighed. "He always did have a big mouth."

"Well, shoot," Joel groused in disgust. "And here I thought it was the wings that were the dead giveaway."

"Are you going to stand there all night grinning

like an idiot,'' Reed demanded. ''Or are you going to let her come in?''

''Give me a minute. I'm thinkin'.'' Reed made a threatening move and Joel burst out laughing, fending him off with an upraised hand. ''Okay! Okay. You wanna marry my brother?'' he yelled down to Angie.

''Well, he's a pretty crummy date, but I think I can work on that. I guess I'll take him on, if you agree, that is.''

''Well, he—*heck,* yeah!''

Reed held out his hand. ''Come on, sweetheart. Come on home.''

She took a deep breath. *Thank you, Good. I'll make you proud. You'll see. I'll make the best da—*dang! *wife and mother heaven has ever seen.* The gate blew open at her touch and she started up the walkway. Then she was running, flying into his arms. Reed caught her, wrapping her in a tight embrace, holding her like he'd never let go.

''Don't leave me,'' he ordered against her mouth. ''Don't ever leave me. I love you, Angie. I love you more than I believed possible.''

She sealed his vow with a kiss. ''I love you, too, Reed. I love you so much, I swear they'll hear our happiness all the way to heaven.''

Together the three of them crossed the porch and walked inside. Before they could close the door, a black and white polka dot streak rocketed up the porch steps and into the house after them. Scratch barked at Joel and Becca's excited welcome. Reed rolled his eyes, but Angie just smiled. Guardian

Angels might be tricky creatures, but they were also welcome additions to any family.

The door closed, securing them inside.

Home.

She was home at last.

EPILOGUE

"Now you sit here," four-year-old Becca instructed, pulling out a miniature chair for Tiger. Gingerly, he eased his bulk into the fragile seat, accepting the cup and saucer she handed him. She fluttered at his elbow like a dainty butterfly, her wide-brimmed hat clipping his nose. Not that he'd have complained. Not for anything in the world.

"Would you like cream and sugar?" she asked, clutching her white-gloved hands together, not a hint of her usual mischievousness showing—at least for the moment.

"Er, just sugar, thanks."

Joel grinned, looking frighteningly adult in his suit and tie. "Aw, come on, Tiger. Have some cream. And for cryin' out loud, get that pinkie up. Don't you have any couth?"

Tiger struggled to contain the fragile bit of china within his meaty hand. "Don't give me any lip, boy," he growled, glancing up from his juggling act long enough to shoot Joel a threatening glare. "Or I'll have you in the office doin' bookkeeping for the next week."

"Can't do it next week. College starts, remember?"

"Oh, yeah?" The foreman tugged at his bow tie,

crumpling it beyond repair. "Well there's always spring break."

Becca continued around the table, stepping between her two grandmothers and pouring invisible tea into their cups and saucers, as well. "Two lumps of sugar for my grandmas."

"Why, thank you, sweetheart," Lorraine said, exchanging a smile with her counterpart. Flowered bonnets topped each gray-streaked head. "You always fix the best tea."

"That's 'cause it's love tea. That's what you always told me." She continued around the miniature table. "And some for Mommy and Daddy."

Scratch whined. Sitting on a leather hassock, he wore his best red bow tie and a hopeful expression.

"I'm coming," Becca said with an exaggerated sigh. "I still have to get the baby, first."

Angie frowned as she watched Becca pretend to pour tea into a spare place setting. "Darling, I think you miscounted. There's only eight of us, not nine."

"This is for the baby," she repeated.

"What baby?" Reed demanded.

"My new baby brother." Becca offered her father a sunny smile. "He's coming next summer."

"Brother?" Reed's brows shot up and he glanced at Angie, an odd glitter gathering in his eyes. "Something you neglected to mention, sweetheart?"

"I just found out myself," she whispered. "I was going to tell you tonight." She raised her voice. "Becca? How did you know about your new brother, darling?"

"An angel told me," the little girl answered promptly with a sly glance at Scratch.

"I told you that dog has a big mouth," Reed muttered.

But Scratch just grinned. After all...

Guardian Angels were tricky creatures. Especially when it came to accomplishing their missions. Fortunately, this mission looked well on its way to being successfully completed. Perhaps in another forty or fifty years, he'd know for certain.

A BETTY NEELS Christmas

What better way to celebrate the joyous
holiday season than with this special
anthology that celebrates the talent of
beloved author Betty Neels? Bringing to
readers two of Betty's trademark
tender romances, this volume will
make the perfect gift for
all romance readers.

*Available in October 2002
wherever paperbacks are sold.*

HARLEQUIN®
Makes any time special ®

Visit us at www.eHarlequin.com

PHBNC

HARLEQUIN®
Romance®

Receive 75¢ off your next Harlequin Romance® book purchase.

75¢ OFF!

Your next Harlequin Romance® book purchase.

RETAILER: Harlequin Enterprises Ltd. will pay the face value of this coupon plus 8¢ if submitted by customer for this product only. Any other use constitutes fraud. Coupon is nonassignable. Void if taxed, prohibited or restricted by law. Void if copied. Consumer must pay any government taxes. For reimbursement submit coupons and proof of sales to: Harlequin Enterprises Ltd., P.O. Box 880478, El Paso, TX 88588-0478, U.S.A. Cash value 1/100¢. Valid in the U.S. only.

Coupon expires March 31, 2003.
Redeemable at participating retail outlets in the U.S. only.
Limit one coupon per purchase.

109928

5 65373 00075 5   (8100) 0 10992

HARLEQUIN®
Makes any time special®

HARLEQUIN®
Romance®

Receive 75¢ off your next Harlequin Romance® book purchase.

75¢ OFF!

Your next Harlequin Romance® book purchase.

RETAILER: Harlequin Enterprises Ltd. will pay the face value of this coupon plus 10.25¢ if submitted by customer for this product only. Any other use constitutes fraud. Coupon is nonassignable. Void if taxed, prohibited or restricted by law. Void if copied. Consumer must pay any government taxes. Nielson Clearing House customers submit coupons and proof of sales to: Harlequin Enterprises Ltd., 661 Millidge Avenue, P.O. Box 639, Saint John, N.B. E2L 4A5. Non NCH retailer—for reimbursement submit coupons and proof of sales directly to: Harlequin Enterprises Ltd., Retail Marketing Department, 225 Duncan Mill Rd., Don Mills, Ontario M3B 3K9, Canada. Valid in Canada only.

Coupon expires March 31, 2003.
Redeemable at participating retail outlets in Canada only.
Limit one coupon per purchase.

52603857

HARLEQUIN®
Makes any time special ®

Receive
MOULIN ROUGE™
on VHS video

with two proofs of purchase from any four specially marked Harlequin® collector's editions.

Special Limited Time Offer

YES! Please send me my *MOULIN ROUGE*™ VHS video without cost or obligation, except for shipping and handling. Enclosed are two proofs of purchase from specially marked Harlequin® collector's editions and a check or money order for $3.50* shipping and handling fee made payable to Harlequin Books.

*New York State residents please add applicable sales tax.
*Canadian residents please add 7% GST.

Name (PLEASE PRINT)

Address   Apt. #

City   State/Prov.   Zip/Postal Code

097 KJL DNC9

MOULIN ROUGE VIDEO OFFER TERMS
To receive your *MOULIN ROUGE*™ VHS video, complete the above order form. Mail it to us with two proofs of purchase (one of which can be found in the upper right-hand corner of this page) from any four specially marked Harlequin® collector's editions. Requests must be received no later than March 31, 2003. Your *MOULIN ROUGE*™ video costs you only $3.50 for shipping and handling (plus applicable taxes for Canadian and N.Y. State residents). It has a retail value of $14.98 U.S. All orders subject to approval. Terms and prices subject to change without notice. **Please allow 6-8 weeks for delivery. Offer good in Canada and the U.S. only.** Offer good only while quantities last. Offer limited to one per household.

© 2002 Harlequin Enterprises Limited

Visit us at www.eHarlequin.com   PHNCP02-OFFER